The Obit Man

THE OBIT MAN

F.F. Langan

mosaic press

National Library of Canada
Cataloguing in Publication

Langan, F. F.
    The Obit Man / Fred Langan

ISBN 0-88962-829-7

    1. World War, 1939-1945 — Canadians, French-speaking
— Fiction. 2. World War, 1939-1945 — Underground
movements — France — Fiction. I. Title.

PS8573.A5534O73 2004   C813'.6   C2004-902809-X

Published by Mosaic Press, offices and warehouse at 1252 Speers Road, Units 1 and 2, Oakville, Ontario, L6L 5N9, Canada and Mosaic Press, PMB 145, 4500 Witmer Industrial Estates, Niagara Falls, NY, 14305-1386, U.S.A.

Mosaic Press acknowledges the assistance of the Canada Council and the Department of Canadian Heritage, Government of Canada for their support of our publishing programme.

**Canada Council
for the Arts**

**Conseil des Arts
du Canada**

Design by K.S.Daniel
Author photo by Peter Rehak

Mosaic Press Canada:
1252 Speers Road, Units 1 & 2,
Oakville, Ontario
L6L 5N9
Phone/Fax: 905-825-2130
info@mosaic-press.com

www.mosaic-press.com

Mosaic Press U.S.A.:
4500 Witmer Industrial Estates
PMB 145, Niagara Falls, NY
14305-1386
Phone/Fax: 1-800-387-8992
info@mosaic-press.com

To Grant Bush and Anthony Carter, two friends of mine who died while I was writing this and whose obituaries I never wanted to write.

obit, *n.* *Obs.* *Exc.* **Hist.**

1. a. Departure from life, death, decease (of a particular person). *Obs.*

b. A record or notice of a person's death, or the date of it; an obituary notice. In mod. *colloq.* (esp. journalists) use usu. regarded as an abbrev. of OBITUARY *n.*

OXFORD ENGLISH DICTIONARY

One spy in the right place is worth twenty thousand men on the battlefield.

NAPOLEON BONAPARTE

PART ONE

1

We live in a great age for death.

That thought came to Jack as he was bumped on both sides, one a rather harsh poke in the soft part of his back — was it the kidney? He turned and saw it came from a wooden umbrella handle.

"Sorry," he said with a pained smile, even though he had nothing to be sorry about.

He stared out at the people in the subway car and thought each one of them is going to die, some soon, some later. A few, maybe none of them, might be worthy of his notice upon their death. The woman with the sharp umbrella handle was pretty enough, but what had she done with her life so far?

An older woman at the end of the car moved and he thought he caught a spark in her eye as her head turned. She was sixty, maybe older, slender, erect and about five foot eight. She had a handsome face, a shock of white hair with some black still left on the sides, and was well dressed. When the subway car moved she grabbed for a hand strap and when she turned he saw a trace of pearls round her neck.

Would her life be interesting in death?

Maybe she drove an ambulance or a staff car during the war; she might have worked close to airfields when they were being bombed or carried intelligence officers from the Admiralty on their secret trips, headlights taped over, just little slits of light to bounce off the cat's eyes as they sped almost blind down dark country roads.

He started to write her obit in his head.

Maude Worthing, who has died at the age of 89, was awarded an OBE for extraordinary bravery while serving with the Motorised Transport Corps. She drove three badly burned pilots and two injured airmen to a hospital during a Luftwaffe raid on North Weald in August of 1940.

She looked as if she might have been in the MTC. Not that he'd been there, but he'd just done something on a man who flew out of North Weald, and his widow had told him about the incident with one of the young things from the MTC. It was a rather fashionable thing to do, drive ambulances and trucks and things. Even Princess Elizabeth was part of the motorised corps, though she was too young to have done anything during the Battle of Britain.

During the war women had to do men's jobs so the men could fight. While working-class girls went to the factories, as they had done in the First War, the women of the middle and upper classes drove cars, lorries and ambulances. Maude Worthing did two out of three, starting her life in the MTC, driving a heavy lorry, and then shifting to life as a chauffeur for MI6.

She was driving an intelligence officer to North Weald when the raid began.

Just then the train stopped, the doors opened and the imaginary wartime driver pushed her way through to get off at Knightsbridge. The way she moved showed her a confident upper middle-class woman. Jack was tempted to follow her and ask a few questions, but it was a stupid idea and this wasn't his stop.

Maude Lacey married Group Captain Henry Worthing, DFC, in April of 1941. He had been one of the men she saved at North Weald. They had three children.

A little Jane Austen in the ending department, but still a good story. He didn't have time to make up the part about the air raid and how she had trained as a nurse before the war. All of a sudden the car seemed more crowded. People stuffed on at Hyde Park Corner, something that almost never happened. An elbow stabbed him from the side and another umbrella handle caught him again, this time in the hipbone.

It hurt. There wasn't much padding on his bones. A few years of living on his own had left him thinner, and he didn't weigh more than 165 pounds even though he was almost six feet tall.

Jack pulled his cuff back, rubbing the red hair on the back of his hand as he looked at his watch and changed his mind about work and decided to get off early. He struggled through the silent sea of grim-faced office workers and got off at Green Park.

It wasn't total whimsy. He remembered the current woman in his life. He knew her morning routine, and thought he'd see if she went to her usual spot, a rather smart coffee bar just past where Bond Street changes to New Bond Street. He was ahead on the story he was working on and all of a sudden sick of crowds. He'd take a cab to work in an hour, or maybe jump back on the tube when it was less crowded.

The streets on the other side of Piccadilly from the Ritz seemed almost empty, at least compared to the crush of commuters he'd just left. He crossed the road to look at what was being served today at that famous restaurant in Stratton Street. The one Michael Caine had a piece of. At the top of the menu was a watercolour of three rather louche men, one of them the famous actor, another a famous Irish drunk and the other an unknown. Jack thought he might have lunch there later in the week.

Around the corner there were three workmen doing no work outside a half-renovated building. They milled around a couple of funny looking yellow bins full of earth and construction junk. The workers were smoking, laughing and talking in loud voices. Jack thought the little dumpsters were rather odd.

Clouds moved by fast, and light seemed to come and go. A rain shower half an hour earlier had left the streets wet and shiny, the way film crews like them. The sun lit up the colours on the buildings, pulling reds out of signs, things that might seem to disappear with the clouds. And the morning light seemed to turn the grey road a sharp black. When the sun went in the air felt cold and fresh, though not cold enough to make him move any faster.

Huge pictures of landscapes hung in a gallery window. Jack stopped and looked at a few of them. A woman walked out of a discreet hotel and flagged a cab. Jack smiled and wondered what she had been up to. He took his time, having his first cigarette of the day, looking in the windows of a print dealer as he thought he should give up smoking. He promised himself he'd quit tomorrow.

He stopped at a newsstand outside Sotheby's and bought another pack of Marlboros and an *International Herald Tribune*. He never cared about baseball scores at home, but now, five and a half years away, they seemed an odd kind of link.

The coffee shop was just a few steps down a small street. There was a crowd by the cash, office workers and clerks from the shops picking up a morning fix. Only people who didn't have to be at work by nine could take their time. There was space in the back where he could keep an eye on the door and see if Claire walked in, which he guessed she did at the same time every morning. Then he worried, thinking maybe she isn't that regular in her habits.

Jack ordered toast and a regular coffee and the waitress almost frowned. According to something he'd read in *The Economist*, the British didn't drink as much tea as their self-image told them they did. Coffee was cutting into tea drinking, but his accent and the order for what passed for an American drink brought on a little xenophobic scowl.

It amazed him how the English could not do coffee shops. The delis and drug store counters he hung around as a kid had more to them than this. The English were good at pubs, but Jack was tired of pubs, except on weekends.

The places for coffee or tea were one extreme or the other. Most were grungy caffs, but this one had white tablecloths, a kind of halfway house for people who didn't want to splurge at Brown's Hotel down the street.

Just as his coffee arrived, Claire walked in. The sight of her still made his stomach hurt. Blonde hair, thick lips and an unusual face, beautiful to him, and a rather exquisite bottom, though some people might think it a bit oversized on such a flat-chested woman. Every movement, her hand, her head, her walk, seemed so feminine. Too bad they'd been fighting a bit for the past few weeks.

He waved and smiled, and she smiled back. He was glad of that since her reaction to a surprise was not always predictable. She motioned to the girl behind the counter to make her a tea to go. Strange for a Frenchwoman, she couldn't stand coffee. The people here knew her since she worked in the office above the smart shop across the street, doing publicity for the jeweller. Claire's boss thought it wonderful her boyfriend was a journalist, but he was too stunned to know Jack's main interest was in dead people.

Claire sat down with some drama and put her face forward to be kissed. She didn't often kiss back.

"Hello, my darling, what are you doing here?"

My darling, thought Jack. Why wasn't this happening at night, or at least on a weekend afternoon? She clasped his hands with each of hers and leaned across the table. Seemed romantic, but then she might have been warming her hands. She hated the cold. He started to tell the truth, that he had been on the way to work, but she interrupted him. She knew why he was there.

"I have something special for you," said with such emotion it was starting to scare him. Was she pregnant? She opened her large bag and pulled out a book.

"*The Dirty Weekend Handbook*," she laughed, and she knew she had him. "Pick one and we're off this weekend. My car is working again. I couldn't stand the train." She slipped the book across the table, or did he grab for it? "Pick something today. And ring me later."

She got up and kissed him a public kiss, on the lips. Brash French girl, thought Jack. A teasing wave and "Goodbye, my darling," from the door and she carried her tea across

the street. His eyes never left her skirt as it grabbed her round-
ness as she walked.

Jack wondered why he had wasted his time, twice so far
today: once with the false economy of taking the tube in rush
hour; the other taking an hour out of the day to wander around
just to bump into this crazy girl. Now in the street outside
the coffee shop, he smiled at his own weakness and her crazi-
ness and flagged a black cab. In the back seat he turned on
the heater, a trick Claire had taught him, since he never knew
cabs had heaters. Seemed almost un-English.

He thumbed through the book. *The Dirty Weekend Handbook* had different sections. One told women about the type
of men they should go out with, rating lawyers, soldiers, journalists and other types. He laughed as he saw that last cat-
egory came low on the scale. Unreliable, given to melodrama,
heavy drinkers and often broke.

Naughty drawings hinted at the possible delights of a
weekend away. But the best part was the actual names of places
to go, a rating system of the hotels along with phone numbers and rates that looked as if they weren't too out of date.

Such a practical girl, thought Jack.

2

There was no set number of obituaries the paper ran every day. Sometimes it might be just one, as long as four thousand words with a big picture. Most days it was three, with the most British subject getting the biggest art, as editors called photographs or even sketches that would go with the obit.

War heroes were big, along with offbeat artistic types: writers, sculptors, actors or just plain ne'er-do-well bohemians who had spent half their lives drinking themselves to death in Soho. It helped if they'd been to public school.

Brutal honesty was part of the new obituary. Even Jack was still shocked when some roué was described 'as a womanizer and a cad.' Not shocked in a prudish way, since he was both those things at times, but because the paper had the nerve to call a cad a cad.

Jack's beat was Canada, the United States and Latin America, though if the Americans were halfway famous, or the Latin American artsy enough, it would be plucked from his basket. He didn't mind. It was interesting work, and no one ever bothered him or much cared when or if he showed up, as long as he produced the copy on time. He was paid by the word, but they gave him a desk, a phone and a computer terminal, though he had better gear back at his flat.

Today's dead man was an American baseball player, a colourful drunk who was in the Baseball Hall of Fame, not that that would mean much to British readers. But because of the war there was a British connection. Cowboy Rhett had spent two of the best years of his baseball career sitting in a B-17 while strangers shot hot metal at him. He could have wangled a dispensation and sold war bonds. That would have meant staying at home and playing a few exhibition baseball games on tour, but he'd volunteered for active duty.

The baseball part would be easy for Jack. Since Englishmen, and the particular type of Englishmen who read this paper, knew nothing about baseball, he could do the baseball from memory and the stuff he scalped from the sports pages of the *International Herald Tribune*. A few phone calls to an American sportswriter who worked for *The Gazette* in Montreal should give him an anecdote no one in Europe would ever read.

The plane was where he needed the edge. The Americans loved the B-17, the Flying Fortress, and thought it the greatest bomber of the war, at least until the B-29. But Jack's audience would disagree. While the B-17 might have had more armour and an extra gun turret, his readers would know the Lancaster carried a bigger payload and could outfly the B-17 – higher and faster.

Phone calls wouldn't be enough. This meant a visit to his air force expert. Jack looked over to see if the obit editor, Christopher Langton, was busy. On his desk was a row of reference books, things such as British political biographies and, of course, *Who's Who* and *Debrett's*, the encyclopaedia of the aristocracy and a must for this newspaper. Behind him were stacks of newspapers, theirs and the competition's, all kept in a messy sort of order the way they are in a library.

Langton was on the phone. Jack waited a minute. He knew Langton would hang up soon enough since he didn't like long chats on the phone. Odd for a newsman.

"When do you want to run Cowboy Rhett?" asked Jack, though he guessed the answer would be sometime next week.

"Tuesday."

"Right. I'm off to North Weald."

At the mention of the address in the outer suburbs of Essex, Langton looked back down at what he was working on. It was a genealogy of some noble family scribbled on a sheet of paper with details cribbed from *Debrett's* on things such as how the title started life. It would be translated into the story-telling prose of the long newspaper obituary later in the morning.

Jack closed what he was doing, picked up his Death Book, his nickname for the notebook he used for obituaries, then left. On the way out he pinched the first edition of a morning tabloid and last week's *Economist*. One of the perks of the news biz: free newspapers.

As he was about to leave the beard-and-checked shirt caught up with him.

"Oh, there you are. Glad to have caught you." Langton was breathing harder than usual from the rush to find Jack who wondered if there was a new policy about cadging *The Economist* and the *Daily Mail*.

"What is it?" asked Jack a bit nervous.

"Just some French fellow. Canadian French. DSO, *Croix de Guerre avec palme*. You can do him?" asked Langton, with the emphasis on the can, which had the effect of turning a question into an order.

"Sure." Jack never turned down work.

"No rush. Just came through. Do the American first and I'll have everything you need on this French-Canadian chap. Talk to me tomorrow."

"Right. I'll be here," promised Jack who hadn't planned to come in at all.

Langton handed him one slip of paper, a fax of a cryptic death notice, and turned to walk back to his office. Jack walked over to the reception desk and opened his Death Book. He borrowed some scissors and tape from the girl behind the desk and, leaving six pages for Cowboy Rhett, taped the death notice into his book. He'd think about it later.

Now he was off to see his air force expert, a man with memories of every plane flown in the last war and books to back up every memory. Without people like him, obituaries would be little more than death notices.

Before leaving Jack had called his air force man to make sure he was in. No use making the trip past Epping for nothing. Though rural Essex, or at least the edge of rural Essex, might seem a long way from the newspaper office in the centre of London, it was only one change and fifteen stops on the Central Line. It should take forty-five minutes, thought Jack, maybe an hour if there's a problem.

His first trip to North Weald was in 1970, to an air show. He'd been back many times since, at first to see a girl he'd met there, now always just to see Nick Mason.

"Cowboy Rhett was nothing special, and neither was the B-17," said the retired Wing Commander, a man who had flown Spitfires at the beginning of the war. After being shot down twice, and almost bleeding to death the second time, he went to Canada as part of the Commonwealth air-training programme, putting pilots through their stuff at bleak, frozen airfields. Places with names like Rivers, Manitoba. He didn't return to England until late 1944.

Mason's cottage was almost on top of the North Weald airfield, and although the tube stop was five minutes from his door, the place seemed part of the English countryside. Even Langton might approve. Mason was a neat little man, short with a slight build, a jockey custom made for a Spitfire or a Gloster Meteor, England's first jet fighter that he flew in the last days of the war and into the 1950s.

"He was another pilot who arrived here in 1942 with the United States Army's Eighth Air Force. When I say here, they couldn't fly from here of course," as he motioned in the direction of the North Weald airfield. "They needed room for those B-17s."

Mason walked over to the bookshelf in his study and pulled down a big book on bombers of the Second World War, one of dozens he had on Allied fighters and bombers. He flipped through to get comparisons between the American and British bombers.

"You know they didn't even start flying bombing raids until August of '42." This was said with the disdain of the Little Englander, who liked to feel the British won the war almost on their own. Jack thought without the Americans the Germans would still be in Paris, but he liked Mason and wasn't about to argue with him. Maybe later.

The old fighter pilot thought he knew the bomb loads of the B-17 and the Lancaster, but he wanted to be sure. "Flying Fortress. Boeing's always been top notch at marketing. I think they could carry ten thousand pounds tops. Wait a minute, there's one version that carried seventeen thousand, even a bit more with external bomb racks. Not many of those made. At the end of the war the Lanc was carrying the grand slam. That was twenty-two thousand pounds."

He looked in the pages for confirmation of what he already knew. His once perfect eyes now helped by half-slit glasses held by a string around his neck. His distance vision was still better than 20-20, even at 64 years old.

"The Lancaster had the same engine as the Spitfire. Four Merlins. The B-17s took a terrible pounding on the long-range missions. Flew in broad daylight, you know. At one stage they had to call them off until the P-51s got over here."

His finger moved in a dramatic flourish to the chart he knew was in there somewhere. "There it is. The numbers are right. Dangerous business, bombers, Lancs or B-17s. But the Yanks overestimated these things. Brave men flying them though. They took a terrible drubbing in those daylight raids."

Mason closed his book. Once started, he was impossible to stop. Jack reached for it and started looking through. He took notes from what Mason was telling him, but noticed a chart that showed the B-17 had a longer range than the Lancaster. And it had more armour plating. The Lancaster was stripped down to carry a maximum bomb load.

"Now the B-25. There was an adaptation," added Mason, as if to prove he wasn't anti-American. "Fully armoured it was a real weapons platform, as they say these days. An incredible amount of firepower. And of course the B-29: but we never had those in Europe."

Just then Mrs. Mason came in, carrying tea. She liked Jack, since he reminded her of home. She was a beautiful Icelandic woman from Gimli, Manitoba. Her blonde hair had turned grey but she still had the striking light blue eyes that had captivated her British pilot during the long prairie winter of 1943.

Mason kept talking but Jack stood up.

"You're much too thin Mr. Devlin. Eat this cake and put some meat on those bones."

"You're too kind Mrs. Mason. If you made it I'm sure it'll be wonderful."

She smiled at his flirtation, even with an older woman. "So charming. It must be the French blood." Since Jack was from Montreal, she was convinced he was French though the only French blood he had came from fights with French boys a few streets over.

She called her husband Nicholas. Jack noticed most women do that, call their men by their long-form name. He never let on there was any other name but Jack on his birth certificate. As Mrs. Mason left, Nick Mason started talking about bombers again.

Jack interrupted. He knew Mason well enough, so he could get away with it. And Mason knew Jack's father had been in Wellingtons for two years, a place where the odds were worse than for a soldier in the trenches in the First War.

"Enough with the hardware," laughed Jack, putting up his hands as if asking for mercy from the torrent of statistics, comparisons and real war stories from this walking encyclopaedia. "Give me a bit of stuff on how American pilots would fit in, and where did he fly from?"

"Somewhere in Norfolk, according to this," looking at the death notice and small obit Jack had brought from Cowboy's hometown in West Virginia. "They were all over the country, of course, but this lot seemed to have been in Norfolk."

Mason talked about how the Americans had a lot of money and how some Englishmen resented their success with the English girls. As Mason spoke Jack remembered one of his trips up there. He'd been doing a television piece and walked into a shop to get a key made. The shopkeeper snubbed him and as much as threw the key back at him.

"Thinks you're American," said the older cameraman he was working with. "Still angry at how many of their girls the Yanks knocked up during the war."

Just as Jack was ready to leave, Mason started talking about the dead American pilot. "Bit of waste using someone like Rhett in a bomber. A baseball player. He was the same as a bowler in cricket, wasn't he?"

Jack mumbled yes. "A pitcher. It's more like rounders than cricket."

Mason ignored him.

"Should have put him in fighters. Fellow probably had first-class eyesight. There was another baseball player, Ted Williams, I think. They had him in fighters."

The stuff of the perfect obit. Jack shook Mason's hand and got ready to walk back to the North Weald tube stop. It ran on a weird timetable, but Mason assured him there would be a train within half an hour.

Now came the payoff. "Could be longer. But let me run you down. We can stop in at the Fiddler's on the way." An excuse to get out of the house and drink. Jack suppressed a smile and thanked him for the offer of the lift.

The car was a bit ancient, a late '60s Rover 2000TC, quite advanced in its day. It looked as if it had been bought yesterday, except the red leather upholstery had creases and wrinkles, but then so did Mason. For a man who flew some of the fastest machines in the world in the 1940s, Mason was a danger to shipping on the road in the 1980s. He was slow, deliberate and absent-minded, all at the same time.

They managed to get to the pub, run by a caricature of an old army man, complete with a thick, white moustache, cavalry twills, a checked shirt and a brown knit tie. Jimmy was his name.

"American, are you?" Jack thought right away, another Little Englander. Better to humour him or he was in for a boring lecture. Humour him by being short and telling him what he wanted to hear.

"Yes."

Jimmy didn't even look up as he drew a couple of pints. "Over here on a trip?"

"You might say that," Jack replied, though he had been there since the late 1970s.

Mason interrupted as Jack paid for the beer.

"Canadian actually, Jimmy. Father was in Wellingtons during the war. Hard to tell the accents apart. Rather like Aussie and Kiwi to the untrained ear," Mason smirking, enjoying the dig at the snobby publican. "Got to know the nuances of all four after a couple of years in Rivers, Manitoba."

A laugh from Mason, a grudging smile from Jack and a worried look from Jimmy who wasn't sure whether or not the whole exchange had been a put-down. But it didn't really matter. To Jimmy the fly boys weren't the right class anyway.

Just before they walked over to a table by the door, Jack snapped up a London Underground timetable sitting on the bar. It gave the local times for Ongar and North Weald. Not all trains went to the last two stations on the Central Line and there wouldn't be a train until around four. That meant almost an hour in the pub then an hour back to London, all the way back to his flat. Mason had told him a bit of a fib, but he didn't mind. He'd work tonight, then finish off Cowboy Rhett by early tomorrow.

"It's actually easier to tell Kiwi from Australian than Canadian from some Americans," said Mason, this time with Jimmy out of earshot. "We had a few Americans in the squadron, just before and after Pearl Harbour. Chaps from California sound just like you. And we had someone from Nebraska who trained in Rivers. Went back to the American Air Force. Killed over Ploesti in a B-24 Liberator. Long trip that."

"Romania, wasn't it?" Jack asked though he knew the answer. Mason seemed to sense that and plowed right on.

"Now if a B-17 was making that run they would have to cut the bomb load down to maybe 4,000 pounds. I think your dead friend Cowboy Rhett was in on one of those, according to that clipping. They always talk up anyone famous who did something brave and lived. Good for morale and recruits. Dangerous business, as you know."

Jack took out his pen and scribbled a note about Ploesti.

The conversation drifted to the Mosquito, the safest bomber the British flew. A combination of speed and altitude kept the plywood fighter-bomber out of reach of almost everything the Luftwaffe could throw at it, except maybe the Me-62s, the German jets that flew towards the end of the war.

Three pints took their toll. Jack took a leak at the pub and planned another at the station. It would be hard making it all the way back with a full bladder. Then he could always change at Mile End to the District Line and, to use Mason's expression, 'shed a tear' part way home. Jack was 40 and found his bladder didn't have the endurance it once had.
The white Rover dropped him off just a few minutes before the train arrived. Mason seemed sad to see him go and waved goodbye before heading back to his books and his view of the airfield.

3

LONDON, 1943

Seemed senseless to have washed the car, Jane remarked to the minder as they drove through Admiralty Gate. The Buick was an odd sight in London. A big American car, on loan from the Americans rather than the British models 'borrowed' from their owners for the rest of the war.

Early autumn storms were never like this at home, thought the minder's charge in the back seat. Here the rain lasted all afternoon and the dark sky made the air seem much colder than it was. Where he grew up, when rain made it this cold in a hurry you could expect lightning. Not here it seemed. The windshield wipers kept the street in view though his eye was drawn to the driver whose blonde hair was brought up in a rather severe bun.

He took in her unlined neck and the straight line of her chin. The hair was almost perfect but one strand fell away. When she spoke he watched the side of her face and the redness of her lips as they parted. She moved her hand to push back the wisp of loose hair. It would look better let down, thought Henri.

The longer his life of celibacy lasted, the better women looked to him. He looked out the side window to the street and laughed to himself, thinking of the boys he went to school with who had joined the priesthood. He wasn't much better off.

The driver didn't say much but he could tell by her accent she wasn't British. The minder travelling with him frowned when Henri spoke. Everyone worked on the no-talk rule, that the less people knew, the better.

"Are you American?" he asked her.

"No, Canadian," she answered. "What about you. French, I suppose?"

It was one of the first times he had been out of uniform, at least when on official business. No shoulder flashes or badges to tell the world which country he came from. He decided to practice deception.

"Yes, French," he said, trying to modify his accent to sound more like Maurice Chevalier in English and less like the son of a bourgeois family from Montreal. "You, where are you from in Canada? I hear it's a big place."

"Montreal." He decided to say nothing and she too stopped speaking. The minder glared at them both. They were in any case near the address in Baker Street where he was to be dropped off. She might be the one who would pick him later, and then it might be someone else from the car pool. She stared at his taut profile as he slid across to get out of the car. Sharp blue eyes, impossible hollows on cheekbones so sharp they seemed almost carved by a sculptor.

He looked back at her and she smiled at him, in a way that seemed to say she wished they could meet tonight. That was against the rules. But they'd have so much to talk about since she knew they were both from Montreal. Much later she would tell her flat mate the forced French accent didn't fool her.

Beautiful boy, hope he doesn't try anything like that in France.

The door opened for Captain Henri Foix without his even having knocked. A stern-looking woman in a harsh woollen suit and mannish shoes greeted him without using his name. After a short wait he was shown into an office where one man in uniform sat behind a desk, another in civilian clothes sat on a couch against the wall.

Henri knew the drill. He saluted and stood at attention in front of the desk.

"Do you know why you're here?" asked the man in uniform, a brigadier. He told Henri to stand at ease. As he did he thought about how this was a bit of charade. He had already trained as a commando and had been before two selection boards, one of which seemed concerned with his mental health. He was able to deal with them; he could deal with this.

"Yes. I volunteered for special duty and I assume because I am here in civilian clothes the special duties are those of an agent. I also assume since I am a native French speaker you want me for work in France."

Seemed an odd conversation. Stiff on his part, but then his English went downhill if he was a little edgy. He was just stating the obvious to the two other people in the room. They must already know that he had trained at an American Special Forces base in Helena, Montana. He thought the British wouldn't trust the American training and he knew he might have to go to Scotland for a while. He wasn't supposed to know that, but he did.

The civilian on the couch switched to French.

"Have you ever been to France?"

"No, the only foreign country I have visited is the United States." Then he thought and added, "That is until I arrived here."

The civilian continued in French, which Henri thought sounded more Belgian than French, though with an English accent. An Englishman who went to school in Belgium. Henri always made a game of parsing accents. Countries were easy. He almost always knew which region or even small town people came from in Quebec, or in which district in Montreal they grew up. And he knew French accents too. Boys from France had been sent to his school and there were several French professors at university and a couple from Belgium.

The man continued in French and asked Henri what he thought was an odd question. "Why do you want to fight the Germans? Do you have anything against them?"

Henri thought, for maybe five seconds, before answering. He knew the answer, he'd thought about it.

"No, I don't hate Germans. I think it's wrong to hate any one nationality. That's what the Nazis do. When I was at school and then at university, I always read the papers. I followed the Nazis. *Kristallnacht.* There are Jews in Outremont, the part of Montreal where I grew up. I never knew too many, but I tried to imagine how I'd feel if mobs burned synagogues and smashed shops."

No expression crossed the civilian's face. "Nothing about France? You're French. Do you have feelings for France?"

"Well you might think I would. I love French, the language. And I love my own people, but I've never been to France, so I have no love for the country. Some sentiment, no love. There are people I grew up with who feel we shouldn't do anything for France. Or England. I'm not one of them."

Like his inquisitor Henri spoke without emotion. He wasn't clipped, just answered the questions without excitement. In part it was his nature, but he also did it on purpose, thinking *sang froid* might be something they'd look for in a man.

The motive side of the inquisition was over. They switched to English, with the uniformed man asking a question or two. He seemed to be the kind one, the civilian the hard case. There were a few generalities until they returned in French to a part that Henri knew was important.

"Tell me why you think you might be useful to us if we were to choose you to work in France?"

Henri was ready for this too. He had thought about it, in Helena, hoping the special assignment would be working in France ahead of the invasion in northern Europe everyone knew had to come. But he wanted to make a good impression so he spoke in an even more deliberate way than he usually did and tried to make his French precise, as he had in debating at school. He'd been to the best private school, the best university; he knew the language of Voltaire better than this Englishman sitting watching him, waiting for him to make a mistake.

"First, I'm a good soldier. I'm trained and have my wings as a para. I speak French like a native. My accent may be a bit strange to someone from Paris, but it is not much different from that of people from Normandy." The priests had told him that in the first years of school.

But he had thought ahead, knowing this was not enough. There were thousands of young French-speaking officers. What they needed was someone who wasn't just brave, but clever.

"I have a university degree in science, which is unusual. I'm a trained chemist. If I had to, I could make explosives with things you find in a farmyard. Fertilizer contains nitrates. I also took some courses in electricity and worked with the signal corps when I was in the militia. I understand radios and I know telephones."

That was an understatement. He knew more about phones that most men in the signal corps. He had worked two summers as a lineman with the phone company, and he worked in the country, not the city. But more talk might sound boastful so he stopped.

The man on the couch stared at him, saying nothing. He took a pipe from the table in front of him, pulled a box of wooden matches and lit it.

"You even worked for the phone company in the summer, isn't that true?"

He's done his homework, thought Henri. "Yes. Installing phone service in farms and small villages." He decided to leave it at that. He didn't want to ruin his chances by seeming too cocky. He felt he was close.

"Captain Foix," said the brigadier, speaking for the second time, and switching back to English. "Please sit down." Henri thought his accent a little odd. The way he pronounced vowels seemed almost familiar. The brigadier motioned for Henri to take the chair in front of his desk. Henri thought the chair looked out of place. It was ornate, French, and the building was so ugly. A utilitarian lump in the middle of London. He thought it looked like a department store from the outside.

"Have you ever heard of the Special Operations Executive?"

"SOE. Yes, I have." Until that moment Henri didn't know what form this special assignment might take. His heart started to race a little. This was beyond his dreams.

"Do you know much about it?"

"Well, only that it drops agents into occupied Europe. I think its most successful operation was the assassination of Reinhard Heydrich." Henri had read of the Czech operatives of the SOE who had parachuted into Czechoslovakia. They shot Heydrich, and thought they had killed him, though in fact he died of blood poisoning from his wounds.

Heydrich might have become Hitler's successor, a blonde, ruthless sociopath, SS commander, the 'protector' of Bohemia and Moravia and the perfect Nazi. Henri would like nothing better than to be given such an assignment, even though he knew all the men who went to Prague died, all except one traitor who gave his friends away.

But Henri knew he wasn't going to central Europe. All this flashed through his mind as he waited for the brigadier or the pipe smoker to speak. The brigadier kept talking.

"We've had other successes, though Heydrich is perhaps best known. We don't really like people to know who we are, or that we even exist," and he reached into a drawer and pulled out a folder.

"What we want you for is something similar. But we don't want you to go after one man, but many. We need trained officers such as you to lead men in skirmishes in France. One day there will be an invasion. We need trains blown up, phone lines down. And we need dead Germans. Every dead German is one less to point his weapon at a British, or Canadian, soldier. We also need information."

Henri sat in his chair. He seemed to have passed the audition. But he kept quiet until he was asked a question.

"SOE is not really the army, you know," said the brigadier. "Thus my civilian friend over here. No, SOE reports to civilians. You'll keep your rank, of course, but you won't wear a uniform. Oh, I forgot to ask, are you on for this sort of thing?"

"Yes, sir. For me, it's a great honour." His English became a bit formal again. He spoke only French until he was about eight years old. The Gallic sentence structure slipped in with the excitement.

"Good. I liked what you said about phones and radios. We'll need a lot of that." The brigadier paused. "The odds of you making it through this alive are about even. It's a dangerous business. No one will think you a coward if you want to back down. You don't have to answer now."

"My decision would never change," said Henri, cursing himself inside for interrupting.

The brigadier stood up and so did Henri. The man in the suit put down his pipe. The brigadier saluted, Henri saluted back.

"Fine then. They'll deal with you outside. Good luck Captain Foix."

Henri never did get their names.

The paperwork didn't take long, surprising for a government-run operation. They gave him train tickets to Scotland. He wouldn't even have to return to his base. They didn't want him speaking with anyone, or having anyone guess where he was going. He was just gone.

"This is all secret of course," said the stern lady in an office a few rooms down from the brigadier. She looked at him and said in a matter-of-fact way. "Tell anyone what you're doing and you'll be hanged, shot if you're lucky."

He didn't register any emotion.

"There's a car waiting for you outside. You have four days to get to Scotland. Now we've lost your minder. There are too many of you to deal with this week. So don't say goodbye to anyone, just get there. There's some money in here, as well. You'll be met at the train station, no matter what train you arrive on. They'll know who you are."

She looked down at her desk, which he took as a signal to leave. A porter opened the door of the house and the driver was standing by the back door of the car. He looked at her legs, which had some shape even in those shoes. And the uniform couldn't hide her figure, the waist and the round-ness it promised. She opened the door and he got in.

"Hello again," he said smiling at her. Well they did say he had four days.

Henri watched her walk away as she went down the hall to make some tea. Her soft curves clinging to her thin cotton nightgown, something she had brought over with her. He only knew her first name and she knew only his code name, Pierre, from a remark the minder made in the car. They hadn't talked much, but he liked her, though it was doubtful he would ever see her again. Celibacy was over, for a while anyway.

Later she would pick up the car and take him the rest of the way to King's Cross Station.

4

Carlyle Square, London, 1986

There wasn't much space for Cowboy Rhett. Someone had shot Olof Palme, the Swedish Prime Minister. With the picture he would take up two thirds of the page. Earlier at the newspaper, Jack had listened to the talk about Palme from the next desk. The English, or at least the type of Englishmen who read this paper, despised Palme. The obit would have to take a hard line; there would even be some mention of his wife's efforts at social engineering.

There were rules about the new obituary: don't lionize the dead; never mention how they died, unless it's part of the story; there are no brave battles with cancer, no soppy quotes from the family; and if the dead man, or woman, was a shit, say so.

For the obit editor, Olof Palme was a shit, the worst type of sanctimonious European politician. And a socialist to boot. Just last fall a writer in *The Spectator* had done a hatchet job on Mr. and Mrs. Palme. Now that same writer would be given the commission to write the obit.

The real secret of the new newspaper obit was it must never read like a newspaper story, but more like an essay or even a short story. There were few newspapermen who could knock them off; most were too stuck in their old ways. Fact, quote, fact, quote, piled in one paragraph after another, and all built on the inverted pyramid where the whole story is in the first paragraph and each succeeding paragraph has less information. Easy to chop from the bottom.

And sentiment. All dead people were good. Jack thought often that Shakespeare was wrong. In Mark Antony's obit for Julius Caesar, he said the evil that men do lives after them, the good is oft interred with their bones. Well not in the average American or Canadian newspaper. Everyone is a great guy - once he's dead.

As Jack made himself a cup of tea in his flat, he laughed to himself. He remembered an obit from a small town south of Montreal. There was an oddball English immigrant who ran a pub there. There were a lot of phoney pubs in the city, but an hour outside town, near the American border was a bar that seemed like the real thing. Even the sign was genuine. But the best part was a small room where people just drank at the bar; the restaurant, such as it was, was in a bigger room through the door.

Fred, that was the Englishman's name. He sat behind his ersatz saloon bar pulling one Labatt 50 after another out of the fridge. He smoked Buckingham plain-end cigarettes non-stop. The man never moved from his chair from opening to closing, his smiling face covered in red lines so tight they looked like an ordinance map of County Durham, which was where he was from.

One day Fred dropped dead.

"Fred Cooke's death came as a surprise to all who knew him," said the story on the front page of the *Huntingdon Gleaner*. A sentimental lie. If anyone looked ready to die, it was Fred Cooke. It was the worst thing you could do in an obit, tell a sentimental lie.

Jack might have had some fun with Fred Cooke's death. He must have been in the war. He would have had to find someone who knew him, since his wife never seemed to know much about him. She was wife number two, maybe even number three, young and Canadian. But there must have been a story about how a drunken Englishman managed to end up running a bar a couple of miles north of the border with New York State.

The hardest obits were the ones of people who weren't famous. With Fred Cooke you would never have to mention how he died, just how he lived. That would give them the picture. Details of his early life might have been hard to find. This morning Jack's job was easy. He only had to fill a 650-word space. He won the fight to use a picture of Cowboy standing beside his B-17. It was the one everyone would use, with the pilot's head right beside the decal at the front of the plane, almost nestled by the big tits of Daisy Mae, the sexy blonde hillbilly wife of Li'L Abner, the comic strip hero.

Cowboy Rhett, who has died at the age of 66, was an American baseball pitcher and then television commentator who flew B-17s during the war out of airfields in Norfolk and the Midlands as well as Italy. During the war he was well known to newsreel watchers in this country for starring in the U.S. Army Air Force baseball league, a game that few Englishmen ever understood.

Captain Rhett was the pilot of a B-17 on the night of April 15, 1944 when the Americans made one of their longest-range penetrations into German-occupied Europe. The B-17s of the 15th U.S. Army Air Force flew 1,200 miles from a field in Italy to make a bombing run on the Romanian oil fields at Ploesti. The raid was aimed at denying fuel to German divisions then in retreat along the Eastern Front.

Casualties along the route were high and Rhett recalled one of the B-17s in his formation exploding beside him when it was hit with flak, chunks of metal fired at high-flying bombers. The tail gunner of Rhett's plane, the Daisy Mae, was lost in heavy action against German fighters.

The losses would have been higher, but the American bombers were by then covered on long trips by the P-51 Mustang which, with its drop tanks, almost matched the range of the bombers and was more than a match for the ageing Messerschmitts in use in that theatre of the war.

American and British attacks on oil targets had reduced the Luftwaffe's fuel supply to 10,000 tons a month by September of 1944. The Germans needed 160,000 tons a month. Floyd Rhett flew 25 missions in the Daisy Mae and left combat in January of 1945.

After his tour of duty the Americans used Rhett for propaganda. He gave speeches to raise money for war bonds. Audiences knew him from baseball and now they could see the ribbon of his Air Force Star on his chest.

After the war his baseball career lasted only another two seasons. In the fall of 1947 his team played in the World Series and Rhett pitched a one hitter, where the other team only managed to make it to the bases once. His team won the game, but lost the series.

Floyd Polk Rhett was born on August 19, 1914, in Wheeling, West Virginia, the son of a local radio station owner. On his mother's side he was descended from James Polk, the American President. He never liked the name Floyd, or Polk for that matter, and concocted the nickname Cowboy, though West Virginia is a state better known for coal and hillbillies than heifers and steers.

Not much of a scholar, young Floyd was a hotshot baseball player. Before he finished high school he left to play in a minor league team in Indiana. After two years he was called up to the major league, the equivalent of football's First Division. He was a major figure in American sport until he joined the U.S. Army in 1943.

Floyd Rhett was a rich man in the 1930s, from baseball and his father's growing business. He owned and flew a Beech stagger-wing, a high performance four-seater biplane that got him to most cities well ahead of the rest of the ball team. He was flying a B-17 out of England before the end of 1943. Later that year he moved to Italy.

A few years after the end of his baseball career he was named to the Hall of Fame. He also became a radio announcer at one of his father's stations. It was more than nepotism. He had a way of massacring the English language while being crystal clear to his baseball audience. English teachers wrote letters asking that he be fired, but he remained on air until 1981.

Floyd Rhett married four times, the third a dancer whom he divorced the morning after the wedding night. He had one son *from his first marriage.*

A little more than 650 words. They might have to cut a
bit, but Cowboy Rhett was dead and buried. Jack fiddled with
the dip switches on his modem and logged into the paper's
computer. Off went the file into the ATEX system. He was
one of the few reporters who had mastered the art of filing by
phone.

Five minutes later Jack's phone rang.

"Got your story. Clever you Americans with your technology," said Langton. "By the way. Something came up on
your SOE man. Seems there are a few Germans who don't
like him. Take your time. This might be better than we
thought."

5

Inside, the station seemed shrouded in fog. Some of it was a grit-filled mist rolling across the open platform, but most of it was steam, hissing from the hoses that ran all the systems in the passenger cars. More steam and smoke from the big coal-fired locomotives added to it, and particles of soot hung in the soggy air.

Henri looked at the trains lined up across the station. He thought it looked like a scene from a movie. He remembered its name, The 39 Steps. He had seen it in Montreal just before the war. "How far is it from Winnipeg to Montreal?" the hero of the movie had asked Mister Memory on the stage.

There was the desperate woman he took home. The hero slept on the couch. The woman had a sleepy European accent and she was murdered in the man's apartment. Henri loved the movie. Later the hero, a Canadian in the movie version, took the Flying Scotsman north to dodge the police.

Now The Flying Scotsman was taking Henri north to another training camp, to learn more of the arts of war. He already knew how to kill, the Americans had taught him that at the commando camp in Montana. And the Canadian Army had trained him to obey orders and make soldiers obey his. Henri figured the British were going to show him how to run a network of agents, and if the brigadier's hint was right, an armed force of guerrillas.

The Underground, the Maquis. He couldn't wait to get to France. As he looked out the window he thought about his father who had been in France in 1916. A young officer, wounded in August during the late stages of the Battle of the Somme. This would be different, thought Henri, no trenches, no mud.

Henri was like his father, taut and slender and intense. Neither ever showed much emotion, though they were not morose and enjoyed a drink. There had been some pressure for Henri to study law, like his father who was by now a judge. There were frowns of disapproval when he took science at university.

The war worried his friends from school and university. Some of them demonstrated against it, many refused to serve overseas. Henri found the idea of war exciting. The last several months had been filled with adventure as he learned the finer points of killing, first in Canada then in the United States.

But this morning things were more mundane. With no minder along he had to remember to be quiet, though he wasn't that gregarious even after a drink or two. He looked innocent enough and had the smile of a boy, which helped. Henri found it easy to be secretive; he was a private man and in his way quite tough.

The trip from King's Cross to Edinburgh took eight hours on a good day. He remembered the Flying Scotsman from books he had read as a boy. For some reason he knew it was the longest non-stop train in the world, with enough coal and water to produce steam for almost four hundred miles.

But today the trip to Scotland would take more time. Ammunition trains rushing to supply the ships of the Royal Navy at Scapa Flow or bombers in the Midlands would shunt the Flying Scotsman aside. The naval officer sitting opposite him told his children it might take as much as sixteen hours. Henri didn't mind. It would give him an excuse for being a bit late. And he loved trains ever since he used to listen to them at night or count freight cars as they passed by his family's country house south of Montreal. That was near the main line that ran through Quebec and then into the dense backwoods of the state of Maine on its way to the Atlantic coast.

The sign on the window said first class, but the heat in the car was third class. The English children complained to their mother. Not much of a hardship for Henri. It seemed cold, but his greatcoat would keep some of the damp away.

And he was used to cold. He'd been a skier from an early age and just walking five blocks in a Montreal winter was harsher than this. Still he was amazed at how the wetness in the air made it seem colder than it was.

British trains were different from those at home. Here he was in a carriage with six seats, five of them full. He sat across from the navy man, a plumpish man with salt and pepper hair who looked as if he might be a bank manager in another life. His wife was quite pretty, with auburn hair piled high on her head as well hanging in a pageboy at the side.

The daughter, a bookish-looking thirteen, sat beside them. There was an empty seat between Henri and their son who he guessed was about nine or ten. The boy never stopped fidgeting and talking, but Henri smiled and took no notice. He had younger brothers and could read or sleep though any commotion.

He did notice the officer looking at him in a strange way. Henri wondered why until he realized he was out of uniform. Even the greatcoat he wore was a civilian number, not the khaki one he had been issued at home.

Good training, thought Henri. Maybe he thinks I'm a coward. Or a spy. I'll see if I can carry it off. The easy thing would be to hint at what he was doing or even make up a story about his military life. Instead he smiled. The train gave a shudder as the giant green locomotive strained to move the carriages from a standing start in the station.

Henri laughed to himself. He would really surprise them when he spoke; they would never guess his accent. He pulled a novel from his bag and started to read. It struck him that the novel was a rather absurd giveaway. *Sick Heart River*, by

John Buchan, who had been Governor-General of Canada. Unlike Buchan's *The 39 Steps*, it was set in Canada, in the far north. He noticed the man across from him was doing the cryptic puzzle from *The Times*. Henri stared at the pages and thought to himself, if this naval man has any brains he should be able to figure it out.

The book had been on the table beside the bed this morning and the blonde driver had lent it to him. It might have been a way of making sure he came back when he was in London. He had memorized her address and would post the book to her from Scotland.

Now he looked inside on the title page and saw her name. To darling Jane, Happy Christmas, 1942. Jane. Rather an ordinary name for such a beautiful woman. Odd, but they hadn't spoken much, just the gibberish of passion and not much else.

He leaned his head back and looked out the window at the smoke-blackened cottages beside the railway line. Henri thought of how he and his friends used to laugh about the coldness of English women, the ones at home that is. He smiled at how wrong they'd been. Then he shook his head, to blot out the daydreaming, and started reading again.

But Henri read only about ten pages, and then closed his eyes, leaning against the window side of his seat and then falling asleep, the book dropping into his lap.

"Funny sort of book," said the naval officer when Henri's eyes reopened after what seemed to him a few minutes later but was, in fact, half an hour.

"*Pardon*," said Henri, not yet awake enough to answer in English. The naval officer gave a slight smile, seeming happy to elicit a piece to the puzzle from his travelling companion. *Pardon*, indeed.

"Your book. It seems an odd type of book for a foreign gentleman to be reading?"

What little flesh there was on the side of Henri Foix's face wrinkled as he ground his teeth. He suppressed a glare when he saw the subtle smile on the naval officer's smug face. A commander, thought Henri reading his rank from the stripes at his wrist. Equal to a lieutenant colonel. Of course

Henri was in civilian clothes and headed north to some of the most secret places on this little island.

Again Henri tried to disguise his accent, giving it a French ring, though only an English-Canadian, or someone who had lived in French Canada, could tell the difference between him and a Frenchman from France, even when speaking English.

"Yes, a friend lent it to me in London. Interesting. About the wide open spaces in Canada."

Henri looked out the window. There were no more towns now, and the fields were all tilled for next spring or still covered in crops. What was green was speckled white with the remains of last night's frost. He hoped there was snow farther north, for some reason he was feeling a bit homesick.

"Have you been there?" asked the Commander.

Henri turned from the window and gave his quizzical little boy look. "Where?"

"Canada?"

Now was the time to play games, thought Henri.

"Only in books. I love stories about the open spaces. People hunting caribou like our ancestors did thousands of years ago. What about you?" said Henri turning the tables? "Have your travels ever taken you overseas?"

Expand the question and force the busybody sitting opposite to reveal a little of himself.

"Yes. I was based in Halifax for a couple of years. Helping build up the Royal Canadian Navy for the war. Big job, you know. They started with almost nothing."

Henri gave a tight smile, as if to say, I don't know what you're talking about. He thought to himself, this man is mad or a liar. He was giving Henri far too much information and on one of the most sensitive areas of the war, the place where the convoys start. Could he spot Henri's accent? He'd have to be really good since there were few French-Canadians in the navy and almost no French-Canadian officers. Men of his class, who spoke almost perfect English, went into the army, or politics.

"Where is Halifax?"

Henri wanted to see how far he could take the man. In Canada it was a crime to mention the name Halifax. It was always referred to as 'an unnamed eastern Canadian port.' The naval man must know that. "Is it an important place?"

The commander was trapped into talking but adjusted in his chair. Maybe he knew he'd said too much. His probe had bounced back at him.

"Well, yes. Main port on Canada's east coast. In Nova Scotia. Damn fine harbour. Natural harbour, you can see why people went there."

Henri felt he had his man on the run. "How do they use it in the war?"

Now the commander's son was staring across at his father, beaming with pride that he knew so much about the war. Henri smiled, as he knew the boy was forcing his father's hand.

"Well, it's all quite hush-hush. But it's no secret many of our convoys leave from there. The city's full to the brim. Population doubled with all the sailors, soldiers and airmen there."

"Airmen?" said a surprised Henri. He put a marker in his book so he could listen to the naval man. "Why would they need airmen in a seaport?"

Now the commander knew he had gone too far. He bristled as if he thought this Frenchman was badgering him, which he was.

"Yes, why daddy? Why do they need planes in a sea battle?"

The wife, oblivious to the tension in the small car, reached over and patted her son on the head. What a clever boy to ask such a question. She looked over to her husband and a raised eyebrow shot over the unspoken command, 'Well, tell him.'

"Well I mean, submarines. They have planes escorting the convoys out into the Atlantic. And then there are planes that search for submarines. Hudson bombers and Catalinas. Tough work, twelve hours in a plane over that rough sea. Catch a few Gerries too."

The train slowed now, just outside York. The Flying Scotsman had its wings clipped by another ammunition train. The naval officer got up and smiled and walked down the corridor. Henri smiled and nodded at the boy and his mother and went back to his book.

After twenty minutes the train jerked back to life, the clouds of steam and smoke rolling past the window. The naval officer came back to his seat five minutes after the train restarted. Henri looked up just enough to see the commander motion to his wife not to talk.

Henri knew what he'd been up to. The naval man thought he was a spy and was getting off a message while the train was in the siding. He was in for a shock when they arrived in Edinburgh.

It was just past seven in the evening when the Flying Scotsman pulled into Waverley Station in Edinburgh. The two children were shivering in the car. The commander and his wife sat next to each other for warmth. The girl had changed places with her brother a couple of times but was now snuggled deep in the folds of her mother's fur coat.

On the platform, a lot of men in uniform, official dress and the unspoken uniform of the men in the secrets business. They were so obvious they might as well wear caps and badges, thought Henri. One of them would be his new minder. As the train came to a stop, the commander pushed down the window in the car and reached outside to open the door. From several yards away the group of men moved forward, two of them military policemen. The commander gave Henri an evil glare and smiled the smile that said 'I have you now, you little frog.'

Henri closed his book, picked up his case and waited for the family to move outside. A man who was straight from intelligence central casting came over to the commander. The two soldiers stayed a few paces behind.

"There's your man," said the commander. "The one I wired you about. Asking the most dangerous questions."

Henri surprised the commander. Instead of running away he walked straight over to the group. Henri nodded at another man, and said something in his ear. He looked over at the other intelligence officer and nodded to the soldiers.

The commander thought he had him when in an instant he was grabbed by both arms, a soldier on each side. Henri's minder whispered something to the other intelligence man.

"You'll come with us, sir."

"But that Frenchman?"

"I think you've done enough talking already, sir. Please be quiet." He looked over at his wife. "Your husband will be back with you tomorrow madam. Please go to your rooms." When the commander looked up, he could just see Henri disappearing into the mist and smoke. It reminded him of the weather at an unnamed port in Eastern Canada.

6

The French girl would have to wait. Jack jumped on the tube and rumbled off to Oxford Circus. When he came up the stairs to the street, he stopped and looked around. Some of the time he had to see the church to know which way to start walking. He could still get lost in London and the streets around Oxford Circus were too crowded for him.

People filled the sidewalk most hours of the day, and now they jammed what the English called the pavement, from the curb to the store windows, moving like a train of ants. There was no way to move out of the herd without ducking down a side street. It was a strange feeling for someone who grew up in an empty space, or what was empty compared to this.

Beside the church was the old BBC building. There was a legend in the radio business that during the Blitz a bomb had gone in one window, slid across the floor, straight by a studio and out the other wall without blowing up. The announcer, dressed in a dinner jacket, never stopped reading the news. Jack didn't know if it was true, but it came up every month or so in the pubs around here. There were two businesses in this district - the rag trade and the talk trade.

Jack was in talking. He did some stringing for Canadian radio and the occasional voice-over for TV News, on a week-

37

end when no one else was around. It had nothing to do with his newspaper work. Although he told some people about his two jobs, he found it was better to keep things separate. It was a trade where people were jealous of the extra money or the status of the extra work.

Then there was the politics. The newspaper was right wing, as was Jack, and the network left wing. The radio and TV people mocked the paper, some thought it was down-right evil. If they all knew he worked for it they would con-coct bullshit ethical reasons why having two jobs was a con-flict.

For a hustler like Jack, it was easier stringing on the European side of the Atlantic. There was less political nonsense, at least for a Canadian freelancer. And being five hours ahead of Toronto and New York gave him a real edge. When the desk was just getting into work, around noon or one o'clock London time, the likes of Jack had already read two or three of the best newspapers in the world and had listened to the BBC, where radio had everything a reporter needed to know. British Television was still in the Stone Age.

Today Margaret Thatcher had spanked one of her ministers in public and Jack would have to relate it all to the Canadian public. They might not care, though he thought he could make it amusing. Maybe he'd even use the word spank.

Michelle was the tall English girl with the French name who did research for radio. She had striking blue eyes, though her lids were droopy and she always looked as if she had just woken up or was just about to go to bed. She liked Jack and he her, but they had never done anything about it. Michelle made Jack's radio life a snap.

A few hours ago she had called the desk in Canada suggesting the story. Now she had a sound clip of Margaret Thatcher from the House of Commons and a bit from the naughty schoolboy the Iron Lady had just ruined, all pulled from the BBC news. Jack just had to fill in the blanks.

Writing the script took him ten minutes. Michelle had even typed out transcripts of the clips he had to read into. A hundred dollars Canadian, or about seventy pounds. Enough for Saturday night at The Bear at Woodstock. He'd already made his choice from *The Dirty Weekend Handbook*. Jack laughed to himself as he waited for the studio technician to come back from the pub across the street. If only Maggie Thatcher knew what she was financing.

It was still only 5:30. The streets would be crowded and the tube a crush of sweating bodies. As he thought of sweating bodies, he looked across at Michelle who was bending over, packing a case of tapes.

"Want to got out for a drink?" asked Jack. "I need to brush up on local gossip."

"Sure," said Michelle, smiling back over her shoulder and catching Jack staring at her round ass. "Give me ten minutes until I pack these. Why don't I meet you across the road?"

"Right," and he shot her a smile mixed with a short laugh, as if to say 'guilty' for his leer. She smiled back. Jack went to the phone in the lobby and called Claire. It was Wednesday and he'd want to sleep with her at least once before the weekend.

"What are you up to," asked Jack.

"I want to play tennis," she answered.

"Is that *pension tennis* or *tension penis?*" asked Jack, making a French play on words that she had taught him.

"*Pension* first, *tension* later," teased Claire.

They agreed to meet at nine o'clock in a wine bar in Holland Park, near where she lived. He knew he had lots of time since she was always late.

He hung up the phone and walked across the street to another wine bar and he thought about how different this one was from the one he would be at in a few hours in Holland Park. There the crowd would be middle class and, to use a local phrase, very English. Here, a block or two in from Oxford Circus, it was a real mélange.

This place was full of men from the rag trade in their modern, well-cut clothes. They were as brash as the stunning women they sat with. Jack had a thing about Jewish women; he found them sexy, though he always thought they found him rather boring.

And speaking of boring, there they were. Sitting at the bar, power drinking, four Australians, all from the television news agency around the corner. If Jack had a prejudice, it was Australians. For some reason they got up his nose. An entire country of people trying to be cute with phrases such as 'I'm up to my tits.' All happiness up front, but shifty in the corners.

Jack sat down beside an American stringer, someone who made a living writing for a paper in Kentucky and filing for a couple of radio stations. It wasn't much of a living so Jack bought him a beer.

"I've scraped together enough money for a trip to Ireland," said Homer Lamont, a man with a million dollar name and an empty bank account. Homer was white and pasty, a bit overweight but handsome enough in spite of it all. He had a voice that was even deeper than Jack's and a civilized way of speaking that hinted he might not always have been this broke.

Every country has its myths. The American myth about themselves was they thought only the British had a class system, but Homer was a down-on-his-luck preppy American, though he tried to hide it.

"The paper is paying for the ticket and the radio stations are picking up the hotels and per diems. I might even sell something to your network." Then Homer realized Jack might not want him on his turf, so he started to backpedal. "It's a radio feature. You don't mind do you?"

This guy was so polite Jack couldn't help but like him. Why should he mind? Jack hated radio features. Too much work for too little money. More efficient to just do radio news hits.

"No, I don't care Homer, really. I hate features. Sitting there with a razor blade cutting tape. It's demeaning. I'll stick to death and news." Jack meant that as a bit of a joke, but Homer didn't get it, or ignored it.

"Not much travel in death, though," mused Homer.

While he never name-dropped, like many freelancers working in London, Homer was a place snob. Getting an assignment to an exotic place was better than making tons of money. Homer was into city dropping. Beirut, Athens, Prague and Gdansk. All those names might make it into just one conversation.

"Hell, if you're going to be over here you might as well get around," Homer once told Jack. "It's all so close." Like many Americans, and Canadians, he liked living here but it was almost certain he would die at home.

Travel, other than for pleasure, was not for Jack. He had worked out the most efficient way to make the most cash. And as far as he could see, wars were inefficient and dangerous.

"Well you know Homer, I don't do wars. But even the death business travels. I have to go to France soon. The World War Two guys are all starting to die now and I want a look at the beaches and some of the battlefields. No rush, though. And no desk screaming for deadlines."

Homer was an old draft dodger or, to be more accurate, a deserter from the Vietnam War, though he was allowed to go home now. He covered wars for money, though he hated them in principle. And he thought Devlin glorified war, or at least warriors, in his obituaries. But Homer was too sober to argue and even when he did he never became nasty. Too civilized.

"Don't you do anyone besides World War Two veterans?" asked Homer.

"Sure," said Jack. "When anyone from the First War dies they're almost guaranteed a spot, if only for longevity."

This time they both laughed and Michelle came in. Jack knew she wouldn't want to talk to Homer, since he was so desperate for cash he would try to slip in a pitch for his Irish features or some other project he was working on. Jack ordered a gin and tonic for her, paid for another round and made his excuses to Homer as he and Michelle headed for a table.

"He drives me crazy," said Michelle. "I like him, and he's such a nice man, but he's always on the game. Pick, pick, pick. Always an angle."

Jack, who'd been through similar periods in his own life, felt sorry for Homer.

"I guess it's just because he's so broke. Those strings of his are so cheap, it's amazing he can live. Thank God he's a vegetarian. That must make life cheaper," said Jack.

Michelle laughed. "I'm not so sure. Have you ever been to any of those organic places? A head of so-called pure lettuce costs three times what you pay for the regular stuff at Waitrose. The booze and the brown-rice diet are probably bankrupting him."

Enough of Homer. Jack decided to change the subject. He knew Michelle from work, but they had only been out together a couple of times before. As she looked away he gave her the once over. In the old days he would have tried to get her into bed tonight. But he was smarter now. He knew it would just complicate his life. Still, he'd like to try. Maybe just flirt to the brink.

"Where do you live?" asked Jack, London real estate always being a safe topic.

Turned out she lived in Camden Town, the poor man's Hampstead. Owned her own house, since the Canadian network had been overpaying her for years.

"It's small, just two bedrooms and a sitting room but it has a big kitchen. Do you still have that place in Chelsea?" Jack thought, strange what people remember. She would have known it from packages she'd sent round by motorcycle courier. Still, he thought, women seem to have a dossier on every man who comes in the office. He was sure she'd know about the French girl. Nothing seemed secret.

"Yeah, but who knows for how long. My landlord is a little tricky. I'd buy a flat, but who can afford it?"

The conversation drifted until it came to obits, which she knew he wrote, and then to the war. Unlike most women he knew, she didn't think writing obits was morbid. And she liked talking about the war, and what her father did in it. He had been in bombers.

"There are a lot of clippings my mother kept. I learned he flew Halifaxes and completed thirty missions by the start of 1943. Most of the early flights were over the Ruhr, not too far, but then they went on the thousand bomber raids, to Hamburg and even Berlin. When I got him to talk about it he told me the horror of being trapped in the searchlights. He saw planes blown from the sky. His plane was hit more than once, but they always managed to make it back."

This guy would make a great obit, though Jack wouldn't be allowed to get his mitts on him. There was an obit specialist for Bomber Command, someone who had flown Lancasters, and Jack was only allowed the Canadians and Americans. Even those could be snatched away if they had a DFC with bar.

"Didn't he ever run into night fighters?" asked Jack.

Michelle gave Jack a flirtatious look and waved her empty glass at him, rattling the ice in the bottom.

"Any more obit material will cost you another drink," smiled Michelle. Jack almost blushed and with a weak smile grabbed her glass and decided to switch to gin himself.

"Two doubles," he said to the barman. A single shot wasn't worth much in England, one sixth of a gill, whatever that was. Two sixths of a gill was more like it.

After settling back in, Jack took up her father's story. "So he did one tour of duty and then stayed on?"

"You've been watching too many American movies," said Michelle, not in a mean way. "British aircrews almost always stayed on. It's why Bomber Command had the highest death rates. My father took another job though. He switched to dropping spies instead of bombs."

"Spies?"

"Poland one night, France the next. He missed the biggest drop of all, when they sent those poor Czech SOE agents to assassinate Heydrich."

Jack interrupted. "You mean the guy who planned the Final Solution?"

"The very one. They managed to get Heydrich in Prague. But they were all killed, or committed suicide. Except for one Judas who was hanged after the war."

"Sorry to be so dumb, but what's SOE?" asked Jack. Though he had some idea, he wasn't sure.

"Special Operations Executive. Weird group. They didn't even come under the military. They were part of some bizarre economics ministry. It was Churchill's idea, apparently. Take the war to Europe. I'm not sure how much of a success it was. A lot of people tortured and sent to camps or just shot."

"What's a nice girl like you doing knowing so much about spies?"

Michelle raised one eyebrow. "Clever boy. One of my best friends growing up, her father was in it. And he talked more than they usually do. When we were 18 or 19 it seemed so glamorous. He would stay up and tell us stories at night. A wonderful man. Died last year."

Jack took a sip of his drink and stared at Michelle, who was looking off into the distance. A walking encyclopaedia.

She looked back at him. "There were even some Canadians. Most of them French I think, but a few English-Canadians and some Chinese Canadian agents who were used against the Japanese."

"How do you know all the Canadian stuff?" asked Jack.

"I'm reading a book on it. A history of the SOE by a man who was in it. It's a freebie review copy that floated into the office. I'll lend it to you when I'm finished, if you like?"

Jack grunted a yes and then went back to questions. Maybe reading about spies was her father's idea. "Your father wasn't a spy, though?"

"No he just dropped them into Europe. Everything left from some secret airfield in the Midlands. All bombers and some Lysanders, little planes that look like a Cessna. I have even more books on this stuff. You can borrow them too if you like. You can even have them tonight. It'll cost you though."

Forward girl, thought Jack. This is taking it to the brink. "What?"

"One more gin and tonic and a cab ride home." She stared at him and smiled. "And don't get any ideas. I saw you staring at my bottom earlier. You are a very rude man."

In the old days Jack would have poured on the charm, and the booze, in an effort for a conquest. Closing in on 40 he was a bit smarter. Sex with Michelle would be a disaster.

The first night would be great, but then he'd be expected to be back for more. She would find out about Claire, if she didn't know already, and pressure him to dump her. If he didn't it could hurt his freelance work at the network. Altogether a crummy bet. Flirt, but don't touch, for now.

Back at the bar Homer was finishing another pint. Not much the worse for wear. He had an amazing capacity for beer. Jack thought it must be all the lentils and rice soaking up the alcohol. Homer was chatting up a redhead who was half drunk. Not a vegetarian on the sex front.

The bar was crowded now and it was hard to push through without spilling things.

"Are they on bombers or the SOE?" asked Jack as he put down two more double-gin-and-tonics.

"What?"

"The books. Are the books you're going to lend me on bombers or the SOE?"

Michelle laughed. "Lateral thinking Jack. You can't assume people know what you're talking about just because you've finished the first part in your head. I only have one on the SOE, the one I told you about. I'm not finished it yet. But I have three or four on bombers. Maybe more."

"I just finished an obit on a bomber pilot. An American. He flew B-17s."

Claire interrupted. "My father goes crazy when he hears about B-17s."

"Don't tell me," said Jack. "He thinks they're overrated. All American propaganda. Low bomb load. The only thing they had going for them was sheer numbers."

Michelle looked a bit shocked, then laughed. "That's exactly what he says. Almost word for word. How did you know?"

"I spent yesterday afternoon with an old RAF man. Fighters, not bombers, but he knew enough. Too bad I didn't know about your father, I could have used some more detail."

The war talk stretched on for another drink, a final. Jack guessed Michelle was an only child, or that she had no brothers, which was why she knew so much about her father's war record. Right on the second guess, she had one younger sister.

"Where did the fighter pilot live?" asked Michelle.

"North Weald."

"That's on the tube. End of the Central Line, isn't?"

"How'd you know that?" asked Jack.

"Stand in front of the tube map long enough and everything registers. I've never been to Cockfosters either, but who could forget it." They both laughed. "And I haven't forgotten you promised me a cab ride home."

So it was a cab ride to Islington, half pissed, well maybe just a quarter, and then the same cab to Holland Park for an attempt to mount Claire, though Jack thought that should be an easy climb. Michelle talked about the book on the SOE, though as he was to learn many people dispensed with the article and talked of plain SOE.

At Michelle's door it had been a kiss on the cheek from him, returned with a close-mouthed kiss on the lips from her. That had him thinking. As he waited she ran inside and came back with a kind of spotter's book on bombers, a little thing filled with pictures and statistics of British, American and German planes along with a few Russian and Italian.

"Just a sampler." And she closed the door.

As he headed off to Holland Park he thought, thank God it was a mini-cab; a regular black cab all this distance would have bankrupted him. Back home it would have been tax deductible, but he hadn't got around to paying tax in England so he never bothered with receipts.

But the cab ride paid for itself. The driver had the news on. There was a flash about the death of a B-29 pilot. Jack didn't catch his name but he was one of the men on the atomic bomb raids on Japan. He also heard he was in one of two planes that dropped bombs on Hiroshima or Nagasaki. Jack looked at his watch, 8:30 GMT, so it was 3:30 in Toronto. Enough time to file an obit on the guy by tomorrow.

He'd have to rush with Claire.

For once she was on time, even early and they bumped into each other as his cab pulled up. The wine bar was another world from the one he'd left and he wanted to leave this one as soon as he could. He ordered white wine for Claire and an orange juice and soda. No more booze. He was going to need some stamina, both for Claire and for work.

She kissed him on the side of his face when he sat down then from the next chair threw her legs over his lap and started talking.

"That woman at work is driving me crazy." Claire was always *en colère* with the Iranians who ran her swish jewellery shop. Good expression, *en colère*, thought Jack as he watched Claire's white face redden with anger while she spoke of the people she worked for.

"That woman is such a peasant. If they didn't have me there, no one would ever buy any of that overpriced rubbish." Claire was always called down from the office to model jewellery for rich customers. On her, anything looked good. And she told him she spent at least one morning a week on the phone with a drunken woman from California who called in the middle of her night to buy jewellery. "Next week I'm going to tell that lunatic from California to save her money." Good news thought Jack. When Claire was this emotional she liked to burn off her anger with sex. I can be home in two hours. Sure enough. After another glass of wine she suggested they leave. Her house, the one she shared with another woman, was down at the end of the road.

The other woman in the house was already upstairs with her married lover. Jack and Claire slipped into the room on the ground floor, the one with the television. Right on cue, she turned rather passionate. They kissed standing up and then she gave a little signal, turning sideways and almost purring. She bit at his ear. He knew what it meant.

Claire moved over to the couch and lay on her stomach. Jack pulled up her skirt and massaged her, while taking off all his clothes. She moaned and lifted her round cheeks in the air to make it easier to slip into her. Some nights she loved it this way and Jack wasn't going to complain.

Jack kept one eye on the clock in the VCR. He didn't want to rush things but he knew he had some work to do. He gave her a few sharp slaps on her ass and she thrust her hand between her legs and made herself come. After five minutes it was over. Claire seemed happy, so he wouldn't fuss. After a little kissing, he threw his clothes on, leaving some buttons undone and stuffed his tie in his pocket. He went up to bed with her and then kissed her goodbye, saying he had some radio work to do in the morning.

It was an excuse for not staying the night. If she knew he was rushing off to do an obit she might not have spoken to him for a week. She thought it morbid to write about the dead.

7

A SOUTHBOUND TRAIN,
SOMEWHERE IN THE SCOTTISH HIGHLANDS

There were so many different ways to kill people. Henri wondered if the Americans or the English were better at it. The Americans were tough, and their drill sergeants knew the theory of death. But Henri thought the English were meaner. They were like ratting terriers cornered in their little part of Europe and now they could feel they were about to win. They weren't going to give the Germans any quarter.

Wire garrottes, balanced throwing knifes, even makeshift ice picks. In a pinch you could make a weapon out of anything. Noses could be broken and cartilage pushed into the brain. Knees and ankles smashed with a club or a boot if you needed a moment's advantage.

But Henri had spoken to men who had fought the Germans in France and North Africa. Frenchmen, Englishmen and Scots. And he learned how the Americans underestimated the Afrika Corps when they first came up against them in Tunisia. He did not plan to make the same mistake. He didn't hate the Germans yet, but he did know they were the enemy and he knew they were magnificent soldiers.

At camp in Scotland Henri learned it was the German soldiers he had to kill, but it was the Gestapo who were out to capture him, torture him, send him to a camp and then have the SS think of some terrible way for him to die. The garrotte. Maybe just starvation and constant work. He stared out the window and looked at the snow and promised himself he would die rather than be captured.

"There's someone out to supplement his rations," said the minder pointing out the window at an old man fishing in a fast flowing river, not even lifting his head to look at the passing train. "A fat salmon. And venison too, I'll wager. He's eating better than we are."

It was the same minder who had travelled with him in the Buick back in London and who had met him at the station in Edinburgh. Henri had grown to like him. They talked, not as friends, but then not in the formal military way they had at the beginning. Henri guessed the minder knew he was one agent they didn't have to worry about.

Henri couldn't wait to shake him when they got to London. Now they had at least 12 hours alone in a compartment together. No security risks, no children, no talkative naval men.

Henri decided to find out something that had been eating at him.

"I wonder whatever became of that naval man?"

"That fool. I should think he's on the slowest ship in the North Atlantic for the rest of the war. A Commander too. Well I shouldn't think he'll be commanding anything, just an old tub, if he's lucky."

"No. I meant what happened to him after the railway station?"

"Oh, simple. They took him to safe house and talked to him for twelve hours. He told them you were a French spy. They never told him what you were, except he was lucky you weren't. A French spy. All that talk about Halifax. God's teeth. What was the man thinking?"

That was a new one for Henri. God's teeth. But he knew what he meant about Halifax. Back home in Canada people never mentioned it by name, at least not in public or over the telephone. "We're going to play bridge," was one family's code word for a trip to Halifax to meet relatives. The code was for telephone conversations, but some people he knew even used it in private.

Henri thought of the man's wife and two children. "Poor fellow," he said to the minder, even though he hadn't liked him much.

"Idiot. Lucky he wasn't court-martialled. But the rest of the war in a corvette or frigate for a man who was with the home fleet is almost as bad. Convoy duty might be important, but it's the low spot on the totem pole. They call it the senior service. Should be the snobbiest service."

Just then the minder moved his hand to the window. "Look there. There's your man's venison."

About a dozen deer poked into the snow looking for grass. The does and fawns started to run from the train, but the stag just looked straight at it in cocky defiance.

Henri thought how small they looked compared to the big white-tailed deer of the Appalachians.

Good thing there was something to look at. The trip from Inverness to Edinburgh was wartime slow. It wasn't just the ammunition trains causing the delay, but weather and the old railway equipment shunted off for use in the Highlands.

Remote Scotland was a perfect place to practice the black arts of war. For one thing it was quiet. Special passes were needed to get as far as Inverness, and then more passes to get into every zone. Henri and the minder had to get off the train in some remote spot where a spur line took them to a more isolated speck of Scotland. At the small station they stood alone with a smiling Scot in a kilt, no uniform. He never asked for their passes, but then he didn't have to. There could be no secrets here.

Silent killing, simple codes for sending messages and the art of using the radio in short bursts. For weeks they practiced parachute drops. Henri already knew about parachutes and guns, but he was trained again and issued his own weapons: commando knives, garrotte wire, a Sten gun and an American 45 automatic.

He liked the Sten gun and the way it could break down into separate pieces, the clip and the barrel. It was perfect to hide under a coat. A small submachine gun, not too accurate over any distance but a killer in close-up fighting. The 45 could blow a huge hole in just about anything. But for Henri it was too heavy. He wanted a 9-mm Luger. Used the same bullets as the Sten gun. It was one of the first things he planned to pick up when he was in France, though he might have to kill a German soldier to get his Luger.

When he left the camp, none of those weapons were with him. Just the minder.

Henri didn't know when he was going to France, but it would be soon. He knew his mission. He was to land near Lyon, meet with members of the Maquis, the resistance, known in the newspapers as the Underground. Romantic figures, but not great fighters. His job was to transform them into soldiers and kill as many Germans as they could. Every German they killed was one less to meet the Allies when they landed on the beaches, maybe this summer, maybe next fall.

Right now his mind drifted from war to the memory of the curved, white form he saw leaving the bedroom in London. The Canadian woman, the one from Montreal. He wondered if she spoke any French.

She knew he was coming, but she didn't know when. She had left him a little *billet doux* in the book she had lent him. He wondered when she had time to write something so tender. It impressed him. He had written her a rather cryptic note when he posted the book back to her flat in London.

Dear Jane, I too had a wonderful time in London. And I long for the touch of the beautiful angel with the golden hair. I will see you soon. H.

He couldn't sign his own name, but now she knew he would be back, and knew he wasn't Pierre. As he sat looking at the frozen Scottish countryside, he dreamed of a warm couple of days in London before he flew to France.

"Where are we staying?" asked Henri.

"I'm staying with my parents. A place you wouldn't know, just outside the city. You're staying in a safe house in London." The minder laughed, "Or as safe as houses can be in London."

Henri decided on the direct approach. "I'm not under house arrest am I? Am I allowed to go out?"

"Security isn't that tight. I have someone else to watch over. Just make sure I know where to find you. Call in every few hours, say every four or five. And..."

Henri cut off the minder. "Don't talk. Don't worry I don't talk much at the best of times."

A smile from the minder.

"And wear your uniform. You'll attract less attention that way. Your civilian clothes were what worried our busybody Commander."

Three hours later they were in Edinburgh. They had half an hour to catch the Flying Scotsman, so they spent most of it in a pub beside the station. They didn't talk much. Both of them looked around at what passed for normal life. In the corner a soldier was kissing a woman, who was making a weak attempt to resist.

"Aye, you men are all alike," said the girl, who was about 18, in an accent so thick Henri had a hard time understanding it. "You're only after one thing."

Henri smiled, since he had heard this same thought expressed by girls at home. It had no effect on the soldier who pressed his attentions even harder, putting his hand on the girl's thigh. She feigned disgust but didn't move.

Across the u-shaped bar stood a couple of men more interested in drink than women. Glum-looking boozers of about forty, Henri's guess, they stood with two glasses each, one whiskey, one beer. They seemed to have a rhythm, three good slugs of beer to a sip of whiskey. The whisky seemed to last about three sips before they would just make a slight nod at the barman who would refill their glasses.

They were sailors. Hands hardened from work, faces lined from exposure. Their coats were on so he couldn't catch their rank. He guessed they were career men, and the equivalent of a sergeant major. He didn't know many naval ranks.

They were too old for conscription. No telling whether they were on their way home or going back to sea.

Money didn't seem a problem. Henri had seen this type at home. There was a tavern near the university where he noticed men started drinking beer and tomato juice at seven o'clock in the morning. He watched the larger of the two sailors. His neck muscles moved as if massaging the beer on the way down, pulling in as much as he could.

The two of them never spoke, then neither did he and the minder. Except for one last exchange.

"Ten minutes to the train," said the minder. "Let's take a page from their book."

He nodded at the barman. "Double whiskies. Neat."

They bundled into a first-class compartment, once again left on their own. The soldiers, sailors and airmen going down south didn't have the money for first class. Henri had a little money of his own, from home, and would have paid for the upgrade, but the minder handled everything. The conductor kept people out of their compartment, and Henri figured he'd made that arrangement too.

"Bloody cold," said the minder. "We'll be thankful for those whiskies." He was right. Within 20 minutes they were both asleep, huddled under their greatcoats. They didn't awaken until the train pulled into a siding near York to let an ammunition train pass.

Moonlight bounced off the snow outside. Henri didn't even have to look at this watch, he could tell by the angle of the moon it was about four o'clock in the morning. They had been travelling six hours. Not bad. They might be in London in another three.

"Here's the address. Take a cab. I can just catch the next train to my parents' place. Haven't seen my fiancée in a while, getting rather anxious, if you know what I mean," and the minder gave one of his infrequent smiles. "I shouldn't really leave you alone, but there you are. I'll meet you at the safe house at noon on Monday."

"I'll see you then," and they shook hands.

On his way to the cab rank, Henri stopped at a news-stand and picked up some writing paper, and a packet of envelopes. He gave the driver the address of the safe house. In the back seat he wrote a note.

Jane, meet me at the Admiral Coddington at 7:30. H.

He printed her address on the envelope and, when he arrived at the safe house, looked at the driver.

"Like to make some extra money?"

"Who wouldn't, guv?"

Henri handed him the letter. It wasn't a long trip and he looked at the meter.

"How much, for the trip from the station and the delivery."

"Three shillings should handle it."

Henri gave the man a ten-shilling note and his eyes widened.

"Just make sure this is delivered. In the next ten minutes," said Henri with an air of conspiracy that scared the driver. Henri knew he'd go there straightaway. He knocked on the door, and another stern Englishwoman in grey itchy clothes showed him to his room. She never said a word. Didn't even ask his name.

A bath would come later. Now he wanted more sleep.

8

Death was hot that night.

The cab dropped him in Carlyle Square. As he fumbled with the Banham's security key, Jack's mind was racing trying to sort out how he was going to do the B-29 pilot by the morning. He walked into his basement flat, the alarm beeping and he punched out the code to turn it off.

It was just one bedroom, a tiny kitchen and a fair-sized sitting room that doubled as his office. Here gadgets made his life a lot easier. Television, VCR, tape recorder. All stuff to justify the alarm, which the landlord who lived upstairs insisted he put in. The rest of his electronic gear: a fax, a computer, a printer and a telephone answering machine. The light was flashing on the message counter. Push the button.

"You have one new message."

Hit 1.

"Devlin. Langton here. Good work on the baseball player. Works well with the big picture. Seems three pages of *Debretts* have died in the past couple of days. Real interest in your Canadian though. Ring me in the morning."

Jack was going to be busy. Well he wasn't tired so he might as well stay up late. For Langton, the morning meant ten at the earliest. He had only glanced at the death notice of Henri Foix, so now he took out the fax from the birth and death pages of *The Montreal Gazette* and gave it a thorough read.

War hero at a glance. Medals, children. Mention of service in France. SOE. The service Michelle mentioned. Wonder what the German connection is? He'd get Colonel Foix in a minute, right now, time to let technology round up the B-29 man.

Jack had a better computer than they had at either the newspaper or the network. He'd spotted about five years ago that computers were something that could make his life a lot easier. No more tearing the paper from the typewriter and throwing it in a crumpled ball into the wastebasket after three typing mistakes. Now the spell checker did the work.

He disconnected the jack from the bottom of the telephone and clicked it into the back of his Hayes modem. It worked at 2400 baud, which was a lot faster than his original 300. The network had given him some passwords to let him use their wire services. In less than a minute he was in the 'Urgent' file where he found the latest news stories on the dead pilot. There was even a point-by-point history of the two A-bomb raids. He printed them all.

The original news story had it wrong. Patrick Francis O'Brien was the tail gunner in the B-29 that dropped the second bomb on Nagasaki. Fat Man it was called and the tail gunner's job was not to defend against fighters, there weren't any at that altitude and that late in the war. The Japanese Air Force was running on empty.

O'Brien was there to take the picture of the mushroom cloud, in case the chase plane which was meant to take the picture messed up for some reason. O'Brien was famous for being human. After he saw the flash and the cloud, his words over the plane's intercom were: "My God, what have we done?"

After the war he went back to Malone, New York, and sold real estate. Be a nice touch if he turned out to be a drunk. Irish name, like Devlin. He had to make a few calls, but not too many. Overseas long-distance rates from England were a killer.

He did call a friend of his on the night desk at *The Gazette* in Montreal who managed to drag up something from an old magazine article. He called Jack back around one in the morning, London time. O'Brien had taken to the booze. But then so had just about everyone from the war it seemed to Jack.

While he had him on the line, and on *The Gazette*'s nickel, he might as well move on to the next victim.

"Have you got anything on a guy called Foix? F-O-I-X?"

The Gazette man didn't even pause.

"You're in luck. It's right here. The Army, or excuse me the Armed Forces, sent out a release on him. I can fax it to you with the magazine article. Christ, Devlin, you're going to owe me," said the man at *The Gazette*.

Jack thought fast. He needed this guy.

"Well take your choice. I can zap you a cheque for $100 or you can stay here the next time you're in London." Jack hoped he'd pick the free room.

"Alright. I might come over next year. I'll take you up on it."

"Okay just let me switch over to my fax machine," said Jack. "It'll take me a minute or so. Thanks and your bed is waiting."

Jack hadn't a clue where he was going to squeeze him if he did arrive. Be better if he moved in with Claire for a week.

After he hung up he unplugged the telephone and plugged in the fax and waited. From his shelf he pulled a book on aircraft of the last war. He would leave the obit on the new man until the morning. But he knew if he didn't knock off a couple of hundred words before bed he'd never get to sleep. The unfinished work would eat at him and he would lie there stringing words together in a new lead or thinking of a clever way to say something.

The fax machine made its high-pitched whine as it kissed and linked with *The Gazette*'s fax, 3,255 miles and one ocean away. The first stuff was the magazine article he needed. The release on the new obit would come at the end of the roll.

While the fax came in he started work on the dead American airman. There was an off chance they wouldn't take this, but when he had an obit half done they almost always bought it. The atomic bomb angle would be too much to pass up.

Pat O'Brien, who has died at the age of 61, was the tail gunner on the B-29, the 'Superfortress' with the rather Germanic name of Bockscar that dropped the atomic bomb on Nagasaki on August 9, 1945.

"My God, what have we done?" were the words O'Brien spoke into his pressurized mask as he saw the mushroom cloud burst into flower over Nagasaki. Since the plane could fly higher, almost 32,000 feet, and faster – a top speed of 365 mph – than the few fighters the Japanese had left, the tail gunner didn't have much to do. It was Sergeant O'Brien's job to take a picture of the blast as the plane raced away.

The B-29 was the most advanced bomber of the Second World War. The Germans had planned a four-engine jet bomber—with the range to hit New York—but it never made it into production.

O'Brien had trained on B-29s at an airfield in Texas before being transferred to a fighting airfield in Guam. Before the Nagasaki trip, O'Brien had flown on 15 raids on Japan, carrying out the firebombing tactics of General Curtis LeMay. Although not as dramatic as Fat Man, the bomb dropped on Nagasaki, the firebombing raids were more effective than the atomic bombs, killing 100,000 people or more in one night in Tokyo.

Patrick Francis O'Brien was born on September 4, 1925, in Malone, New York, a small city surrounded by dairy farms that ran up to the border with Canada. His father was an insurance agent and young Pat sold insurance for a few months after high school before joining the U.S. Army Air Force. He started training on B-17s, but managed to talk himself into the B-29 program.

After the war he returned to Malone and took over his father's insurance agency, selling policies to local dairy farmers. His notoriety as the man who dropped the bomb was always good for business, though it might not have been great for his health. O'Brien was fond of drink, and people who knew him said he could become morose about the war after the fifth shot of Southern Comfort.

Jack's WordStar program told him he had written 360 words. It was two o'clock in the morning. He wanted to go to bed but he couldn't resist peeking at the other fax. He leaned over and ripped the funny fax paper from the machine, then set about cutting it into single pages with a metal ruler that never measured anything.

He went over to the couch and started reading, first the piece from the Canadian Armed Forces, as the combined army, navy and air force were now called. Jack looked at it and mumbled to himself, "What a mess that asshole Trudeau made of the army."

A great Canadian hero has died read the start of the release. A bit much, thought Jack. I've never heard of this guy and here he is trotted out as a great hero. He scanned the rest of the release and took in the list of medals. That impressed him. Then he flipped through to the magazine piece and started reading.

Weekend Magazine, August 1955. He did owe *The Gazette* man a free bed for the week. He read the cutlines below the pictures, which showed the hero home from the war. His eyes were too tired to read the whole article. Then at the end there were a couple of clippings from 1945, one from *La Presse*, the largest circulation French newspaper outside France, the other from the old *Montreal Star*.

The headline in the *Star* caught his eye.

French-Canadian's Maquis clubbed so 58 Germans lined up and shot. Jack thought this obit might be more interesting than he thought. Maybe this was why Langton mentioned Germans. But he was too tired to think much. He read one more sentence but his eyes closed and the paper slipped from his hand. That was it.

He walked back to his desk, leaned over and pushed the two keystrokes to make sure his story was saved. He shut down his computer and put the soldiers and the bombers to bed for the night.

9

TEMPFORD, A BOMBER COMMAND AIRFIELD, MARCH 1944

More than sixteen hundred horsepower rattled the airframe as the first engine of the bomber came to life. Then another lit up and soon all four had the plane straining at its blocks. Inside, a crew of six. Tonight the bomb aimer was off. The load was just one paratrooper on a mission to southern France along with a couple of containers for the Maquis: Sten guns, ammunition, grenades and radios.

The Halifax taxied to the end of the runway, the three bladed props champing at the air as the new air-cooled Bristol engines gave the pilot more power than he was used to. In the back there was talk between the crew. Soon there would be radio silence as they left their airfield at Tempford in the British Midlands and headed south across the Channel, dodging the radar stations which were looking for streams of bombers headed to Germany.

The German air defences were interested in masses of bombers. Fuel was too scarce to waste on a sortie of Messerschmitt 110s or JU 88 night fighters to search for a single plane, even on a bright night like this one. The German fighters could get lucky, but they were better off hanging around a British airfield in the dark, flying a 'reverse box' against the traffic of landing bombers. Easy to pick off when they switched on their landing lights a hundred and fifty feet above the ground.

In the back of the plane no one spoke to the man in civilian clothes, the stranger they were taking to France. There were a few grunted pleasantries as they helped him aboard, but the crew had been briefed beforehand: no one was to speak to the passenger, unless they wanted to spend the rest of the war in a military prison. The orders came from a Wing Commander who had a Lieutenant Colonel from a parachute regiment standing beside him.

No one did speak, at first. The navigator who like most Englishmen had a thing about accents, later told his girlfriend he noticed the passenger wasn't English. He could have been a Pole, but he almost sounded like a Frenchman when he spoke English. That would make sense, but he wasn't a Frenchman, at least not any type of Frenchman he had met. He was tempted to speak to him in French; he had lived in France before the war, but decided maybe the Wingco meant it about prison.

The bomber flew low across France. The crew could see moonlit rivers just a thousand feet below. Flying at this altitude ate up fuel and would test the range and endurance of the Halifax, though it would be able to move to the thin air at 20,000 feet on the way home. Inside the plane the crew and its passenger were almost numb from being cramped in what little space there was for humans in a plane built to carry bombs. The navigator once figured his on-board living space was one square yard, like spending six hours in an outhouse.

They were now a little more than an hour from where the passenger would leave. He started to go through a checklist of what he had to do and whom he had to meet when he landed. He knew that many agents dropped into France were captured within an hour of landing, tortured and then shot. There was no uniform, no flashes on his French-looking clothes to identify him as a soldier. The Germans had every right to shoot him. His side did it. The British had hanged at least one German agent dropped into Yorkshire or Norfolk. Though he would love to land with a Sten gun, it was too dangerous. His only weapons would be his knife, the thin commando blade he had learned to use at the training camp in Scotland and an American automatic pistol. He checked inside his pockets for his forged papers, the French passport which used his real family name but a false first name. Here in France he would be known as Pierre. His cover would be he was an army officer, retired since the French defeat in 1940 and now living near Lyon.

Strange name Foix, which is why they let him keep it.

There were many ways for an agent to get into France. Perhaps the best way was in a small single-engine plane called a Lysander. It looked like a Cessna with its overhead wings and with its robust fixed landing gear it could land on a grass strip, marked at night by a couple of portable lights.

Then there was the parachute drop, either from Dakotas, converted American DC3s, or from the Handley Page Halifax, a second string bomber, without the payload of the mighty Lancaster but with range and the space to carry equipment for the men and women on the ground. And, in a pinch, the Halifax could shoot back.

An agent could be met by two or three members of the resistance, known as a reception committee. That could be dangerous and tonight Henri Foix was happy to be parachuted blind into Burgundy. This was to be his sector for six months, maybe longer. It was where he would blow up bridges, derail trains and kill as many Germans as he could.

Henri preferred to land blind, that is without a reception committee. The Germans had done a brilliant job infiltrating the resistance. He wasn't meant to know that, but he did. The SD, the police branch of the SS, was at work all over France, having moved south into Vichy. Apart from torture they also used more subtle methods, such as turning agents, or making traitors out of men and women who had lovers or relatives in camps or working in German factories.

The most notorious of that type was The Cat, now living at Holloway Prison near London. A beautiful woman, she had turned in a string of British agents and members of the French resistance and had the cheek to return contrite to England. It wasn't just the agents who died. A phoney radio transmission sent to London convinced the British that three German warships, *Scharnost*, *Gneisenau* and *Prinz Eugen* would stay in port at Brest for repairs. It was a lie. The three ships escaped into the North Atlantic, sinking dozens of Allied ships in the spring of 1942, leaving their crews to freeze to death in the North Atlantic.

The navigator came back to talk to Henri, or at least give him some information.

"We'll be over the drop zone in half an hour."

"Thanks," said Henri. "Want a smoke?" he asked passing a crumpled packet of Gitanes, which he had been smoking for the past several weeks. Not only had he changed his brand of cigarettes, he had even changed his table manners, his minders being careful to see that the knife and fork went back on the plate the French way, not the English way or, in his case, the Canadian way.

Since Henri started the talking, Billy Todd, the navigator, decided to brave a little conversation with his Gitane.

"Thanks," said Todd, almost coughing on the first pull of the odd-tasting French cigarette. He looked at the agent, his slight wiry form, and his gaunt face, which without the moustache must have looked no more than 20. "I don't envy you. It'll be pretty dangerous down there."

Henri didn't want to talk much, but this man wasn't the enemy. He'd just make small talk without telling him anything. He waited for a while, using his cigarette as an excuse not to speak.

After a minute he replied, "No more dangerous than it is for you. You have a lot of enemies up here, and even some down on the ground." Henri knew, just from speaking with his friends, that flying slow bombers over Europe was as dangerous as being in the trenches in the last war. Maybe even more so.

Curiosity was eating away at Billy Todd. He decided to be bold.

"*Est-ce que vous êtes Français?*" he asked.

Henri wasn't even ruffled. This was good practice, he thought. His friend the navigator couldn't figure out his accent from the way he spoke English. He wouldn't speak French and give him anything more to go by. The navigator's French was better than just university French and he might have an ear for accents.

"You might say that," said Henri in English, with a smile to show he wasn't angry. "But I don't think I should say anything else. Thanks my friend, but I think I'll get ready to leave." He handed Todd what was left of the Gitanes and shook his hand.

"*Bonne chance,*" said Todd.

"Thanks. You too."

The pilot took a bearing from a light a kilometre from the drop zone. A little more than a thousand yards away, he kept his air speed low and his altitude at about 1,500 feet, enough for the chutes to open for both the agent and the canisters.

Henri then checked his parachute harness, and patted his pocket to check that his money belt was strapped to his waist. He had 100,000 francs and 50,000 marks ready to grease his agents and make sure he could live what would pass for a normal life so the Germans wouldn't catch him. He took a deep breath. He was ready. He checked his pistol, the 45 automatic that he thought far too big, and the slender commando knife strapped to his leg and moved to the door.

The pneumatic doors opened on the bomb bay. The canisters would drop first, then the agent was clear to leave, though not through the bomb bay. The navigator and one of the gunners opened the side door for Henri as the pilot made a pass over what he hoped was an open field.

"Now," said Billy Todd and Henri Foix dropped into the near darkness, the earth lit by an almost full moon.

10

The moon lit up early on Friday night. The start of March in England means the sun still doesn't stay up too late. Jack sat in the right-hand passenger seat as Claire piloted her hyper-Gallic Renault R-4 on its way to Oxford. Funny little car, it had the gearshift sticking out from the middle of the dash. Jack had the toughest time working the thing and much preferred that she drive.

A light from an oncoming car lit up her face and Jack looked at her reflection in the mirror, then over to her.

"You really have beautiful eyes."

"Yours aren't so bad either," said Claire. Even her flattery had a cocky edge to it.

The Dirty Weekend Handbook described Woodstock as a quaint village in Oxfordshire. Its biggest attraction was Blenheim, the palace built for the first John Churchill. He had won a string of battles against the French, including one at a place in Europe called Blenheim. That victory allowed the British to pretty much do as they pleased for the next 60 years or so. Jack was looking forward to a walk in the grounds.

"See those walls?" asked Jack as they drove past the estate. "Built for a man who beat the pants off the French almost 200 years ago." That didn't get a rise out of Claire, who wasn't all that patriotic. She preferred living in England to

France, though she never went out with Englishmen. Lucky for Jack.

He pointed at an old brick wall that ringed in the eleven thousand five hundred acres of the Blenheim estate. "Look at that pheasant. Wonder how they get them to pose on the wall like that?"

"Don't be so stupid," and she laughed, knowing it was a joke. Apart from the sex, it was one of the reasons Jack liked her, she laughed at his jokes. It wasn't that she was that great in bed, but she was so good looking it drove him crazy. Thick blonde hair, sleepy green eyes and a wonderful smile. She was 12 years younger and he always thought he'd won some kind of lottery to have ended up with her.

"How are the dead people?" she said, making light of it.

"Not that good. The weather must be warm and sunny back in America," said Jack. He had given up describing the distinction between Canada and the United States. For the French, and most of the English, there wasn't one. It was just America. It drove most Canadians nuts but it didn't bother him. When people mistook him for an American, he carried straight on talking.

Jack gave Claire his rather unscientific theory about why people didn't die when the sun was shining. "People don't die in this good weather. An old girlfriend of mine worked in a hospital, doing tests on bits of dead bodies, and she told me there was less work at the start of spring. If they can, people wait until the weather is crummy. Weird, isn't it?"

"For God's sake, I've never heard anything so stupid. People die every day. The weather doesn't make any difference," she shook her head, and he knew she was thinking he couldn't reason, that no one could teach Americans how to reason. Sure enough, out popped the following jewel: "You Americans believe the craziest things. Ghosts, flying saucers. Look at your movies for God's sake? Everyone believes in creatures from outer space. It's ridiculous."

No use arguing. Just let her have a rant and hope they arrive at the hotel soon.

Woodstock looked as if it were designed by a committee, but one with some taste. It wasn't too cute, but had everything you could want in a weekend retreat. Shops, newsstands and restaurants.

And there it was, The Bear at Woodstock, named in *The Dirty Weekend Handbook* as a gem of a spot for two days of sex and food. It looked like an overgrown pub from the front, but their room upstairs came with a large bed and a separate bathroom, two key ingredients for a successful dirty weekend.

Claire kissed him and took her clothes off, not to make love but to have a shower. He thought of following her in, but he knew her habits. She'd be in there for half an hour making sure she smelled all right. A little over the top thought Jack, but better than the other way around. He decided to nip downstairs to look for some newspapers.

Jack's mind raced as he walked downstairs. Without the distraction of Claire, he started to brood about work. He needed the weekend to relax.

Turned out doing the A-bomb obit on spec was a money maker. The obit editor had wanted the story, but it could hold until sometime next week. He started working out the logistics in his head. Since he had started writing it on his computer at home, he wouldn't bother to go to the paper on Monday, he could send it in over the phone line. The paper had just figured out how to handle electronic filing and it made his life a lot easier.

That morning before leaving London for Woodstock Jack had found out there were a couple of people in from Canada doing a documentary on Hiroshima and the A-Bomb. Bit of a fluke. The Dolan brothers. He knew them from Montreal and called the TV office in London to see if they were in town. Only one of them was available, the younger one, Mike, or Michael as he now called himself. Sounded more grand.

"Time for a quick beer?" Jack asked over the phone. They agreed to meet at noon. Jack had walked to the Sloane Square tube station and was at the office in half an hour.

The Dolan documentary was a classic bit of TV. Write the script and go out and fill in the blanks to match your prejudices. Never let a fact you find in the field, or an idea from an interview get in the way of the pre-sold story. Forty-five minutes with Michael Dolan was enough to make Jack glad he'd left Canada and television.

All this went through Jack's mind as he walked down the stairs to the newsstand. He was still boiling at the patronizing treatment from Dolan that afternoon. Jack had hoped to pick up some colour that one of the brothers might have gleaned in all the research for their big project.

Fat chance. Mike, or Michael, knew everything and knew the Americans were wrong to drop the bomb. "There was no difference between the Germans and the Americans," said Dolan in a tone so smug Jack thought about belting him in the chops, just on principle. "They killed women and children and hardly any soldiers or sailors. Pure terrorism."

Jack ordered a whiskey to go with his beer. The information session almost turned into a bar fight.

"The kill ratio in the Pacific was 20 to 1, for the Americans," argued Jack. "If the Americans were expecting a million casualties, that would have meant twenty million for the Japanese. Less than two hundred thousand dead in two bombing raids seems a cheap price to pay."

"You're such a fascist," said Dolan the younger. "There were women and children there."

"They should have thought of that before they started the fucking war. Like your brother should have thought of it before he started beating up his wife."

And so it went for another 15 minutes. No information. Dolan didn't even know the name of the plane that dropped the bomb on Nagasaki. *Enola Gay* at Hiroshima he knew, but so did everyone else in the world. Useless. All opinion, no facts and a sanctimonious prick to boot. Instead of punching Dolan, Jack just decided to hate him for life.

Which was why he needed the dirty weekend. He pushed Dolan out of his mind and cursed himself for even thinking about him. Waste of bile. Downstairs most of the English papers were gone. There was one *International Herald Tribune* and the local paper for rural Oxford. An addict, he bought both. He was back in the room, undressed and in bed and Claire was still in the bathroom.

There wasn't much going on in the paper and since he preferred British politics to American—much more Machiavellian—he skipped to the baseball stats. The Yankees had beaten the Blue Jays. The Expos were in second to last place. He looked at the averages and tried to calculate where they might be if each won the next few games.

Then a quick spin to the death notices, though there wouldn't be much in here worth reading. Wrong. There was a short death announcement of a Canadian diplomat who had been quite a rake in his day. He had written a rather indiscreet book in which he described bonking sessions during the Blitz when he was in London. Jack had read it and might even have a copy in his flat.

He picked his watch off the table beside the bed. Eight thirty. The obit desk would have gone home for the night, no use calling them. Shit. Why hadn't he picked up the *Trib* earlier in the day? He would call Langton at home tomorrow. He wanted to make sure he nailed this one.

Claire came out wearing only a towel, but with her hair dried and as coifed as it was when she went to work. She dropped the towel and slipped into bed beside him. He had put down his newspaper but was still a bit distracted. She changed that in a hurry.

Claire liked to sleep in the morning. Maybe because she was younger, maybe because she worked more regular hours during the week and felt staying in bed on Saturday morning was cheating the system. Jack ran his hands over her naked body lingering for a while on her ass. Her head slid into the pocket on his shoulder but she mumbled that she wanted to sleep now.

"Later." There was a smile with the later, so he decided to go for a walk.

It was a little after eight and there was a full-blown news agent within a hundred yards of the hotel. He looked in at hotel breakfast and decided it was too formal. He would grab his papers and find a down market caff, what at home he would call a greasy spoon. A cup of coffee and some toast. He could have room service later, after he had Claire.

He wondered if the big papers would have any more on the Canadian diplomat. He had been in London during the war, so there might be something. He doubted if anyone had time to do a full-blown obit. The man was too obscure for anyone but a Canadian.

Newspapers were one of the things Jack liked about living in England. Here he was a few hours out of London and he could find as many papers as he could five minutes from his flat in Chelsea. There was a *Paris Match* in the corner so he snapped that up for Claire. He picked up the *Telegraph*, the *Times*, the *Daily Mail* and this week's *Economist*.
"Going to read all day, luv?" asked the woman at the cash.

"No just until noon," laughed Jack, thinking he was going to read until he thought Claire was ready for a morning refresher. Just a few doors down the street was the caff of his dreams. They would never be able to produce a decent cup of coffee here, so he ordered tea and toast.

A quick scan of the headlines. There were still horror stories about the nuclear accident at Chernobyl, two months after it happened. Jack had covered the accident at Three Mile Island, which was nothing compared to this. He thought back and remembered all the hype. He smiled as he remembered the airhead CBS reporter fretting over a script, and the producer, pacing like a straw boss behind him.

"Throw in some shit about the China Syndrome," a reference to a hysterical movie with Jane Fonda about a nuclear disaster. It had nothing to do with what was happening in rural Pennsylvania, but who cared. TV News, all emotion, few facts.

In the paper this morning there were new pictures of the men who put out the fire more than a month ago. Some of them looked like patients in a cancer ward. They were gaunt, and their hair was falling out. The *Telegraph* had a piece on the investigation into the Challenger disaster.

Old deaths. He flipped to the important stuff, today's deaths. He wanted to see who had done what and in particular if anyone was on to his Canadian diplomat. They might not know the British connection, or at least he hoped they didn't. It was too early to call Langton.

Without Jack noticing, an old man had sat down at the table next to him. Jack had moved to the weekend section and was reading another anniversary feature on the war. British papers took any excuse to celebrate victory, even more than 40 years on. It might bother some people, but it didn't bother Jack. His mind was filled with wars. Some years he was obsessed with the First World War, others with the Second. For a short while he had read everything he could on the Crimean War. A woman with the androgynous name of Cecil Woodham-Smith was the big expert.

Today the *Telegraph* had a four-page spread on the Battle of Britain. Our planes on one side, theirs on the other. Jack knew they were missing a lot. He could name every type of fighter and bomber used by both the Germans and the British, and most of the American planes that appeared later. The maps in the paper showed the distances across the Channel to Luftwaffe airfields in France. Six minutes it took to cross over from one side to the other. Not much time for planes to scramble. Even though he knew all this, he read every word and studied every diagram, like a kid so fascinated by a story that he reads it over and over.

"You can have the few, we were the many."

Jack was startled and almost knocked his tea over. The old man beside him had seen what he was reading. "Sorry, what did you say?"

"I said there's two much fuss about those who fought in Spitfires and Hurricanes. Lot more soldiers killed in the First War. More people killed in the Second, but that was the bombs. More soldiers killed in the First. British soldiers."

The old man lit a Woodbine, a funny-looking little cigarette with no filter. Amazing he made it this far, thought Jack. But he liked the old guy.

"You know how old I am?"

Jack thought. He had to be at least 86.

"Well if you were in the first war you would have to be at least 86. So I'll guess 87."

"I'm 88. I was born in 1898. I worked on the estate here from 1912 on. I wasn't allowed to join up until 1916. Said I was needed on the land. Well they got other people to do that work. Women, a lot of them. I missed the Somme though, at least the first part of it."

Jack knew about the Somme. Fifty-seven thousand British casualties on July 1, 1916. Worst day ever for the British Army. There were Canadians there, he remembered. A whole regiment from Newfoundland wiped out.

"You Americans weren't there yet."

Jack smiled. "Got you there. I'm Canadian. We were there. There was a regiment from Newfoundland... more than 900 people were killed. And that from a place where the population couldn't have been more than a quarter of a million." The old man was not about to apologize for not knowing the difference between an American and a Canadian accent. He even got a little shirty at being corrected.

"I fought with a lot of Canadians. Most of them were lads who spoke proper English. Went over for the good life and all of a sudden they were back here."

"My grandfather for one," said Jack. "He only came to Canada in 1911 and was in France four years later."

That warmed up the old man and he told a few war stories. Said he had an award for bravery, but didn't name the medal. Was a soldier in a Guards regiment. Jack looked at him and thought this guy would make a great obit. He felt his jacket pocket to see if he had a pen.

"Oh, my name's Jack Devlin," he said reaching out his hand.

"And I'm Will Tup," said the old man. Jack felt his hand disappear into the old man's grip. His fingers were huge and hands rough and hard as an old board. "It's spelt T-o-u-p-e, and it's pronounced Tup. Know what it means?"

Jack thought for a minute. He wished he did know. He loved word games. "Tup. Tup. Can't think of anything."

"Well Tup means sheep. A ram and I guess they used to spell it the long way back a long time ago."

Jack pulled out his pen and started to doodle the name Tup and Toupe on the blank white space at the top of the section of the *Telegraph* he had open. He could take a few notes and the old man would never know it.

While Willie Toupe talked about the Battle of the Somme, Jack ordered more tea and toast. Then he ran out of space on the top of the paper and pulled out a small notebook he had in his pocket.

"Mind if I take notes? It's interesting."

"No. I figured someone with so many newspapers might be a newspaper man," said Will Toupe with a smile to let Jack know he might be old, but he wasn't dumb.

The old soldier loved to talk. Jack watched his hands move in slow circles when he described a battle. "It wasn't always hell, you know. Sometimes there'd be nothing but a few shells for a couple of weeks. And there were all those French girls." The lines beside his light blue eyes helped light up his smile.

Jack nodded at the women behind the counter and she brought them two more cups of tea. Will never stopped talking. He sat there in an old brown jacket, which might have been bought for someone else 40 years ago. He had a soft yellow scarf around his neck and the outside pockets of his jacket bulged with cigarettes and boxes of Swan wooden matches.

After fifteen minutes, Jack had enough, including phone numbers of a few relatives. He'd told Will what he did and the old man rather liked the idea. Jack told him he'd show him a rough copy of the obit in a few weeks, maybe a month.

"Might seem odd, but better to get it right," said Jack. "And fish around for some old photographs from the war. I'll make a copy and send them back to you."

Willie Toupe laughed. "You don't waste much time do you? We haven't been here thirty minutes."

As he walked back to the hotel, he wondered how long he could make it, the obit on Will that is. Six hundred words. No, nine hundred. They were running out of First World War men.

It was now well past ten, and Jack started to think as he walked up the stairs to the room that he might have left things a little late. When he opened the door the light was on beside the bed, and in it, propped up by pillows at her back, was Claire, reading *Le Canard enchaîné*, the French version of *Private Eye*.

Her eyes lit up. "Bonjour chéri." Odd thought Jack, she almost never spoke French to him.

"Here's *Paris Match*. I was just out reading. I didn't want to wake you up."

She smiled and threw her magazine on the floor.

"Stop talking so much for God's sake. Take your clothes off and get into bed and make love to me."

The eiderdown had slipped and her small breasts poked above the covers, her pink nipples standing at attention like little soldiers. Jack was getting undressed as fast he could.

11

VICHY FRANCE, MARCH 1944

As Henri Foix floated down in his parachute, he hoped there would be no welcoming committee. He worried about betrayal. It wasn't death. He'd prepared himself for that, though of course he wasn't anxious to die. What worried him was the frustration of getting caught before he had a chance to fight.

The people in the resistance knew he was coming, but they didn't know which night and the exact spot of the landing, though by now they would have heard the plane. Still, it might have been just canisters and not an agent.

Henri was going to be careful. He had heard stories at camp about men being captured within hours, or even minutes of landing. Two of them, English Canadians from Toronto and Winnipeg, were betrayed, though one of them was reckless enough to land in France as an agent without being able to speak enough French to pass.

Both had ended hung from a meat hook, as piano wire strangled them in a slow agonizing death. Hitler had ordered film sent to him so he could see the deaths he ordered. Henri was determined not to give the Fuhrer the same satisfaction.

He rolled with his wiry body as it hit the grass in an open field. Billy Todd and his friends in the converted Halifax bomber had done their job. Now it was up to him. The French Resistance had a romantic image in propaganda, in particular in Canada where the government wanted to appeal to young French-Canadian men to join in the war to free France. But Henri knew not to trust the Resistance. In the camp in Scotland he learned the Resistance harboured as many traitors as heroes.

The new agent had memorized this patch of land and thought he knew it almost as well as his neighbourhood in Montreal or the lanes around his father's country house south of Sherbrooke, just a few miles from the border with the United States.

It was four thirty in the morning and there was no sign of the sun, though it would come soon. It was colder than he'd expected, about 6 degrees. He'd taught himself to think in Centigrade, though he'd grown up with Fahrenheit. He also had to think, and speak, in metres not feet.

A few weeks ago the *Times* had reported the temperature in Montreal was almost minus 40, the same temperature in Fahrenheit or Centigrade. Henri thought at home a man lying around outside might be dead from the cold in less than an hour. To him, this was like Florida.

He gathered up his parachute and started to fold it into a neat bundle. Then he headed for a silhouette about a few hundred yards away, a copse of trees. There he would stash his parachute and decide whether to wait for someone to come to him or head into the village later in the morning.

The pack around his neck held a small crystal radio. He had memorized the two encrypted bursts he was to send, one to London, one to Lyon. Within an hour his reception committee should arrive. They would not only look for him, they would have to pick up the canisters of arms and supplies that were a few hundred yards away in the same field.

Henri made his way across the field and towards the woods where there should be an unused barn or tool shed where he could hole up for an hour or so. It wasn't a barn, but just a building with a roof covering hay. He had seen these in England and thought them bizarre. At home all the fodder was inside a weather-proof building and near the cattle. He threw some loose hay over his parachute and then sent his messages in two short bursts.

The sun was starting to give the sky in the east some colour. He didn't like the idea of waiting in a building where he might be surprised by French police or the Germans. He pulled out his pistol and headed fifty yards away to take cover in some trees until the reception committee arrived. He was dying to smoke one of his Gitanes, but worried about the light giving him away. He figured out a way to huddle against one tree so no one could see his cigarette.

Then he heard some noise, bicycles coming down the lane. A man and a woman went over to the barn and called the name Pierre. That was Henri's working name, for now. He let them search in the barn and watched as they found the parachute. He wanted more light before he walked over. He looked at the crest of the hill and worried there could be others just beyond there. He then looked the other way and saw he could escape through the woods to a road on the other side, though that was something he hoped wouldn't happen.

He pulled his American 45 from its holster again and walked over to the hay shed. They were talking and making a racket pulling at his parachute, maybe thinking the canisters of arms and supplies were in here too.

Christ, thought Henri. What amateurs. I have a lot of work to do here. His mind went through a checklist of the things he learned at the commando school in Montana and then the rules of life as an agent from his masters in Scotland. Before they could hear him he was about ten feet away.

"Don't make such a racket," he said and they turned, startled to see a small man with a large gun pointed at them. The woman pressed against the hay. The man frowned, not used to being challenged. Turned out he was the leader in this sector.

"Are you Pierre?"

"Maybe. Who are you?" asked Henri.

"Philippe," and looking over his shoulder, "Florence. Put that gun away." He said it in a voice of command.

Henri looked at him. He didn't appear to have a weapon. The woman wasn't carrying anything that might conceal a pistol. He put his pistol back in its holster and walked toward Philippe who now decided to give him a lecture.

"You left your drop spot. It was difficult to find you. We have our work to do here." His officious manner was irking Henri and the sides of his jaw moved as he listened to a man who called himself Philippe. "And why did you challenge us? This is not how things are going to work. You'll have to learn to take orders."

He was a big man, who had maybe six inches on the agent. He had the air of a bully, or at least someone who was used to having things his way.

"No. That's not how it's going to work," said Henri who now took one step forward and brought his fist into Philipe's solar plexus, drawing all the breath out of him in an instant. Then kicking his ankle, hard, he brought him to the ground, at the same time producing his commando knife as if from nowhere.

"Don't move, mademoiselle," he said giving her just one quick glance.

"Look, Philippe, if that's your name, " Henri spoke with almost no emotion, "I am here to command a troop of Maquis. I work for the British but I'm as French as you are. You're making too much goddamn noise. What's your job? To try and attract the Germans?"

Henri decided in a hurry that he could trust no one here. He scraped the blade of knife along Philippe's neck. The bully backed off.

"No."

"Then let's get moving," and he jumped up with the agility of a circus performer, moving toward Florence as he did. "There are canisters with precious equipment in that field. Where's the rest of the reception committee."

Philippe had moved from officer to corporal in a flash. Florence, who wasn't too keen on Philippe, gave a light smile. Later she would recall how Philipe had almost got them killed and more than once.

Henri now changed his tone. He gave orders and Philippe obeyed.

"You and I will locate the canisters and you, Florence, will bring up the rest of the reception committee. Are there many Germans around here?"

"Not that many, at least until the last month or so."

That fit with what he already knew. The Germans had troops on the ground, working with the Milice, or French police, and the Gestapo. But the increase in activity was because the Germans were preparing for the invasion that every school child knew must come. It was Henri's job to make their lives a misery, and let London know what the Wehrmacht was up to.

"Do you attack them?" asked Henri as they walked across the field of winter wheat.

"No it's too dangerous. We concentrate on blowing up rail lines."

"When the train is there?" asked Henri.

"No. Again, too dangerous. And we might hurt the driver and the train crew. They are French, after all."

Henri didn't speak right away. He was taking it in, not believing what he was hearing.

"Too dangerous? It's too dangerous not to attack. From now on at least ten Germans will be killed every time they come into this sector. And the trains will stop running on time. I hear the Germans like their trains to run on time."

Henri drew his 45 from its holster. Philippe looked at the weapon, he'd never seen one before. He asked about it.

"An American 45. That means it's 45 calibre, American measure. Bigger than a 9-mm. Blows a hole the size of grapefruit in a man. Hit him just about anywhere and he dies."

The reason a British agent was carrying an American gun had to do with bureaucracy and British Army prejudices. They didn't like automatic pistols and in any case didn't have any in their stores. Henri knew that but he didn't bother telling Philippe, to whom he had taken an instant dislike.

Philippe looked more concerned as the barrel waved in a circle, sometimes pointing at him. He thought, this man doesn't do things by mistake. He was right.

"I don't really like it though. I want a Luger. We'll have to find a German officer and take his Luger and his knife. They're mostly SS here, are they not?"

"Yes, we call them the Gestapo, but they're really the SD. The police arm of the SS." Philippe spoke with a hatred mixed with fear. "We can hate them, but they're ruthless. Kill one of them they execute dozens of us."

Henri Foix's eyes brightened, and an almost boyish smile lit up his face.

"Then," he said staring straight at Philippe, "we will be more terrible. Our job is to kill Germans. We'll kill so many they won't have time for reprisals. Every dead German is one more who won't be firing at our troops when they come."

By this time they were back at the rendezvous spot. The woman heard their conversation and Florence spoke for the first time. "And when are they coming, Monsieur?"

"Pierre. I'm not Monsieur," said Henri. "And they are coming soon."

"Not soon enough," said Florence. Henri looked at her. Too bad he couldn't put her spirit in Philippe's body.

12

Claire was more uninhibited than usual and in fact put Jack through his paces. For once he felt a bit older. They lay in bed for a while afterwards and Jack smiled to himself and wondered about what he and his friends back home referred to as a second shot on goal. Another half hour and he might be ready.

He started fooling around, trying to fire up Claire's desire in advance. But all of a sudden she bucked him off, throwing him to one side of the bed.

"Leave me alone, for God's sake."

She headed for the bathroom where she would stay for at least twenty minutes. She did smile back at him before going in, a kind of peace offering, which he accepted. There was always the afternoon. Before getting into his newspapers, he debated calling room service for a surprise breakfast, if there was room service. But the room was too small and he didn't feel like tidying it up.

He read *The Economist* as he waited for Claire.

The restaurant downstairs did know how to make coffee and Claire was happy to see they served croissants, though she gave a running critique of English cooking, and baking, as she ate two of them. A big eater, she never seemed to put on a pound.

"Did you find any interesting dead people in the newspapers?" She didn't wait for an answer. "I can't believe I'm in love with a ghoul."

Jack smiled. He was amazed at how well she had mastered the English idiom. She'd been in England for just three years and didn't speak much English when she arrived. A miracle when compared to the pidgin French he'd been speaking for most of his life. He put it down to English being an easier language to speak.

"There was one. It was in the *Trib*. A Canadian who was a diplomat in London during the Blitz. I have his book at home, or I used to. He went on about his love affairs. Quite a passionate guy, though he didn't look it on the surface," said Jack.

"I think it must be the weather."

Jack screwed up his face at this non sequitur. "What are you talking about?"

Claire, who had never been west of Brest, started on her weather theory. And she made a rare geographical note of the colder part of North America.

"You Canadians. It's so cold over there you have nothing to do in the winter but huddle in bed. Look at you. It's all you ever think about. This old man, the same thing, chasing the women during the war."

Jack laughed and wondered how she had the nerve to come out with some of this stuff.

"It's true, for God's sake. And don't laugh. It's one of the reasons I love you. You're so warm in bed, the warmest. Let's go for a walk and then make love again."

Jack didn't know if she was kidding, but he could use a walk.

Good morning for it. A little past ten o'clock and the sun was out but it wasn't yet hot. It might get steamy later in the day. They went through the village and followed the signs to Blenheim Palace. They didn't talk. She tended to walk too fast for him, he was lazy and didn't like to walk faster than he had to, but she wrapped her arm through his and leaned into him from time to time. He rather liked that.

There were huge gates at the Palace and a man sat in an ornate ticket booth looking like a London bus conductor. He was in a uniform, complete with cap, and had one of those machines they use on buses to dispense tickets.

"Inside the house or just the grounds?"

Jack didn't like poking about in other people's houses, even if they were big museums like this one. Seemed envious, almost an admission of failure that you had to gawk at some rich man's house.

"Just the grounds thanks."

He sorted out a few coins and they made their way inside.

Blenheim Palace was huge. Not a castle, but a giant red house out in the farmland. "I think it's rather ugly. Big, but not delicate or anything. At the risk of sucking up to you, I think those French châteaus are much nicer."

Claire corrected his French, "You don't need an s on that word."

"What?"

"Châteaux. The plural sounds the same as the singular. Like deer in English. Or moose in Canada. "

She knew more about English than he did, he thought. She studied it, making sure she didn't make mistakes. Her accent she could not change; it was almost a perfect stage French accent. He thought it rather sexy, but she got angry if he brought it up. She thought his French so abominable she refused to let him speak it.

There was a statue at the end of a long stretch of grass. He assumed it was John Churchill, the first Duke of Marlborough.

"Winston Churchill was born here, you know," said Jack. She didn't answer, maybe because she already knew that. "Funny it's all due to war and a war with the French. I don't suppose you study it much in France?"

She wasn't much of a nationalist but she rose to the fly. "We study the victories. Napoleon only lost one big battle. And we won France back from England. Remember Jeanne d'Arc? We won the Hundred Years War."

The wars of his own century were the ones that fascinated Jack. He wondered if Claire's family did anything. He shared the general Anglo-Saxon prejudice that the French did nothing in the Second War. She surprised him by answering his question before he asked.

"My family doesn't like the war. Sometimes I hate to even talk about it. I see sometimes in those obituaries of yours that people have had what you call a good war. Well we didn't have a good war. My grandmother was half Jewish. So even though we didn't practice, to the Germans we were Jews."

Jack said nothing. He did some mental arithmetic and figured she must have been born in 1960, maybe 1959. That meant her parents survived.

"Only one person in our family was murdered in the camps. My uncle, my mother's brother, I never knew him. Obviously. But the Gestapo were after the rest of the family. They were saved by a Canadian. Someone who worked with the Underground."

Jack waited. He was curious but he didn't want to start acting like a reporter and asking questions, though he wanted to know the Canadian's name. She was quiet for a minute, and then started talking again.

"My mother is still scarred. She never wants to admit she's part Jewish, she just denies the whole thing. Once, just a couple of years ago, when I went to Israel with my ex-husband, she got angry. She said we should never tell anyone."

Again Jack kept quiet. They were now close to the statue. Jack looked up. The Brits sure paid off their heroes, he thought. They went off to look at a lake before turning around to walk back to the village. It would a bit after noon by the time they got back.

He couldn't wait any longer. "What was the Canadian's name? Do you remember?"

Jack thought she might object to his probing, but she didn't.

"It was a French name. Strange, sort of old-fashioned sounding. I can't remember. I'll ask my father. My mother wouldn't tell me. She might even have pushed it out of her mind."

"Well what did he do, to save them I mean?"

"It had to do with a bargain he made with the Gestapo. He threatened the Germans, and told them he would step up his attacks on them if they didn't leave the Jews alone in his sector. He was some kind of an agent. My father knows the story."

Jack let it drop. But in his mind he was planning a trip to France. A cross-channel excursion in the Renault 4. He wasn't that nuts about meeting parents, it was too close to getting married. She might not like it either, but he'd work on it over the next little while.

The weather changed as they walked back through the gate. Clouds moved in fast, and the temperature dropped. It was going to rain and the dark clouds off in the west meant it might even thunder. He loved storms. They made it back to The Bear just as the rain started.

Claire kissed him as they got inside the door to their room. They fumbled their way out of their clothes and made love on top of the bed cover. She made a little squealing noise when she came and then started to cry. Just as the thunderstorm started they crawled under the covers and went to sleep for an hour.

She slept, Jack lay awake thinking, listening to the storm.

13

OUTSIDE LYON, THE LAST FEW DAYS OF WINTER, 1944

The hired man's room above the shed was a little cold, but Henri was used to it, the cold that is. His mother believed fresh air was the tonic of life and insisted he sleep with the windows open. The Jesuits had kept the dormitory at freezing temperature, with the windows open at each end of the hall. He seemed to remember mornings when there was a thin film of ice in the water glass by his bed. When he was an older boy at school he thought the priests kept it cold to discourage some of the girlier boys from roving at night.

Now he was living in a place almost as primitive as his school dormitory. Florence was his wife. Overnight someone made her a second identity card, changing her name to Florence Foix. He was Pierre Foix.

Florence was already married. Her husband was in a labour camp in Germany. Henri had never met anyone who hated another people as much as Florence hated Germans. It might have seemed difficult to pull off, in a place where you couldn't trust all the neighbours. But Florence had in fact come from another part of France and no one knew her husband by sight. It was dangerous, but they hoped it would work.

Their house was in an industrial suburb, a place of light industry and small houses, each with a patch of land just big enough to keep a kitchen garden or even a few chickens. Both Florence and her husband were Communists. Which was why she wasn't too keen on Philippe. Too bourgeois. He had a villa in a smart part of Lyon and a flat in Paris. It was hard to know what he ever did for a living, at least before the war.

"You listen to the way he speaks," said Florence while she and Henri ate dinner. "He's very grand. I think he might own properties in Paris and Lyon. Rental properties. Imagine, a landlord. The worst type of capitalist parasite."

Henri just nodded. For one thing he was rather apolitical. For another his father owned a lot of land, his uncle some rental properties in the city. At university he steered away from the political groups. He belonged to a club that read the classics and held discussions in the evenings. He played chess. But he studied chemistry and had a keen interest in radios. He once built his own crystal set, a rather complex one, just to see if he could.

Since he came from a rather bourgeois background himself, he wasn't that big on critiquing the rich. Though as he listened to Florence he remembered some of the biggest communists at university came from rich families. He made a note again that if these people didn't trust each other, he wasn't going to trust them.

He had only been here two days. His job was to organize the Maquis into a fighting force, not to get involved in local politics. Let Philippe and Florence fight it out after the war. For now, they were all on the same side.

Last night he had met members of the local Underground. So far he didn't trust anyone, though maybe in a strange way, Philippe. After the run-in on the first night he found Philippe reminded him of a fellow named Latour, one of his friends at school. Arrogant on the surface, but witty in conversation. Not coordinated. What the Jews he knew in Montreal might call a klutz.

Henri looked across at Florence. He smiled at her and she back at him. He thought of how he might like a little distraction to kill time until lunch. But he'd promised himself: no romantic entanglements while he was fighting. Instead he decided to take a tour on his own and check the lay of the land.

"I'm going out. I'll take the bicycle," he said as she looked over at him.

"Do you want me to come with you? You might get lost?"

"No. I have to learn where things are."

He put on one of her husband's berets and took the old bike on the road to Lyon. He figured it shouldn't take too long. He was dressed in a warm tweed jacket, a shirt that was worn at the collar, but with a tie. To keep warm he wore a big scarf, tied like a foulard to keep neck and chest from feeling the bite of the wind.

It was a little before noon when he bicycled along the river Saône. He turned down a street and went by a large cathedral. He had studied the maps of the city, and its history. In a bookshop in London he had found an old Michelin Guide to the place and he knew it was more important to the Romans than Paris ever was.

He leaned his bike against a wall near the cathedral and walked along into a wide square. The streets were made of thick paving stones with a gutter running down the middle. The square opened up, with the Hôtel de ville on one side, a huge statue – it wasn't only the English who lionized their heroes – and cafés along the edge.

Hard to think there was a war going on. The restaurants were half full and some sat outside as the sun had pushed the temperature up to 15 at midday. He forced himself to think in the metric temperature, that child of the French revolution.

The outside table on the sunny side of the square. Henri was hungry from his bicycle ride into town. He ordered a beer, a thick soup and a sandwich. When the waitress came it struck him that this was the first time he would pay for anything in French money.

"Bonjour," came the deep, soft voice of a woman at the table behind him. There was something about the accent he found odd.

"All of a sudden it's so beautiful here. Well, it should be, spring is just a few days away," said the woman, a stunning blonde with sharp blue eyes. Not German, the accent was something else.

"You couldn't have sat out here a few hours ago," said Henri, deciding to turn on the charm with a smile. His stomach was in a quick knot, not because the woman was so beautiful, but because she might be dangerous.

She feigned a lack of interest as she ordered. Henri took a packet of Gitanes from his pocket and then some matches in a yellow box. As he struck the match on the box he noticed the writing on the side was in English.

A stupid mistake. He palmed them like a desk of cards and didn't rush to put them back into his pocket. Had she seen them?

"A beautiful place Lyon, are you from here?" asked the blonde.

"No I'm from Normandy, but I moved here after the end of the war. Our war, anyway," Henri paused, not wanting to give anything else away. "Lyon is, of course, a place of languages and schools. What about you? There's a trace of something exotic in your French?"

"Ah, you have a good ear, Monsieur."

He knew he did. He wondered whether she would tell him about her accent. He prodded.

"And where are you from?"

"Warsaw. I too came here when our war was over and it was over a lot earlier than yours."

"About nine months earlier," said Henri.

"Long enough to have a baby," she said with a laugh, changing the subject to the mundane.

Henri decided not to probe. What on earth could a Polish woman, and one that looked like a movie star, be doing in Lyon?

"Have you ever seen the amphitheatre? The Romans, they were so creative. Now there was a new world order. This was a Roman city, you know?"

"Well I knew there was an amphitheatre. But I've never seen it. I'm a little rusty on my Roman history. I'm a working man, not a thinking man."

Henri spent time eating his sandwich as his new friend leafed through a magazine, in almost a theatrical way. He knew she would speak again, he would just wait.

"I think I'll go to the amphitheatre today. Would you like to come?"

"Not today, maybe another time," said Henri.

"How about tomorrow? If I show you where the funicular is, we can meet there."

If this were happening at a café in Montreal, Henri would be counting the hours until he could sleep with this woman. For now he would follow her to the funicular, the tram that went sideways up the hill from the flat near the square.

About ten minutes later they walked over to the place where it left.

"I live up there too. It's a trip I make twice a day."

Or eight times a day if it suits you, thought Henri.

"You're sure you're busy today?" She leaned over and touched the side of his face. Henri felt his heart race. He smiled and touched her arm.

"I'm sure. But I have to be here tomorrow. So, why don't we say noon?"

He turned to walk away. "I forgot. You didn't tell me your name."

"No I didn't." He smiled and took a long way back to his bicycle, wondering whether this woman was a whore or a spy, or both.

As he rode his bicycle back Henri thought about the woman in the square. She was so obvious, it shocked him. He thought a spy would be more subtle. Even a whore – and he been accosted by some on Pierce Street in Montreal – was not as bold.

It got him to thinking about how precious his time was on the ground. He could be caught any time. Then what good would he be? Henri was anxious to do something. Right now, that very moment. A car slowed as it passed him, a big Citroen, and it made him uneasy. Who else would drive a Citroen?

14

"Is that your railway window?" asked Henri, almost his first words as he walked into Florence's house. He nodded his head in the direction of a window at the back of the kitchen. From there you see the main railway line that ran north from Lyon.

Florence was somewhat shocked by the change in the tone of his voice from the morning. All business. The Citroen hadn't stopped, but now he was on edge. He needed to do something, anything before he was picked up.

"Yes. The Germans like timetables. And I have a good idea of theirs." She looked at her watch. "Wait fifteen minutes and we'll go into the garden."

He knew from just two days of watching Florence that she was an obsessive train spotter, writing down the times trains passed, making notes if they were carrying what looked like military equipment or troops.

She explained to Henri that she did more than take notes. A cousin of hers worked for the railway and left a message for her inside a church outside the convent down the road. The paper was taped to the bottom of the coin box for lighting candles. Simple, and there were few Germans in church.

"This afternoon there will be a goods train with some special cars. If I'm right they will be camouflaged. Probably artillery pieces heading for the coast."

92

Henri looked at his watch.

"How far up the line is the nearest bridge?"

"Why?" asked Florence.

"Why do you think?"

Later she'd tell Henri that as soon as he said that her mouth went dry. She figured it was the mix of fear and excitement. "There's one just past that line of factories. It goes over a narrow road."

Henri was already up and packing his kit. He had some plastique and a length of fuse wire hidden outside. "How long by bicycle?"

'Five minutes, maybe seven. But it's too dangerous." Florence was scared at how fast Henri was moving. He stared at her and gave an order.

"You'll take me there and then you can leave. But madame, we are going now."

They grabbed two bikes from the shed. What worried Florence was that it was a little after four o'clock. There would be people out. They might get hurt. Henri seemed to read her mind.

"Don't worry about your neighbours. I'll try not to hurt them. But this is a war. Every one of those guns that doesn't make it to the coast could mean thousands of soldiers who make it past the beaches alive. Your husband will be home a lot faster."

Florence steeled herself, and pedalled ahead of Henri. They travelled fast, but didn't race. Florence was just a few inches shorter than Henri and, like him, slender. Her dark hair came out from a kerchief. They looked like a married couple, in the way they didn't pay that much attention to each other and because they looked like a matched set.

It took six minutes. The last few hundred yards of road were in behind what looked like an abandoned warehouse. Henri propped his bicycle against a wall.

"You can go home now."

Florence shook her head.

She said in voice that sounded like a wife scolding her husband, "You'll just get lost."

"Hold this then." Henri passed her a wire. He looked at the bridge and saw it was much too massive for the amount of explosive he had. It was a masonry arch, thick and well built. He had another idea. He climbed up the embankment and placed some plastique between a rail and a sleeper, picking the spot where there was a joint between two sections of rail.

They taught this technique in Scotland, and in an instant Henri thought back to playing on the railway tracks when he was a boy. A railwayman, riding on a handcar, checking rails on the line near his father's country house. A man named Buster who spoke in the thick accent of English Quebecers telling Henri where the weak spot was on a rail. And that was just where he put his explosive, on the space where the two rails joined.

Just then he thought he could feel the train coming, vibrating through the rail. He had to hurry. He shoved the wire into the detonator and was careful backing down the hill; he didn't want to break the connection. Now he could hear the train. He trotted backwards for the last fifty yards, rolling out the line. Then the two of them stood just around a corner of the warehouse.

Smoke poured from the locomotive. It had built up speed but was still straining to pull its load up the slight grade. It was doing maybe 40 kilometres an hour. The engine passed over the explosive charge. Florence's eyes opened wide. Nothing happened.

"What's wrong? Why won't it work?"

Henri didn't even look at her. His eyes were pressed narrow, as if he wanted to concentrate the light coming into his brain, to make the whole picture clear.

"Quiet."

The locomotive and coal car crossed the bridge and Henri looked back at the rest of the train. Having come this far he was going for perfection. He'd like to get the artillery pieces or whatever they might be. He could see only three or four cars at a time. The rest of the train was blocked by another building.

So far he had counted twenty regular cars. There could be munitions in them but he didn't know. He told himself the next time he was going to try to get manifests for these trains. He looked at his watch. They had been in the same place for minutes. If anyone had seen them it could be dangerous. He thought he heard something, but it was hard to hear above the racket of the rail cars.

Then he saw them. Two cars, right in the middle of the train, covered in camouflage. From the outline, they looked like big guns. He waited until the first one passed the bridge and then set off the plastique. The sound of the explosion was almost muffled by the train. In a microsecond one end of the wooden sleeper was splintered, flying in a thousand directions, and the spikes holding down the rails were like shrapnel ripping into the bottom of the car.

But the rail itself did the real damage.

As the wheel moved off the joint the rail ripped up and out, so fast it was hard to see it. All of a sudden there was nothing for the wheels to ride on and the next axle rammed into the other half of the steel rail. In a flash the tracks gave way and the axle was pulled straight off the bottom of the railcar, the wheels scoring a deep rut in the embankment as they moved straight down into the yard of the warehouse. The second car derailed, pulling the other one down the embankment.

The huge gun stayed chained to the wooden flat bed, its weight pulling it in the direction the axles were headed. The barrel of the gun arched in the sky, snapping the links of a thick steel chain that held it bolted to the car. There was a symphony of noises, each piece of twisting metal sounding like another part of an orchestra tuning before a concert.

Chaos.

It all seemed to be happening in slow motion for Henri, his little package of plastique pulling down hundreds of tons of metal and wood. He saw the first gun had also fallen, and had even damaged one end of what until a moment ago had seemed an indestructible bridge. The second artillery piece was also doing its macabre dance in the sky. Henri knew he should leave but he was frozen as if watching a fireworks display.

Then the force behind pulling wooden freight cars tossed the second flatbed car into the air like a child's toy and one of its huge axles smashed into the first gun carriage, splitting the barrel away as if it had been hit by a ten-inch naval gun.

Florence grabbed at him.

"Pierre, we have to leave."

Again Henri didn't even look at her. He seemed mesmerized by the destruction. "Just one second. I want to gauge the size of that gun. A hundred and five millimetres at least. Maybe more." He shouted since there was still the noise of cars pilling one on top of the other. He knew they would suspect sabotage, because the cars carrying the guns were first to go.

"Alright. I've seen enough."

He pulled what wire was left in the yard and shoved it under his sweater. Then they were on their bikes pedalling through the old industrial estate. They could still hear the final sounds of grinding metal. In the distance came the honking sound French sirens make. Henri thought of huge flocks of snow geese in the thawing cornfields in the early spring. Pedalling along she was first this time. He thought of stopping for bread. It would seem a normal, domestic thing to do. But he changed his mind. They would be home in four minutes now. The streets seemed empty.

"Slow down, madame. We aren't running from anything." Then he changed his mind and stopped at the baker's a few doors from their make-believe matrimonial home. He thought he remembered the baker was safe.

There was no one else in the shop. "Some terrible noises Monsieur Pierre. And now these sirens. Has something happened?" A hint of a smile on the baker's face as he took the money for two baguettes.

Outside the shop, Henri smiled at Florence. "Let's walk the bicycles back. It's only a short trip. This bread is still warm. Do we have any cheese?"

The baker worried Henri. He didn't trust anyone in France, in particular anyone who had this much information for the Germans. He thought about whether he should go back and try to convince the man to keep his mouth shut.

"Can we trust that baker?" asked Henri.

Florence knew treachery more than Henri. "Him, yes."

As they sat in the kitchen Henri looked out the back window and wondered whether the stalled cars he saw were all on the tracks. Maybe the derailment had shunted this far back.

15

There weren't many people on the platform when the train pulled into the Sloane Square tube station. Jack had already read two papers and was now relaxing with a *Daily Mail*. Nigel Dempster was on about the drug habits of some young aristocrat. Chasing druggies. Waste of time, thought Jack, even though he never touched dope anymore. What difference did it make?

He thought the English had the right idea, which was to pretty much ignore drugs, at least the users. Only the rich or famous addicts made it into the papers. He remembered someone he grew up with who went to jail for having a sandwich bag of marijuana. And the Americans. Putting all the poor black guys in jail for selling stuff to rich white kids.

There were plenty of seats on the tube at ten thirty in the morning and he could ride straight through to the stop for the newspaper office. Though he hadn't planned to go to work that day, there was always a check run late Monday morning. He could pick up any new assignments and do his banking.

Following the advice of *The Dirty Weekend Handbook* cost more money than he thought it would, so he had to put the pedal to the metal and earn some cash. He had stayed up and finished the obit on Pat O'Brien, the Nagasaki man. He filed it before he went to bed, which meant he slept well.

He read the paper, looking up every stop to check where he was. Seven stops later he walked up to the street and over to the office. As usual the lobby was filled with at least one nutter trying to get in to see a columnist. Today it was a 'seer,' one of those prediction specialists.

"You can see by this list that last year I was right about every prediction, right down to the royal baby." Jack thought to himself, the accent is so forced cockney it could be Australian. They'd both hate that, the cockney and the Australian that is. And he could have told her she was barking up the wrong newspaper. They don't do seers here, luv, that's *News of the World*.

Geoffrey Langton was at his desk, looking as if he wasn't doing any work. In fact he was always doing at least three things at once, which this morning would include writing an obituary, fact checking one from the navy stringer and giving Jack enough work to last him a week. He wanted two obits from Jack this week, one on the Canadian diplomat, the other on a minor American rock star with a major drug habit.

The Canadian war Lothario would have to wait.

"Ah Devlin. Got something for you if you want it. Some American druggie has done himself in and one of your old High Commissioners has moved on. You're up for it I assume?"

Jack smiled and reached over for the scraps of paper. He didn't even have to pitch the old diplomat; Langton was already on to him. He wondered if he should tell him he'd already spotted him, but why piss on Langton's parade.

"You betcha," he said using an American slang phrase he might never use at home. But part of his act was that he was their American. He had to act like one, dress like one and talk like one so they thought he was the real thing. He could imagine Langton describing him to his wife, as 'our American expert, a Canadian chap, wears the strangest clothes.'

Jeans were the strange clothes. The fashion hadn't caught on, at least not at the paper, of wearing jeans, a dress

shirt and a blazer. Jack even wore a tie. He considered himself quite conventional.

He moved over to the desk he shared with one of the
military stringers, who was almost never there. He opened
the drawer and fished in the back for the spot where he hid
the yellow marking pencil. He went over the death notices
and highlighted the names of the politician's children. He
had died a senator, so this would be easy, but it would have to
wait until Parliament opened in Ottawa, which was two
o'clock London time. Make it two thirty, he might be busy
over lunch.

His fingers worked what he thought was the awkward
dial on the phone. He waited for the ring. British phone habits
amazed him. This was a company and the phone rang a dozen
times until someone answered it.

"May I speak to Michelle Perry please?"

He waited again while the phone rang another five times.
Last week there had been an article in the *Financial Times*
about New York telephone habits. The reporter must have
just arrived on his new beat, because he was astounded to
find people in Manhattan expected the phone to be answered
on the second or third ring.

"Americans will ring off after four rings, assuming they
have dialled the wrong number," wrote the incredulous young
reporter from the *FT*.

"Have a good weekend?"

"Oh Jack, it's you. Yes. Did you?"

Well he'd had one of the great dirty weekends of the
decade but he thought he'd keep that a secret.

"Not bad. Hate to be so abrupt, but do you want to have
lunch today?" The truth was he needed some radio work, and
maybe even some TV news voice-overs. Better to schmooze
though.

"Sure, I'd love to," said Michelle, who was glad Jack
called for two reasons. She needed someone to do some scripts
that afternoon. Write them and read them. "And I hate to be
so businesslike but I need a few stories done after lunch. Do
you think you can manage it?"

His lucky day. "Can I have the spare office?" he knew he'd need it for the obit work.

Michelle didn't care. "Sure. Shall we meet at Mario's at twelve fifteen?"

They agreed. It was eleven thirty. That gave Jack time for a couple of calls to Paris, where the druggie had died. Next, the library.

"Maggie can you get me some clippings on Matt Harris?"

"Oh the rock star. Should be easy. Anything else?"

"Yeah there was a book on him last year. I think Mark Rose did it. Just let me know which bookshop has it. I'll call you this afternoon. Can you do the clippings in 15 minutes?"

"Should be easy." It was her favourite expression and she never lied.

Langton knew Jack spoke French, so it was another reason he had the Matt Harris obit. He made a call to a friend of his in Paris. Already at lunch. He'd get back to him later. He told Langton he'd do the druggie first, the politico second.

"Could you do him for tomorrow? Six hundred words."

"Piece of cake," one of Jack's favourite expressions and one which annoyed some of the people he worked for. "I'll file it from home tonight. Off to see Maggie the magician downstairs." More smart alec talk.

He read the Matt Harris package in the back of the cab on the way to Mario's. The tube might have been faster, but this was easier. He could get Michelle to pick up the cab if she wanted two scripts done today.

Matt Harris was what they used to call a one-hit wonder. His albums had sold well, but it was his leather pants and beautiful face on the covers that did the job. *Rock My Fire* was his one big hit and the story from this morning's *Trib* said rock stations in the States were playing it twice an hour. Even the boring British rock station was playing it on the taxi radio.

"What did you think of him?" Jack asked the cabbie.

"Too flash for me, mate. Live fast, die young, you know what I mean?"

Articulate prick, thought Jack. But he might get something so he kept on. The average London cabbie was a quote machine, maybe this one just needed a bit of prodding.

"Yeah, well I guess you have to feel sorry for the poor bastard?"

"I'll tell you about Matt fucking Harris, mate. He was a cunt. A drug addict and a piece of fucking rubbish. The world is a better place without him."

Cut out the fucking and the cunt and it wasn't a bad quote. Might not fit in an obituary, but he was sure he could fit it in somewhere. He could do a re-jig of his obit as a news story and sell it to a paper in Montreal or Toronto. Who was he to sneeze at a hundred and fifty bucks?

"By the way, I'm a reporter. Mind if quote you?"

"Go right ahead, mate. Name's Lackey. Vince Lackey."

Then he thought about the radio item. He pulled a small tape recorder from his briefcase, turned it on and pointed through the cab's glass at Vince.

"Just a short bite for Canadian radio. Give me the same thing without the cunt or the fuck." Vince blasted out the short quote as if did this for a living. No cunt, no fuck and a mate.

Jack gave him a couple of pound coins as a tip.

"Here's a receipt. And here's another one with my address," said the cabbie scribbling it down. 'Send me a copy of the article."

And that, thought Jack, is why it's so easy to be a reporter in London. Everyone is a clipmeister.

Michelle, the English girl with the French name, was already sitting at the table in Mario's, smoking what Jack guessed was her third cigarette since noon. He was trying to quit, but since everyone here seemed to smoke it was impossible.

She smiled as he sat down and stubbed out her cigarette.

"Jack, you lucky boy. I now have three stories for you to knock off. The Paris stringer is involved in some crisis, and you'll have to do a Matt Harris obit for the nightly news. The other stuff will run later, maybe tomorrow, maybe on the weekend. I've already written it and pulled some clips from the Beeb, so all you have to do is read."

Jack leaned over and kissed her. "You're making me rich. Are you open to a reverse bribe?"

"What do you mean reverse?" laughed Michelle.

"Champagne. But only half a bottle. I have to read this afternoon."

She didn't say anything so he motioned to the waiter.

After the first glass Michelle went back to their latest conversation. She'd had a gin to start and no food, so her eyes were getting their hooded, sexy look, though it wasn't sex she had on her mind.

"I spoke to my father about the SOE. He knew quite a bit more. I told him we were talking about it and he started telling me stories about the people they dropped into Europe. Most of the agents he dropped, he dropped into France."

Michelle's long fingers reached for a Rothmans. Jack picked up her lighter and lit her cigarette. He thought about having one, but told himself it was too early. Michelle kept talking about the SOE. He thought he might like to meet the father. There could be a magazine piece in it, if Canadians were involved.

Jack interrupted. "Can I ask you a weird question?"

She looked at him, thinking the champagne might have made him decide on a course of seduction. Just then the waiter interrupted, as waiters always do, killing the punch line. They each ordered veal, one lemon, one picata.

"And what did you want to ask me?"

"I'd like to meet your father. This SOE stuff has me interested. I'd like to learn some more. Can I take him out to lunch?"

Michelle was smiling. "I thought you were going to ask him for my hand, Jack."

"Not this week."

"Well it'll have to be on the weekend. My father lives in St. Albans. I'll call him later." She took a dramatic pause, made up of a pull on the Rothmans and a sip of the *Veuve Cliquot*. "Saturday lunch. Though I wouldn't want to spoil your weekend, Jack."

It might have spoiled last weekend, but not this one. Lunch was good. St. Albans was Paddington, thought Jack. Shouldn't be much more than an hour. Lunch would be three hours. He could be back by six and still see Claire.

"Sure. You set it up."

Just then Homer, the American reporter, came over. Michelle winced. He leaned over, asked Jack what he was working on and then came to the real point of his visit.

"Much going on Michelle?" Homer needed work.

Michelle was in a good mood, but she wanted to be rid of Homer so she was more direct than usual.

"There is, Homer. But Jack and I are in a heavy discussion. I'm not sure, but I think he's going to propose marriage. Can this wait until after lunch?"

Homer didn't know where to look.

"Sure, I didn't mean to interrupt. Look, I'll come over around three, that okay?"

"See you then Homer, goodbye."

Jack looked at Homer and shrugged his shoulders. Then when he was sure he was out of earshot, they both laughed.

"Well that rumour will be back at the office before you are," said Jack. "Reporters can't keep secrets, you know. That's why they're reporters."

The veal arrived just then, giving Michelle a chance to change the subject. They did agree that he would make the trip to St. Albans this Saturday.

"Find something for Homer to do, will you?" asked Jack who felt guilty because he was so flush. She promised. Homer owed him, but he could never tell him about it.

Back across the street, Jack had to get to work on obit number two. Matt Harris would be a snap. Famous people always were. Along with the file from the paper, Michelle had pulled out more stuff, including a chapter from a book on rock and roll. It was xeroxed. Even her script was so good that it could work as an outline for the obit.

He didn't have studio time until four thirty. The other two stories he would have to record at eight that night. It was going to be a long day, but then he might not have to work for the rest of the week.

The rock star was easy. The politician would be trickier, unless he got lucky. He grabbed the *Canadian Parliamentary Guide* and *Who's Who* and xeroxed the pages. A senator at the end of his life. Could have some secrets. Jack closed the door to the spare office and called someone he knew in Ottawa.

As he waited for the call to connect, his eyes hit pay dirt. The dead senator belonged to Whites and another club in St. James. An anglophile Canadian. Maybe that's why they wanted this guy. Langton knew everything. It was depressing.

The phone rang. "Hi. Devlin here."

"Devlin, how are you my dear boy?" The man from the Senate affected old-world charm. He was one of those odd bachelors who devoted their lives to the government and were sometimes embarrassed to be caught in raids by the Ottawa police, who were not men of the world.

"We have this senator, Archie McArthur. The paper wants an obit on him. Did you know him at all?" A dumb question. The executive assistant to the leader of the Opposition in the Senate knew everything.

"Most interesting man in the Senate," and Jack scribbled for 15 minutes as the man from Ottawa filled in the large blanks left in the official shorthand life as listed in *Who's Who* and the *Parliamentary Guide*. "And you know he was at Canada House during the war. Big man with the ladies I'm told."

"I do read," said Jack, a reference to the old senator's memoirs. The man from the Senate laughed but, just before he hung up, asked Jack a bizarre question.

"You doing anything on Colonel Foix?"

"How did you know?" said Jack.

"Well a paper like yours should. One of the great heroes of the war. Big funeral planned here."

"I am doing it. Can you fax me what you've got?"

"Yeah the prime minister is pulling out all the stops. Makes the separatists look bad, a war hero from Quebec with more medals than you can count. Separatism started in 1944, you know, spawned by conscription."

Jack was going to argue it started in 1917, with an earlier conscription crisis, but he didn't have the time. He gave him the fax number at the network and said goodbye. Now he had too much work to do and he was cutting it close. He could use the rest of the week off.

As he hung up the phone, Michelle came in and told him they had moved up the studio time. Could he do the rock star in 15 minutes? Easy. It was leading into a clip from a rock journalist from Paris, a voice-over some background sound and into 15 seconds of the refrain of *Rock My Fire*.

"And they're going to take the same thing for television. The Paris guy had to rush to Beirut. So no date sign-off, just your name."

Bit of a cheat that. The audience never knew that no place name in the sign-off meant the reporter had never been farther than the studio door. An announcer rather than a reporter. But in the news business it passed as honesty.

Jack banged away at polishing the rocker script. It came to no more than 200 words. It had to have a featurish spin to it and Jack had no trouble with the closing.

Perhaps a London taxi driver summed it up best. As Rock My Fire played on the English radio station, he gave his rather blunt take on Matt Harris.

"I'll tell you about Matt Harris, mate. A drug addict and piece of rubbish. The world's a better place without him."

Maybe the cabbie is a little blunt but it could be how many people in this country felt about Matt Harris. (Sound up of Song) But the world is certainly a quieter place without him. From London this is Jack Devlin.

Just the kind of sentimental crap he could never get into a real obit. What did Marshall McLuhan say about radio?

Was it the hot, emotional one where it's easy to push all the buttons? The item would run three minutes in radio, two minutes on cooler TV. No cabbie. Then there was the other stuff to voice-over later. Double dipping. And two short political items to feed at 8 o'clock. The bill from the Bear at Woodstock was paid off, and then some.

Lunch with Michelle should always be this good.

16

A FARMHOUSE OUTSIDE LYON, SPRING 1944

Rabbit was on the menu that night, as it was whenever the two farm boys ate meat. Henri looked at them sitting in a damp cellar. They were much younger than he, and back home they would still be in school, though they told him they left school to work on the farm when they were 14.

Jean and Louis. The older joked one of us is named after a saint, the other after a king. Henri decided not to point out there was a King Louis who was a saint.

Even at 18 or 19 their hands were huge, roughened by years of fieldwork. Each wore a cap that looked as if it had a permanent place on their heads. Their father was a tenant farmer on a large estate and they were in a wine cellar near the edge of the outbuildings at the main farm. Behind them were barrels filled with red wine, and they poured glass after glass.

Though they didn't have much formal schooling, they had ideas. Both were socialists, not communists, and both hated the Germans. Their secret cellar was where the local Maquis, the soldiers of the resistance, stored their arms. Behind the barrels were clips for Sten guns, grenades, pistols and some automatic weapons.

"Drink Monsieur Pierre," said one of the brothers. Henri wasn't sure which one was which.

Henri had been on the ground in France for almost ten days now. He knew the leaders of the local resistance, and he was training them in the early mornings and at the end of the day. It was late now and the rest of the troop had gone home. Henri was here to find out where all the arms were. The brothers were in charge of this cache.

"Have you killed many of the Boches, Pierre?" asked the skinnier of the two brothers.

"It depends who was on that train," said Henri, who now wanted to get to the business at hand.

"So, how many places do you have arms stored? Tell me. No one should write it down."

The other brother drained his glass and used it to point. "Up there in the woods beside the vineyard. There are crates buried and covered with leaves. They shouldn't be difficult to find. Then in the other woods, beside the field, where they hunt in the winter. I'll show you tomorrow."

He got up and opened the drawer on the table in front of him, the one on which the rabbit was sitting, took out a knife and started to sharpen it on a stone he pulled from his jacket pocket.

"It's the only good advice the Marshal ever gave, rabbits."

Henri was puzzled. What did Pétain have to do with rabbits?

"What?"

He started to carve the long body of the rabbit.

"The propaganda at the pictures. They tell us to raise rabbits. That old traitor. To think my father fought with him at Verdun. At the pictures they have him riding in a car with outriders on the side. Then the announcer switches to tell us how to live. The only good idea is raising rabbits for meat. "

His brother interrupted.

"Did you see those movie stars? Suzie Delair and Junie Astor. Traitors. The newsreels show them heading off to Germany to make films."

"And the others," said the thin brother. "Happy French workers on their way to Germany. The new order. What about the Jews they send there from Lyon and the village? Never to come back I'm sure."

Talk stopped for a few minutes as the men ate their meal of potatoes, bread and rabbit. Even in the cellar the brothers tried to maintain some sense of dignity, to impress their guest.

"Not bad," said Henri, of his first-ever meal of rabbit. To him it tasted a bit like chicken. He was glad of the bread and the potatoes; he needed the blotting paper for the wine. The brothers poured more straight from the barrel into the ribbed glass and passed it back to Henri.

He thought for a minute before telling them the next story. The camps where he learned his craft were secret places. But he supposed these men were safe and even if the Germans did catch them, he wasn't about to tell them anything they hadn't worked out of other agents who knew more. And he needed the confidence of these men, so sharing secrets with them, even little secrets, helped things along.

"In Scotland we met Poles and Czechs, training to do this work. They told us about the Jews there and how the Germans started killing them almost as soon as they crossed the border into Poland in September of thirty-nine. He stopped talking and waited for them to say something.

Again, he told Henri about the cinéma last week where the Vichy French had trotted out some of Goebel's work before the main feature.

"Around here they are more subtle. But Pétain and Laval, they hate the Jews. At the pictures the French voices talk over the German picture. What was it we saw last week? Sus the Jew? A story that justified killing the Jews. They even put the poor bastard in a cage at the end of the film and hanged him."

"That's what Suzie Delair is doing in Germany helping them make those films," said the fatter brother. "And the newsreels. They tell us not to trust the Jews. We hardly know any here. But there are some living in the village, a couple of children. They learn the catechism so the Milice and the Gestapo can't find them."

For another two hours they drank and talked. Henri liked these men. Simple, intelligent and brave. Targets for the Germans since so many weapons were stored on the farm where they lived. And so many of the people they worked with in the Resistance were traitors.

It was too late to go home, and risk being nabbed in the curfew. Also Henri was too drunk to ride a bicycle. He hadn't been drunk since he left Canada. As he lay down on a cot in the cellar, watching the barrels move in the candlelight, he said to himself he might not get drunk again until he was back home, or at least back in England.

He closed his eyes and thought of Jane. He saw her bare back and the towel around her waist as she walked away. In his dream he pulled off the towel and made love to her standing up, and without ever once saying a word.

The sun hit Henri's eyes when brother number one opened the door to the cellar. His usual instinct would have been to reach for his gun or his knife; he had both with him. But he forgot where he was and the young farmer was beside him by the time he remembered.

Another reason to swear off wine, or at least buckets of wine from a barrel. Henri and the brother laughed. He followed him up to the house and they had a huge breakfast.

"So that's where you keep the rabbits," said Henri as they walked past a pen. "My god, they're big."

"Bred for meat. They're not pets. And you'll see at breakfast why we keep chickens. We even have bacon."

The other brother laughed. "I'll let you in on a secret, Pierre, since you're in the business of secrets. We have enough bacon to last two years. We should be rid of the Boches by then. Don't you think?"

Henri smiled and nodded, but he wasn't sure it would be that fast. No use depressing the brothers. Keep the talk on food.

It was, in fact, the best meal Henri had eaten so far in France. At least that's what he thought at the time, but he was hung over and needed the food. The coffee was better than anything he'd had in two years.

Then he outlined the job he had planned for the day.

"The object here is to outsmart the Germans. And the best way to do that is eliminate surprise, at least their surprise. That's why those canisters that arrived the other night are full of wire. That's telephone wire and we are going to lay our own little network, from here to the village and even to the outskirts of Lyon."

The thin brother was worried. "Surely it's more than just wires?"

"Yes, but I can handle that. I used to work for a phone company. And not in the city but in farm country, like this. We can't use poles, but we can bury the lines, even just a few centimetres under the earth. It will give us an early warning system, something to let us know the Nazis are coming."

The brothers didn't know it, but this was just a small part of the plan. No need to tell them everything. Henri and Philippe had already paid some workers from the government telephone office to help set up the network. This was the one isolated part where the line had to be buried. Later the phone men would come and install equipment they'd stolen from the Germans and the French phone company.

Breakfast over, Henri and the two brothers set to work, burying telephone wires from the cellar to two cottages and then to a spot in the woods close to where one cache of guns was stored. Henri then walked beside the road for the three miles back to the village. It took him four hours to lay the cable, with both brothers spending the rest of the day back filling or hiding it.

To anyone passing by they were two simple peasants working with hoes. Henri now had eight kilometers of phone cable connecting outposts of his little rural empire.

He had to leave a little after noon. He and Philippe had another job to do that afternoon.

17

Lyon, later that same day

The wine seemed smoother than the red he drank straight from the barrels last night. But he was only having one glass, maybe two. He thought the stories about the French keeping the best wine for themselves were true. Henri was sitting in another café along rue St. Jean, just down from the cathedral.

"It was the oddest thing. She appeared like an apparition behind me and started talking as if we knew each other. I turned and she was beautiful. Blonde hair, like that American actress, what's her name?"

"Veronica Lake," said Philippe, a fan of Hollywood movies who still managed to read magazines smuggled from the Americans in North Africa. He laughed at his ridiculous knowledge. "I think in English it's called the peek-a-boo look."

"To me she was either a whore or a spy, and she was too well dressed to be a whore, at least one who picks people up in cafés. Who knows, though, maybe she's desperate. Anyway, she also spoke French with an accent. I couldn't place it. She said it was Polish. Does that make sense?"

Henri had learned to trust Philippe. He might be clumsy in the field but he was clever, didn't seem to be stuck on any particular ideology, except wanting to kick the occupying army out of his country. He was more at home in the city and absorbed gossip and intelligence, sifting it all. The Polish woman didn't surprise him.

"Of course she had to tell you she was Polish. The Eastern European accent is quite clear, at least to me. She couldn't very well say she was Russian, could she? I've heard of her. Polish is her first language, German is her second. There are complicated family allegiances in Central Europe, bur her loyalty is to Berlin, not Warsaw. She is very dangerous. So what time did you say you'd meet her?" asked Philippe.

"Around three. Where the funicular goes to the amphitheatre."

Philippe paused, thinking for a good 30 seconds.

"You can't get in the car. It's a trap. She's seduced and killed at least two of our agents. Hard to resist. You'll have to do something else. Lure her back towards the river. I'm afraid my friend we're going to have to kill her before she kills any more of us."

Henri nodded.

Now the problem was how and where to do it. It seemed certain she would be watched. They couldn't use a gun – too noisy – and a knife too messy. They decided to either do it in a hurry at the bottom of the funicular, or walk down to the river Saone. Philippe would watch, Henri would act.

Philippe walked up a narrow street to enter the square from the other end. As he strolled along he passed German officers in uniform, talking with some French women. They looked as if they were off duty. In any case it would be plain clothed men of the Gestapo who would be working on this.

Both men looked straight ahead while their eyes did the searching for suspicious people. The Gestapo headquarters were across the river, at a hotel beside the train station. There was another police barracks and torture palace on the side of the river where they were walking now.

At just after three Henri walked the five minutes to the café on the Place St. Jean. There, at the same table as before, was the blonde. He had already decided to play the love-struck fool. He smiled at her as he walked over, hoping he wasn't going to be snatched right taway.

"How are you?" He said no more, just stared at her.

A kind of worldly smile as she answered. "*Bonjour*. Are you ready for our little history lesson?"

"Let's have a drink first. I could use some wine."

By now Philippe had come around the other end of the square looking at a statue near the town hall. He could see Pierre, but it was hard to tell if anyone was watching the Polish spy. He decided to move, walking in a slow arc to keep an eye on Pierre, who seemed to have ordered some wine. Cool, but maybe foolhardy.

"What made you come back?" asked the woman who told Henri her name was Françoise. Cheeky, thought Henri, picking such a French name. He changed the subject.

"You seem to have an accent. Where's it from?"

"You have a good ear. My mother was Polish and we lived in Warsaw for so long my father worried I was going to lose my French. But you didn't answer my question," and she turned on the brightness in her eyes. "Why did you come back?"

Henri also turned on the charm, but he knew it was wasted.

"To see you. My wife is dead; I don't get to talk to many women."

"What happened to your wife?"

Henri decided to turn up the heat and see her reaction.

"She was a Jew. One day I came home and she was gone."

No reaction except a look of sympathy.

"What makes you think she's dead?"

"Come now. We all know where they go. First to a camp in France, then to Germany or even your country. And when they go they never come back. I wonder how many have been killed so far?"

"I think you exaggerate. It's relocation. To the east."

Henri smiled as she was making a distasteful job easier. He didn't know if he could kill a woman, even one who had already sent men, and women, to their deaths.

He took a good look at her. She was around five six, but slight, not weighing more than a hundred and fifteen pounds.

He was only a few inches taller, but he was fit. He wondered if she carried a knife or a gun. He tried to avoid looking for accomplices.

"Shall we go to the amphitheatre? It might be dark soon."

Henri stood up, paid the waiter and as they walked to the funicular, the tram that ran up the side of the hill, she slipped her arm through his and pressed herself against him.

As they walked he looked at the ground then up, scanning in an arc in front of him, though he couldn't look behind. All of a sudden the street seemed to become more crowded. He listened for languages. All French. Was that a guttural accent?

Along the way they spoke about Rome. She must have been surprised how a man from Normandy knew so much about classical history. But then it was almost certain she knew just who he was.

"You seem to know a lot about the Romans for a man from the country?"

"We have schools there too, you know."

There were now some grey uniforms in the crowd, soldiers, but without their rifles or helmets. Tourists or at least Henri hoped they were tourists. He thought he saw a leather coat in the crowd and had the feeling he was being watched.

At the foot of funicular a crowd was forming, not a queue but maybe a hundred people massing together. Henri moved to the back of the crowd. He looked deep into her eyes and moved to kiss her as she closed her eyes. He thought of grabbing her jaw and snapping her neck like you would a chicken. No noise and he could set her down and leave.

But he couldn't bring himself to do it. Not all his training could force him to kill a woman who wasn't threatening him, at least not in an immediate way. And before he knew it he was on the funicular car, crowded in with her and other people. His only weapon was a knife.

He looked around. It seemed safe.

"You seem nervous. Don't you like this car?" asked the blonde.

"They make me a little edgy," lied Henri. "I've never been on one before." Also a lie. He had used the one in Quebec City.

The car rose above the city, and then made one stop. Two non-descript kind of men got on. The blonde pressed herself against Henri. He pressed back as the car moved up to its final stop near the amphitheatre.

"Let's go see what the Romans were up to two thousand years ago," said the smiling blonde. It was the last place Henri wanted to go, a spot she had chosen, where she wanted him.

"Why don't we look at the city for a while," and Henri led her to a park just to the side of the cable car's stop. All the other passengers were heading towards the amphitheatre.

They looked out over the city and Henri feigned a romantic interest. When it was clear he had no intention of visiting the amphitheatre, she stepped back and pulled a small revolver from her purse.

"Pierre."

Henri's foot moved in an instant and knocked the gun from her hand as she turned to see Philippe. As she moved to pick it up the commando's blade pierced her dress, her breast and her heart, in that order. Henri stared into her unbelieving eyes and let her fall on a park bench.

"Hurry. Follow me, I know somewhere safe," said Philippe.

They walked around a corner, a place where they would be trapped if anyone arrived. They moved in a hurry, but without running, into the zigzags of the tight lanes going down the hill. It was away from where they were expected, and as they descended they also edged closer to the river.

There were sirens below off in the direction of the funicular stop which was now off to their right. In three or four minutes Philippe had them outside a wooden door that looked as if it hadn't been opened in years. Inside what looked to Henri like an illegal bar, a blind pig as they called them back home.

"It's safe here," Philippe assured Henri. "Or safe enough. It will be dark in an hour. I have a house in Lyon. We'll stay there tonight."

The two men drank a large cognac. There were only three other people in here, one woman behind the bar.

"Did it bother you?"

"What?"

"Killing a woman."

"A bit. But she made it easier. She certainly would have killed us."

They smiled and drank another cognac.

18

Jack made so much money on Monday he didn't have to work for the rest of the week. Langton called on Tuesday to say the aristocracy was almost wiped out over the weekend. Two earls and a dowager duchess. Add to that, a man involved in one of the most famous homosexual scandals of the 1940s, back when sodomy still had a biblical ring to it, and was still a crime.

"We've got your Canadian senator from Whites," said Langton, referring to one of the clubs to which the rich anglophile belonged. "He'll be in the freezer for a few days. If you can get that SOE chap done in, say ten days, it'll be fine. We' running the druggie tomorrow."

A week off. There would probably be some radio or TV work, but in all an easy few days ahead. Time to get to work on that old spy, thought Jack, as he rummaged through the papers on the table beside his desk. He found the roll of fax paper his friend from *The Gazette* had sent him, and took out his big scissors to cut it into separate pages.

Most of the clippings were from just after the war, when Montreal papers, like those in all the countries on the winning side, were filled with pictures and stories of the returning heroes. Seldom any bleak descriptions of the dead. No bodies cut in half, heads blown off, or men bleeding to death in wet, cold fields. It didn't make good copy.

Here on the page of an old *Gazette* were a few paragraphs dealing with Henri Foix and others, though Foix was in the headline and the lead paragraph.

Awards to 12 French Canadians were announced officially yesterday among a long list of army personnel who served in northwest Europe, and others who had been prisoners of war in the Far East. Decorations included the French Croix de Guerre avec palme to Capt. Henri Foix, DSO of Montreal.

Jack kept reading as he walked to the kitchen to pick up his tea. The Distinguished Service Order. He was impressed. From doing all the military obituaries he knew that if a DSO was awarded to an officer below the rank of lieutenant colonel it was second only to the Victoria Cross. This could be a better obit than even Langton knew.

The old newspaper went on.

The official citation accompanying the award to Capt. Foix was as follows: "This Canadian officer parachuted into occupied France four months before the Allied invasion and placed at the disposal of the French Forces of the Interior his fine qualities of intelligence, energy and character.

He organized and armed several important units with which he participated with exceptional initiative in numerous operations."

The DSO was almost always handed out for a string of heroic stuff, Jack remembered, rather than one man assaulting a machine gun nest. He looked through several pages of material. There was nothing about the SOE. Even the recent press release from the Canadian Armed Forces mentioned the SOE, but only once.

As he settled back in the chair in his sitting room and office, Jack thought there were a lot of lies in newspapers. And during a war there were even more. Jack chuckled at the obvious propaganda and the lack of any of the grisly stuff that did in the Americans when their newspapers covered the Vietnam War. In Hitler's war the newspapers were all on side.

There was an article in *Le Petit Journal*, a French newspaper in Montreal, which talked about Foix's early training in the army. It told about how, as a lieutenant, he trained with the American Special Forces at Helena, Montana.

Un officier de Montréal reçoit une rude formation dans l'armée américaine, read the headline with the story on how Henri received his basic commando training in the American Army.

At the bottom of the heap was a front-page story from *The Montreal Star* in December of 1945. It was a 'When Johnny comes marching home' kind of thing. Jack thought if you read the jingoistic hometown newspapers, Canada had just beaten the German Army, single-handedly, the Royal Canadian Air Force had bombed the Fatherland into submission and the Royal Canadian Navy had sunk every U-boat in the North Atlantic.

Well that was the standard line, and when a real hero arrived the reporters went crazy. This one told the story of Captain Henri Foix, DSO, *Croix de Guerre avec palme*, and agent extraordinaire. It carried a photo of his fiancée, a new wrinkle in the story. She was a blond woman, her hair up in the style of the mid-1940s. The story said she too was from Montreal and the couple had met in London.

That was all in the cutlines under the pictures. The story dealt with the fighting from the end of the winter of 1944 to months after the fall of Paris in nine or ten paragraphs.

One paragraph in the middle of the story caught Jack's eye. What his generation called 'a fire fight' – cribbed from the Vietnam War – with a gruesome ending. Soldiers of the Underground clubbed to death. Retributions. Then there was a description of Germans being killed, or executed, as part of a payback. It looked as if it had happened the next day. Pretty detailed. Jack marvelled this made it past the censor, if there still was a military censor in December of 1945.

After two hours and three cups of tea Jack had finished reading all the pages faxed over from *The Gazette*, plus the few items Langton had given him at the office. It was a little before noon. He needed time to think. He also needed to go to France in a hurry. He pulled the phone from the floor.

"Claire?"

"Who else do you think it is, for God's sake?"

Jack almost laughed. At times the woman could be from central casting. The French art of the rude opening. Not even subtle.

"Just listen for a second. I have to talk to you about something." said Jack.

She interrupted, with a hint of panic.

"What's wrong?"

"Don't worry it's just about work. I need to talk to you. It won't work over the phone. Can we have lunch at one o'clock?"

A pause on the end of the line.

"Alright. Brown's. In the lounge. I only have an hour, maybe less. Don't you want to give me a hint?" her voice changing to the coquette, which almost always worked.

"No I'll see you at one," and he hung up before she could talk him into anything. He knew if she thought he wanted to talk about obits, she would have hung up on him. He went into his bedroom and pulled a tie from the closet. It wasn't that warm outside, so he picked a tweed jacket. He knew the old rule of 'no brown in town' but then he wasn't English, so he figured he could get away with it.

Jack cut the other way through the square and headed up past his shortcut to South Kensington. That way it was a direct line to Green Park. He had about forty-five minutes. He might be flush, but no use pissing away money on a black cab. He'd need the cash for an air ticket to France.

As he walked past the Princess of Wales he saw the early drinkers settling in. As a man with a weakness for booze, he had to keep himself away from this place at noon or he'd be there till three and the rest of the day would he finished.

He thought back to the old newspaper clippings. War propaganda replaced by post-war propaganda. Like the myth of the Royal Canadian Navy defeating the U-boats. For some reason he remembered one of his father's drinking friends, a con man with the rather formal name of Alistair. Never Al, always Alistair. Alistair had been one of those men on the North Atlantic, bobbing about on Corvettes, ships designed for patrolling the coastline, not the high seas.

"By the end of the war the U-boats could run faster then we could," he remembered Alistair telling him. "You know you'd last for twenty minutes tops in that water. Better to be in the navy, though, than in the Merchant Marine."

Somewhere he'd read that the Canadian Navy sank maybe three dozen German submarines. Planes were more effective by the end of the war. But Alistair had been right about those poor bastards on the freighters. Target practice for the U-boats in the middle of the Atlantic.

Away, away with fife and drum here we come full of rum, looking for women to peddle their bum on the North Atlantic Squadron.

Jack smiled to himself as he remembered all the filthy verses to the song he and his friends used to sing. It struck him now that it was the sailors teaching their sons and younger brothers the song that kept it alive in every beer hall and Legion in the country.

The captain's wife was Mabel, oh Mabel lay out on the table, and gave the cook and the crew a jolly good screw, oh God how Mabel was able.

He took the elevator down to the tube, a large West Indian woman closing the gate for him. He looked around and wondered what they'd all think if he burst out loud into a few choruses of the North Atlantic Squadron.

The cabin boy, the cabin boy, the dirty little nipper, he filled his ass with broken glass and circumcised the skipper.

Away away with fife and drum here we come full of rum, looking for women to peddle their bum on the North Atlantic Squadron.

They needed the rum. Jack remembered doing an obit on an RCMP sergeant, a Mountie who served part of his war in St. John, New Brunswick. St. John, with Halifax, was one of the great setting-off points for the North Atlantic Squadron. The Canadian Pacific tracks cut across the state of Maine in a straight line from Montreal bringing the stuff of war straight to the freighters.

"We used to have to drag those boys out of the bars. Sometimes we'd have to put them on ships at gunpoint. My God, they were scared shitless. Ten knots across the Atlantic in an old tub loaded with ammunition or gasoline. Anyone would have been scared shitless."

Jack walked into the lounge at Brown's at seven minutes to one. He sat at a table and ordered a Bloody Mary and a plate of smoked salmon sandwiches. He grabbed a newspaper from the table. He'd done so much thinking and humming on his way here that he'd forgotten to pick up his usual *Daily Mail*.

Claire came in five minutes late and he stood up to kiss her. She was in one of her wanting-to-shock moods and made quite a fuss about him, smiling, kissing and pawing. He was embarrassed as a rather good-looking woman looked up from her *Country Life* to take it all in.

"So what's the *crise?*" asked Claire, throwing a French word into her English sentence, something she almost never did.

"Well I have to go to France on a story and I need your help. I want to talk to people about the war. Your father or your mother might be just the people I could start with. You can come with me, of course, but I want to do it this week. I might even leave tonight."

"My God. What's the rush?"

He decided to lie a bit. If he brought up obits, she'd become all melodramatic and say she didn't approve of writing stories on dead people.

"A Canadian magazine wants me to do a story on a French-Canadian war hero. It's good money but they need it in a hurry." It wasn't a total lie. He knew he could sell it as a magazine piece, later. "He was an agent, a spy and he worked near Lyon. That's where your parents are from, aren't they?"

"Close enough." She sat silent for a while, looking away, and then she stared back at him, more serious than usual.

"It's what we talked about in Woodstock, isn't it?"

"Yeah." He decided to let her talk.

"I don't know if they would want to say anything. My mother almost wants to forget about the Jewish side of her life. She pretends it doesn't exist. My father talks more, but I think there's something he's hiding." She moved in her chair and added, "He wasn't a collaborator. He hated Pétain. But there was an incident. My brother told me about it."

"Look, I'm just going to poke around. If they don't want to say anything, I won't press them."

She looked away. The waiter brought more sandwiches and a pot of tea. Then she looked back at Jack.

"You have to promise me one thing." She was almost never serious, and now there was none of the usual flippancy in her voice.

Jack moved forward, "Whatever you want." He could smell victory and he was closer to this story.

"You won't speak French. That accent. It's so terrible. It would embarrass me."

PART TWO

The part which your naughty deeds in war play, in peace cannot at all be considered.

WINSTON CHURCHILL, MAY 1, 1944

19

Lyon, late April, 1944

There had been eight people at lunch, an even number around a square table, though only three women and five men. Now there were seven left talking and resting. It was a little after three o'clock and talk of intrigue was over. The villa in the quiet northern suburb of Lyon seemed an oasis. Some slept in chairs, others chatted about things they might have talked about before the war.

The sun helped set the after-lunch mood. It was lower and cast longer shadows in the room, making it even more relaxed. Almost everyone had too much wine, a way of taking the everyday tension out of their lives. The war, and the Germans, had them all on edge. Anyone of them could be arrested for what they were doing.

It was Philippe's house and he and his latest conquest were upstairs when eight Gestapo men burst in the doors, kicking the knee of one man in a chair, slapping the face of a woman who shot them an insolent look. They smashed one man's head into a wall.

"Outside. Into the cars," shouted a man in a long leather coat. He might as well have had a swastika stamped on his chest. But the swaggering dress code of the Gestapo would be a mistake this afternoon.

Upstairs two Gestapo men caught Philippe as he was rushing to get dressed. One smacked him with a pistol, spin-ning him around. He pushed his head through a window, moving it back and forth, pushing shards of glass into his cheeks and nose. Philippe grunted in pain but refused to give them the satisfaction of a scream.

He fell to the floor, half-dressed, semi-conscious, bleeding and weak. He pulled his braces over his shoulders so his pants wouldn't fall down when he did get up to walk. From one eye he saw the other man sodomize his girlfriend. She screamed as he buggered her, but at least it was over in a hurry.

Downstairs the raid was now quiet, or at least only one man was talking. The leader, the one with the well-tailored leather coat, was shouting at another woman, trying to break the weakest link. She stared straight ahead. He slapped her and she made a whimper.

Smiling, he grabbed her by the sleeve and propelled her towards the door. "You'll talk where we're going." Four men and the three women were dragged outside and squeezed into the back seats of four waiting Citroens. The raid had been a gift and the tip had come so fast they didn't have time to ask for soldiers to back them up. As Philippe staggered across the street he saw the eighth man from lunch, huddled in a doorway. Pierre Lequin. Philippe knew in a flash he was the one who had betrayed them. He spat blood at Lequin.

The barrel of a Luger creased the back of his head as one of the ordinary Gestapo men hit him again and pushed him into the car.

The leather coats had been the giveaway. Almost as soon as the Gestapo left for the raid, one of the Maquis had seen all the leather being stuffed into the cars once owned and driven by the Sûreté. But the French police were not invited on this raid, not even the Milice.

Henri Foix had almost as much time to prepare as the Gestapo. There was one way in to Philippe's house and one way out. It was on a hill and the streets here were narrow. It was a place where they should have waited for soldiers.

Two of the four Citroens passed him as he stood inside a doorway. He was at a curve in the road and, from where he stood, the cars had to slow at a sharp turn before they started up another curving hill.

Henri moved his arm to hold back Florence and another man. They wanted to shoot at the drivers in the first car, but Henri waited for the third. Later he would say it was just a lucky shot, as he killed both Gestapo men with a single burst from his Sten gun. The three of them stepped into the street to make sure the other car, the one with Philippe inside, did not get away.

A bullet then crashed into the wall beside him and two more caught the man beside Florence, splitting him open. The fire was still coming from the reversing fourth Citroen. Henri sprayed the engine block of the Citroen and in a second moved the train of fire to the windscreen. He knew he had killed one man, the driver. His leg must have jammed on the accelerator and the car rammed into a wall, making a sudden stop.

The engine stalled and all was quiet. The Gestapo man in the right-side passenger seat was stunned, but not wounded. Florence shot him three times, all in the face to make certain he was disfigured for his family.

Up the road the other two Citroens were shot up as soon as the Maquis heard the burst from Henri's Sten gun. Two of the people from lunch were dead in the back seat of the first car, killed by bullets, which travelled first through the Gestapo men and then through the soft seats.

Three of the Gestapo were mutilated. Philippe's new woman, a rather violent Corsican it turned out, cut off the penis and testicles of the man who buggered her and stuffed them into his bloody, dying mouth.

He didn't have any energy left to scream. He died choking in blood, trying to spit out his own balls.

The man with Henri in the doorway was dead. Florence pulled Philippe from the back seat. Henri stopped to speak to his friend who whispered Pierre Lequin's name into his ear. Henri tossed them his Sten gun and ran past the next Citroen then up a side street chasing the figure of Pierre

Lequin. He had seen Philippe spit at him and after Philipe's confirmation, Henri decided on the death sentence.

Lequin was 35, overweight and a heavy smoker. The small, lean form of Henri Foix streaked up the hill without any effort as Pierre Lequin slowed to a walk to catch his breath, even in a chase he knew might mean death. Lequin moved into a doorway, but Henri saw him and heard the latch close. There was an outside staircase and Henri bounded like an acrobat to the second storey, slipping through an open window.

He moved as if he were wearing slippers. His knife was in his left hand and he listened like a predator hunting a wounded animal. He could hear Lequin breathing and the shuffle of his fat feet on the stairs. He guessed the landing must be just beyond the open door ahead of him. He decided to wait.

Lequin led with his pistol, using it to push open the door. One tiny step further then Henri kicked the pistol knocking it across the room.

"I didn't tell them, I swear," whimpered Lequin. Then he became a little cocky when he saw Henri's empty right hand. "You'd better leave now. The Germans will be here soon. Soldiers."

With his eyes locked on Lequin, Henri made a slight move with his left hand, and Lequin saw the flash of a blade travel as if by magic to Henri's right hand and then felt the sharp point as it cut across his throat. It wasn't that deep a cut, just enough to keep him alive for maybe another minute or two while he bled to death.

The bleeding man staggered down the stairs, grabbing a towel in the kitchen to try and stop the blood. He watched in horror, as it turned red then redder and became soaking wet.

Henri picked up the pistol, another Luger. He left by the window. He walked past the sputtering Lequin without looking at him. People now watched from windows and doorways as the new commander of the Maquis took charge. When

Lequin looked with his begging eyes to a woman across the street, she closed the shutters.

In the street, there were eight dead Gestapo men, one dead Maquis and two people dead from the lunch. Philippe was still alive, stunned and messy, but it was not as bad as it looked. Henri moved quickly.

"Take the wounded to the farmhouse," and, motioning to Florence, "you and the others come with me. We are going where they don't expect us."

Soldiers were already on their way from the centre of the city below. They would expect the Maquis and the man from the SOE to retreat. As the sun cast afternoon shadows, Henri remembered not so much his training in Montana and Scotland, as his Greek and Latin translation.

"Xerxes, too, was once a mighty man," and the people with him looked at him as if he were crazy. Philippe would have known what he was talking about, if he'd been conscious, but the rest of his troop today were factory workers, communists who hated the Nazis and would now follow him no matter what rubbish he spouted.

Henri thought of the stories he so loved as a boy, of the Greeks taking the fight to the Persians, of the Spartans holding back armies by controlling a mountain pass. His blood was up and he started to plan his next move.

"Like the Hoplites, we will take the battle to the enemy," said Henri. And as they walked through the woods that lined the road from Lyon to the suburb, Henri told them of how the Greek phalanxes defeated their Persian enemies by moving to fight rather than waiting for the enemy.

"When they move into our territory, we move against them. With out shields and our swords we shall batter them."

His hands were waving in the air. It was a moment when he moved our of his stoic character and became rather theatrical. The two women and twelve men with him were quiet as they followed him into the forest.

He was brave, but not delusional. He knew that his half-trained band was no match for what even he admitted was the best army in Europe in 150 years. But the Germans, and the Ukrainians, Belgians and others fighting with them, were just soldiers, men who thought a posting to France meant life, not death. They were not prepared for the unexpected.

The Germans must come by this road, thought Henri. He had a small amount of explosive in his bag. He also had a detonator and some wire. Keeping the others up in the trees, he went to the road and laid the explosive and covered it with leaves. He could hear some half-tracks coming and looked up to see dust. He ran a wire 50 yards back and waited.

There were three half-tracks, troop carriers which protected the soldiers and could make it across most open fields, except in the wettest terrain. Again he waited. This time he blew the second half-track. There wasn't enough explosive to kill anyone inside, but it stopped the vehicle, and the troops came out the back.

Trained soldiers, they moved for cover, while the other two half-tracks manoeuvered for position. Henri wanted just a little kill. Three soldiers were hit before the others began returning fire.

Now the Maquis took off through the woods, a thick park really, to streets on the other side where they knew their way. Henri directed fire away from the main group and then caught up with them. Now he dreamed of a set battle, not just hit-and-run. A real battle, something the Germans would never expect.

20

Jack spent the night in an awful hotel. A bed just big enough for one. A television set up near the ceiling, angled so you could only watch it lying down. And a tiny loo with a hand shower. The place was named after the *Gare de Lyon*, the station across the street where the TGV left for Lyon.

It always amazed Jack that names in England and France were so simple. Battersea Bridge, *Gare du Nord*. Back home they renamed a street every time a politician died.

But this hotel was the shits, in spite of the curt name. The travel agent at the foot of his street thought it would be convenient. It would be harder to imagine a more uncomfortable place. Jack was tempted to call him at home, wake him up and ream him out. Asshole. Instead he saved his money.

He had arrived in Paris around nine at night and decided he would be better to leave for Lyon in the morning. He had a few people to see, including Claire's parents, and he wanted to check out the countryside, and the centre of the city where the Nazi Klaus Barbie had his headquarters.

Michelle had helped him out and he had numbers of a few people from the network files. Langton was even more devious. He had the name of a collaborator, an odd duck named Marcel Duclos who gave interviews, for cash. Jack had already called ahead. It would cost him lunch and 500

135

francs. He agreed. With luck he could get the magazine to pay, if he ever sold them the piece.

Seemed a shame to waste a night in Paris, so Jack went out. Even in this drab part of the city he found a half decent restaurant. The waiter in a long apron brought him oysters and steak frites. He ordered a litre of wine; it would help him sleep.

Earlier he had picked up a *Trib*, so he read the American news and the baseball scores. As he sat finishing his wine he did the crossword puzzle from the *New York Times*. It was Wednesday and it was still easy enough. Then he wandered back to his little dump of a hotel room and the wine did its job. He was asleep in 15 minutes.

Train à Grande Vitesse was the full name of the TGV, which the conductor told Jack was the fastest train in the world, 270 kilometres an hour. Jack flipped open the calculator in his Filofax and figured out that was about 167 miles an hour. The trip to Lyon took two hours.

It was so fast it was hard to focus on anything close to the tracks, though the big picture was clear. Broad, green fields, more beautiful than the English ones he saw on his last train trip. First class wasn't bad and a uniformed waitress came by with an aircraft-type trolley.

"*Quelque chose à boire, Monsieur?*"

"*Une demie de vin rouge,*" said Jack ordering just a half bottle. He figured he would drink enough red wine in the next few days.

"You have a strange accent," said the waitress in French.

"Yes, I'm from Quebec, but I'm English."

"*Ah, oui,*" she said with a knowing nod. Satisfied with placing the barbaric accent, she moved on. He remembered he promised Claire he wouldn't speak French, but he did like to practice.

The train wasn't that crowded. Not surprising since it was a weekday morning. Jack got down to reading about the agents dropped into France. Not many, it seems, were as lucky as Henri Foix who had died in his old age. He had a couple of books with him, one by a Canadian, the other by an Englishwoman on the Germans and how they were clever enough to infiltrate huge sections of the SOE.

The entire Dutch Resistance, or least the part run from London, was taken over by the Germans. They would capture agents and run them as their own. Or they would kill the agents and then use their codes to transmit to London. There was a double game here, since the tapping of the Morse code was like a signature or fingerprint. But if the agents were captured right away, sometimes London never knew since the first message became the fingerprint.

France was what Jack was most interested in. He found quite a bit about Henri Foix in the Canadian book on the SOE. It was a bit jingoistic and gee whiz, but was realistic about the chances, or lack of them, for agents dropped into France. He'd read something like this in the clippings, but the book said there were about 60 French-Canadians dropped into France in early 1944. Only 15 came out alive.

Their job was simple. To make things as unpleasant for the Germans as they could. No one knew where and when D-Day would happen – it wasn't even called D-Day then, of course – but they all knew an invasion of Europe had to come. The French-Canadian agents were to lead the disorganized Resistance in a military way.

There were some amazing stories. One man, a major at 22, led his Maquis group on a killing spree across a sector of southern France. He too was a survivor. It seemed that so long as they managed to survive the landing and the first few days after it, their chances were good.

Before leaving Jack had talked with Homer Lamont, the American draft dodger. He knew a lot about the French Resistance or, as he pointed out, lack of it.

"There were more collaborators than heroes," said Homer. "Ever see that movie, *The Sorrow and The Pity?*" Jack nodded yes. "The whole southern part of the country wasn't even occupied by the Germans until later in the war. Almost 1943, I think. The French did their dirty work for them, including turning in the Jews and sending resistance workers to the camps. Though there was one case where they let a few British agents out of jail just before the Germans occupied Vichy France in November of 1942. The French lie to themselves about the war. The resistance stuff, a lot of it was crap."

Jack looked at the names and ranks of the Canadians dropped into France. There were a couple of English Canadians, one of them a brother of the dotty Canadian Prime Minister's secretary. He was captured, tortured and killed, picked up as soon as he landed. Poor bastard couldn't even speak much French. Brave, but dumb.

Most of the French-Canadian soldiers who worked as agents in France were from the upper end of Quebec society, the sons of judges, lawyers, doctors and army officers. The Germans took many of them within an hour of landing. And once the Germans had them, they were as good as dead. He went into his bag and pulled out a clipping from Foix.

"If my men were caught, they were shot. So what was good enough for them was good enough for me. I didn't wear my uniform and they were thankful for that. That's why they backed me."

And it was also why the Germans shot them. No uniforms, no protection under the Geneva Convention. But as Jack was to learn in the next few days, no one gave a damn about the Geneva Convention on either side. It was kill or be killed and Henri Foix was a magnificent killer.

In the bookstore at Heathrow Jack had picked up a *Guide Michelin* for Lyon. He had never been there before. All he knew of France was Paris. Now on the train he read up on a place he had never really given much thought to.

The *Guide Michelin* gave three stars to Lyon, its top rating. Worth a journey, in the parlance of the book. Jack noticed Clermont-Ferrand, home to Michelin itself, only had two stars, and was just worth a detour. He took this as a sign of objectivity of the guide and settled in to read the 36 pages on Lyon.

21

France was not an easy place to live in war. And it was a little tougher if, like Henri Foix, you weren't supposed to be there. There was a curfew, which meant anyone about at night was a criminal. There were identity cards for everyone and for people like Henri there was a made-up identity or maybe two or three.

Carte d'identité. A false one had to be up-to-date. Beside the words *Carte d'identité* was a stamp, then others all 'postmarked' by the police station. The French police did most of the Germans' work for them.

There was a photo in the bottom left-hand corner and beside it, details of height, weight and eye colour. Above that the series of the identity card and then the family name, first name, occupation, date of birth, place of birth, nationality and address.

Prints of the index finger of each hand completed the *Carte d'identité.*

Any change in routine, a slip in the type of stamp or postmark and cover was blown. A captured agent had little chance of survival. Though in London they told the agent their odds were fifty-fifty, they were in fact a little better. There was just a one-in-three chance of being killed. Still worse odds than in the trenches in the First War.

An agent could be caught by treachery – his or her landing site given away – by bad luck or by a radio transmission. A radio signal leaves a trace. It's easy to locate. The secret is to keep the message short and send it from different places.

A message from London earlier that week had blasted Henri for his freelance sabotage job on the freight train. Another burst went on to thank him, in an offhand way, for taking out the two coastal guns being moved from the south to the north.

Now Henri was working on a bigger plan. Today he was dressed as a working-class Frenchman, in a blue coat and trousers that Florence had helped him dirty before he left the house. He rode his bicycle on a now familiar route to the old part of Lyon.

The narrow streets of this part of the city had been laid out by the Romans. The stone strip down the middle of the road looked to Henri like a gutter. He figured it was from the middle ages, to carry the sewage people would dump from the windows. He'd ask Philippe about it later. But this morning he was meeting a man from the railway.

Jean Gradbois was the ultimate *fonctionnaire*, as the French called government workers whose function it was to go by the book. Monsieur Gradbois wore a shiny blue serge suit, a clean shirt with no sign of wear, and an unfashionable tie, which was a mark of his class. Many of the petits bourgeois, the class the snobby lawyer Karl Marx hated most, learned to live with the Vichy regime. Not Monsieur Gradbois. He thought Marshal Pétain was a traitor. And his Prime Minister was worse.

"That Laval, he should be brought to the main square here in Lyon and guillotined. In public, so we could watch his head tumble into the basket."

It was just before lunch and Monsieur Gradbois looked almost embarrassed to be talking to a working man, even though he knew Pierre was an officer, if only a Canadian officer, an odd sort of British Frenchman. But the object of all this was for Henri to learn the details of railway schedules.

Monsieur Gradbois started talking without being asked a question. In spite of knowing that Henri, or Pierre to him, was an agent with the Resistance, he couldn't get over his working-class dress and talked down to him most of the time. He had started life near the bottom and didn't like to be reminded of it.

"My job is the key one at the railway. The entire system depends on it. And because this is the most important city outside Paris, nothing runs without my knowledge." The train master at Marseilles might have taken issue with that but Henri was not about to argue. With this the proper Frenchman took a sip of coffee, as if for dramatic emphasis. Though Henri was drinking wine, Monsieur Gradbois never drank at lunch. He needed a clear head for his work.

Henri looked at Monsieur Gradbois with an intensity that fed his ego. Part of it was acting, and he saw the flattery was working. He knew this man could tell him all the major troop movements over the next week.

"It must be wonderful to have such power. Now you know what we're interested in." Henri wanted to avoid being direct. "Nothing in writing, just a couple of dates and times."

"What you want are the troop trains. I imagine that would do the most damage." Henri winced and spoke in a sharp but quiet tone.

"Please. Do not be so direct. You never know who's listening," and Monsieur Gradbois moved in his seat, his eyes going to the ground. "The wrong person hears that and we're on meat hooks at the *École militaire*," a reference to the building the Gestapo had taken over. "Don't worry now. And don't look around. I already did that. Trust me, this is dangerous work. Let's walk back towards the station and you can tell me along the way."

Within fifteen minutes Henri was back on his bicycle and heading home to his make-believe wife. He had the railway schedule in his head, at least the bits he needed, which was the timing of two troop trains over the next few days. In his pocket he had a train pass, a document that identified him as a railway worker travelling on official business.

That business was to take him about thirty kilometres or so from Lyon, but that was measured as the crow flies. It might take a couple of hours to drive there, and cars were hard to come by. Bicycling that distance could be dangerous. The train would do it.

Henri leaned his bicycle against the gate and went inside. Florence was in the kitchen. They were like a married couple. She just turned and smiled at him when he walked in and went back to scrubbing potatoes.

One reason they seemed so married was there was no passion. Florence was waiting for her husband and Henri had decided on a course of celibacy for his tour in France. Love, he figured, might be dangerous.

Still, he looked at the way Florence's skirt clung to her and he felt aroused, for the first time in weeks. It wasn't Florence. Just the look of a woman, and the cut of her neck and the roundness of her bottom reminded him of his last night in London with Jane.

He got up and walked to a bookshelf in the other room.

"Do you have a map or an atlas of France?"

Florence didn't hear him, so she walked into the other room. The bookshelves were full of the books she and her husband read, the intellectual armoury of French communists. The room contained so many books it was almost insulated from the sound outside and from the trains that ran along the back of the garden. It felt warmer in here than it did in the kitchen, and warmer than the bedroom where Henri and Florence slept in separate beds.

"I'm sorry, the sound doesn't carry well from this room. I think it's the books. What are you looking for?"

"An atlas of France. A detailed one," said Henri.

"Just a moment." Florence moved over to a bookshelf by the door near the kitchen and moved some books. There, lying flat, as if it were hidden on purpose, was a Larousse atlas of the world. Henri opened it and noticed that as with most world atlases, the pages were stacked in favour of the

142

country where it was printed. This one had the details of France he needed.

Florence smiled and left him alone. She knew if he wanted to tell her the location of the place he was looking for, he would have asked. Henri went to the index and thumbed his way to the 'Os.'

Strange name, he thought. Oingt. The train line didn't go right there, but close enough. He could walk, or even bring a bicycle on the train. For that matter he could steal one, it might be easier.

Henri thought the man of the house, Florence's real husband, organized his small library well, though it would have been Florence who stacked the books since her husband had never been to Lyon. The books seemed to take up a quarter of the space in his little house, or at least a quarter of the wall space, and there were books on the two tables in the little study. All of them were arranged in categories.

Along the bottom row of one section of shelving were a few more atlases, some of them school boy things, others picked up at second-hand book sales. The *Larousse* was the prize of the collection. And beside the atlases were tourist books, almost all of the guides from the tire company, though Henri assumed Monsieur Gradbois would hate the capitalists from Clermont-Ferrand. He pulled out a few to find something about the town with the funny name.

Oingt. Henri laughed to himself. Turned out it was named after a nun.

22

Marcel Duclos was not from central casting. Jack had expected a peasant, someone in a cloth cap and a 40-year-old coat, the French version of his old friend in the caff at Woodstock. Monsieur Duclos, for he was very much a Monsieur, was tall and thin with an angular face that made him look younger than he was. Jack guessed he must be 65 to have been the right age for the war, though he looked 50.

He even wore a cravat and smoked American cigarettes, not the smelly French ones. They started to speak in French and Jack detected a rather smart accent, something he hadn't picked up on the phone.

"Let's speak English, it's easier," said Duclos in an English that was less accented than Claire's. "Nothing personal, but I despise the Québécois accent and with you mangling the language it's even worse."

Jack couldn't hold back the smile. This man was ruder than Claire. A new theory struck him that rudeness rose the higher the Frenchman stood on the social ladder, except in Paris where they were all rude.

"I don't mind. It's easier." Jack paused and signalled for the waiter. "Why don't you choose the wine Monsieur Duclos. We don't grow much of it in Quebec, and what you French ship us leaves us without much to go on."

He said it with a smile and Duclos smiled back. As far as Jack could see he ordered by price. Still, it was nothing compared to what he was used to paying in London.

"So what do you want to know? How I helped the Germans, what a cad I am? How many Jews did I send to their deaths? And while we're at it, let's deal with the money first. Five hundred francs I think we agreed to."

"In answer to your question, all of the above," said Jack.

As he passed an envelope across the table, Jack took one of Duclos' cigarettes, his first in days. He didn't like him, but then who would?

Right now he figured he too could be a smart ass and he rather enjoyed the duelling. "Let's go back to the beginning. Where were you when the war started?"

Duclos tasted the wine, not making too much of a show. "Not in the army. I was too young. I was just finishing my *Bac* by the time the war was over for us. Since I was in the south of France, I didn't even have to run from the Germans. But then I wasn't afraid of them. I agreed with their vision. The New Order. I supported the Marshal and Laval."

He looked across at Jack.

"Don't be shocked."

"I'm not," said Jack. "I'm listening. Go ahead. I don't care what happened, I just want to know."

"What exactly are you after?"

Jack hated questions like that. How on earth could you answer them? He didn't know what he was after. He had a few days off and thought he'd give the paper its money's worth for a change. He supposed he was after the truth, whatever that was. Maybe he was just curious. What are you after? What a dumb fucking question.

"The story. I'm just after the story. You know, to get enough of it so I don't get too much wrong."

Duclos shrugged, meaning either he understood or didn't care. He was getting a little pay packet, a free lunch and some good wine. Everyone in France knew his story, everyone that Duclos cared about that is.

So he started a half-hour ramble, while Jack took notes. Not too many. Duclos detailed how he worked with the Milice, first as a uniformed officer, then as an agent. He even used the modern word 'anti-terrorist' to justify what he had done.

"Some of these people were criminals plain and simple. They seemed to enjoy killing civilians. They didn't get many soldiers, or many of us. And the bulk of them were thieves. They enjoyed the good life in a time of austerity."

And on it went. It reminded Jack of the second half of the *Sorrow and the Pity*, the rather bleak documentary on wartime life in France. At one point he tuned out the words and pictured Duclos in black and white, being asked deadpan questions by some French intellectual.

Duclos must have smoked five cigarettes. He wasn't that big a drinker. The annoying thing was he was hard to read since he wore those sleazy glasses that turned grey with the sun.

"And that," said Duclos, "is my story. Not many people like it but I don't care. The idea was to stay alive and I did. Though it was harder staying alive in 1944 and '45 than it was in 1943."

He explained he'd hidden after the war, taken a steamer to Quebec from Marseille. He left the ship one night and met people whose names he'd been given, French-Canadians who had supported Marshal Pétain and Vichy.

"There were others. Bigger fish who attracted attention. Some count they were really after. I worked in a bookstore for two years. I couldn't wait to leave. The place was so provincial. It made Clermont-Ferrand seem like Paris. And the French. Well I've already told you."

"What made you leave?" asked Jack. This was an unexpected bonus but it was so far off his story he'd have to leave it alone soon. Wait until Duclos dies he said to himself, all the stuff of a good obit here. Not for a Canadian newspaper though. Nazi collaborators living in the open in post-war Quebec. All this ran counter to the Canadian myth. The separatists would go ballistic and anyone who wrote it would be branded a racist, the term white French-Canadians borrowed from black Americans.

Duclos was still talking. "I read they weren't killing everyone and so I returned to France. I got on the same boat back to Marseilles."

The Frenchman ordered two espressos. Jack hadn't had it since a French girlfriend of his used to make it in her apartment in Montreal. He nodded at the waiter and asked the question he should have asked at the beginning.

"Did you ever know an agent named Foix? He was from Quebec and operated around here. He's the reason I'm looking into all this. I suppose I should have told you before."

A melodramatic pause by Duclos, who was a man given to the melodramatic touch.

"Foix. Pierre, or at least that's the name he was known by here. I do remember him. I hired a woman to kill him. A Pole, the Germans had sent me. Good looking. But he killed her, or his people did."

Jack took a few notes.

"Did you ever meet him?"

"I didn't want to. He was vicious. The Germans had a price on his head. They almost caught him a couple of times."

The two coffees arrived and Duclos took a sip then made a movement with his hand, as if he'd just remembered something. It was a movement familiar to anyone who'd seen a B-grade spy movie.

"But, I did meet him once. It was in a farm field. We were exchanging some Germans for some Jews. He was a little shit. There was a real standoff. We all suspected a trap, as I'm sure he and his side did too. I remember his Luger and the way his eyes looked. A psycho. I think he wanted to kill me."

And who wouldn't, thought Jack.

It was a busy afternoon. Before he left Duclos, Jack managed to get the name of another man from the dark side of the resistance. As he drove his rented car to meet with Claire's parents he thought of Duclos living in Quebec City. He spent six months there himself, working in the press gallery. He liked it too, at first, but after a while it was confining and cold, the weather and the people, especially if you weren't one of the tribe. He thought most of them would have despised a fancy pants Frenchman like Duclos.

Here he was working on the story of a war hero from Quebec, a man whose chest was festooned with decorations, one of them planted there by Charles de Gaulle himself and, at the other end, Duclos' friends in Quebec City. These were the same people who rioted against conscription. Not for them the idea of some Gallic bond stretching across the Atlantic.

One of them, an oily shrink by the name of Camille Laurin, had sheltered the bigger fish that Duclos talked about. Bernonville was his name. A count. He was later assassinated in Brazil. Laurin went on to become a cabinet minister in Quebec, the one who wrote the French-only language laws.

The whole language thing was one reason Jack was living in London rather than Montreal. One reason. But he couldn't get the French out of his life. He stopped at the side of the road to check the map. He was only 12 kilometres from the village where Claire's parents lived. Alleuze. An odd family name, nothing Jack had ever heard before he met Claire.

The house was well out in the country and Jack had trouble finding it. When he did, it shocked him. At the end of a line of trees sat this small château, or what he thought was a château. It looked almost perfect. Claire always moaned about being poor.

Jack parked and reached into the back seat to get a book he'd brought as a gift, a book of paintings by Canadian war artists. He had a few of them and liked to give them to special people.

The door opened and he was met by a woman he assumed to be Claire's mother. She was well dressed, smaller than Claire. She had big hair, a few moles on her face and a rather prominent nose. She still had a good figure, and Jack stopped himself when he started to give her the once-over. Forgetting his promise to Claire, he started in French.

"Hello, I'm Jack Devlin. I think your daughter told you I was coming."

She switched straight into English.

"We weren't sure when you would come," said in a cold, almost accusatory way. He realized he should have called ahead. "My husband is out for the afternoon, please come in."

This wasn't going to be easy. Jack handed her the book, which he hadn't wrapped and she looked at its cover, thanked him and put it on a table. He followed her into a comfortable room and motioned for him to sit down.

"Would you like some coffee Mr. Devlin?"

He said yes and she pressed a button beside her chair. When the maid appeared, she asked her to bring tea and chocolate biscuits. They waited, and she finally broke the silence.

"So Mr. Devlin, what brings you to France? My daughter tells me you're a journalist." She smiled in a stiff sort of way and he wondered whether she was shy, nervous or wasn't that keen on speaking to him. It dawned on him that Monsieur Alleuze was out for the afternoon on purpose, or was a recluse, sitting upstairs waiting for him to leave.

"Well, yes I am a journalist. I write for a paper in London, but I might also use this for a magazine in Canada."

Jack stopped talking. She was making him nervous now. He was worried he might upset her and a poor report on his conduct would be waiting for him back in London. He thought she was so reserved, unlike her rather forward daughter.

"Claire mentioned you had an interest in the war. Something to do with a man who was here during the occupation. I lived here then, though I must say I don't like speaking about it."

"You must have been quite young."

"I was. And I will tell you part of my story, but I don't want my name used. It still makes me nervous."

Jack was disappointed, but still happy he was getting some information. "No, I won't even take notes. I just want to hear from anybody who might have had some contact with the man I'm writing about. His name was Foix, Henri Foix, and he fought with the resistance, though he was a Canadian."

She moved her eyes away when the maid came in and set a tray in front of her. She poured tea into a cup and handed it to Jack, while gesturing towards the cookies. He thanked her and helped himself to some sugar. Madame Alleuze had a faraway look, seemingly lost in her thoughts.

"I did know people like him. I may have even known him," she said. After what seemed forever, though it was just twenty seconds, she looked back at him and started to tell her story.

"I was just a little girl, eight years old. The Germans came to our village, just down the road. Someone has told them my grandmother was a Jew. My maternal grandmother. My mother had already been taken away, and I never saw her again. Now the French police, the Milice, came to the school. They lined up the Jewish children, which in this case was just my brother and I. He was nine. There were other Jewish children in the village, but they had left. We hadn't left because we had never thought of ourselves as Jews."

She straightened herself up and poured herself some tea.

"I'm sorry, I never speak about this. I try not to think about it, so you'll have to excuse me."

She looked out into her garden and then gave Jack a weak smile before she started speaking again.

"We were put on a truck. I remember we had to climb up into it. One of the policemen even helped me. In the truck I was crying, but my brother I remember was angry. When we got to the crossroads, about two kilometres from the village, there was shooting. We heard the glass breaking in the cab and men came from the fields. We thought they were going to shoot us there."

Her tone had now lost its edge of fear and was rather matter of fact for such drama.

"One of those men was your Pierre, Pierre Foix. He was in charge and his men, and at least one woman, took us and

150

hid us for the next seven months until the liberation. That didn't happen here until August."

Jack's heart was beating, from the story and excitement of a real life incident. It beat clippings from old newspapers.

"What can you tell me about him?"

"Nothing really. We never saw him again. My brother, who died two years ago, named his two boys Pierre and Henri." She moved in her chair, which he thought was a signal to leave. The subject moved to small talk.

"So tell me, how is my daughter doing in London?"

"Oh very well. I've never met anyone who conquered the language in such a hurry. And she seems to love her job at the jewellery shop. She is off to a dinner in some palace this week. A big PR spread where they rent the place for the day. Photography and food."

"Yes, the princess's father. She told me."

Jack paused, wanting to ask another question.

"What about religion. Did you and your brother become practicing Jews?"

"No. I'm afraid after that we were too frightened. My husband is a Protestant, a Huguenot. I'm a Catholic, which is how I was brought up. I shouldn't think Claire ever goes to mass anymore."

As they walked to the door he wondered about whether Claire looked more like her father, though she had her mother's style. He looked at her shoes and saw they were the latest. Just like her daughter. No!

Passing an open door he saw a menorah on a sideboard and wondered about her devotion to Catholicism.

23

This was a late lunch with Philippe. Funny thing about men, friendships often start after a fight on the first meeting. Henri found Philippe more civilized than most of the Maquis and the two of them could talk about philosophy or science or, at this moment, nothing. They were playing chess.

Both men fancied themselves masters at the game and at each of their schools they could not be beaten. But today there was less tension since the chess was a ruse, a way to let passing Germans, or Frenchmen working for the Germans, think here were a couple of idle intellectuals, the thing the New Order would expunge from Europe.

Henri and Philippe had their eye on a building across the busy street. Once a military hospital, it was now used by the police, the SD, which most people called the Gestapo, and the Milice, the French police force of Vichy France that dealt with subversion.

As they looked up now and then from the chessboard, pretending to think, they were in fact looking for a man they suspected of penetrating the Underground. They sat almost beside each other, sharing the same corner of the table so that while one studied the board, the other could observe the courtyard and its several doors.

Two things had gone wrong. The French police had arrested another farmer near the field where Henri landed. They had raided his cottage and found half a dozen parachutes in the attic. The Milice were almost as brutal as the Germans. They had beaten the farmer, turning his face into a piece of raw meat then sent him to a camp somewhere in France.

There was no saving him. The next stop was Germany or Poland, if he lived that long. But what worried Philippe and Henri was that the police knew where to look. The week before, an agent landing from England had been captured. The reception committee was German. They could have taken the Lysander, the light single-engine plane that had landed in the field to let out its lone passenger. But they waved to the pilot who returned to the field at Tempsford.

The Germans hoped to use the radio and code of the captured agent, sending false messages to London. But Henri alerted London that the agent was in the jail in Lyon. It was the usual. The most gruesome torture you could imagine and then a one-way trip to an extermination camp.

"Your move, Pierre," said Philippe, using Henri's cover name. He was glad he had kept his last name, since Foix was so unusual, so French. For Henri using his real name meant one less lie to worry about. Philippe didn't know his real Christian name, nor did he know that Foix was not made up.

The next move was easy. Philippe had left a black bishop where a white knight could hook in for the kill. Henri didn't bother to take the easy move. He figured Philippe was trying to make things easy while they watched. He waited, then moved a rook so it was open to the bishop.

Just then Henri reached over, turned the bishop on its side, and both men looked up to see Prosper, the alias for the agent they were trailing. He didn't see them, but they knew he had come from the enemy version of a safe house. That he was walking out alive meant he was a dead man.

Philippe got up first, ready to do the job, but Henri held his arm and pressed him back into his seat.

"He doesn't know me. It will be easier." And Philippe was still recovering from the beating he took two weeks earlier.

Henri had to rush now to keep up with the man, who then turned to walk up the hill. That took away his advantage since Henri was the fitter of the two. Prosper turned away and walked up a narrow street.

Lyon was a Roman city and before that capital of the Gauls. Someone nineteen centuries ago had done Henri the favour of planning a narrow street, made dark by the buildings on either side. After a minute or two there were only three people, Henri, Prosper and a woman carrying a few shopping bags. The woman turned into a doorway and Henri knew they would soon be alone.

Then some luck. Prosper stopped to pick up a coin in the street and Henri decided this was the place. He moved up and behind his prey. He had a gun, but again it would be too noisy. There would be no time for drama to let Prosper know why he was dying. Henri had the knife in his hand and Prosper stood up, coin in hand. A few extra steps and Henri tapped him on the shoulder.

"*Excusez-moi, Monsieur*," and Prosper turned to answer. Henri used the technique he learned at the school in Montana and stabbed Prosper in the heart, killing him in one stroke. He gasped, but never even had the breath to scream. A quick feel of Prosper's pockets produced a wallet, stuffed with notes.

Henri couldn't resist one piece of melodrama. He stuffed a bill into Prosper's blood-filled mouth and left him in the doorway. It might be half an hour before anyone reported Prosper's body. The sight of the bill in his mouth would make most people turn away. They might not be brave enough for the Resistance, but they weren't calling the Germans.

Keeping a close eye on the windows and exits from the street, Henri turned down a steep lane and in a just a few minutes had time to disappear into a crowded street. He walked back to where Philippe and he had agreed to meet, another café a few streets away. They made their way back to the suburbs on bicycles.

In his pocket was Prosper's blood money, about 250,000 francs, with one note missing.

24

"A Monsieur Omer is waiting in the bar," said the man at the front desk. At first Jack thought they were talking about lobster.

"Homard?"

"No, Omer. He left a message that you were to see him as soon as you arrived."

Christ, thought Jack. It's Homer. What's he doing here?

Drinking was the answer.

"What the hell are you doing here?"

Homer looked as if he had never left the bar in London. All he'd changed was his drink. His white, pudgy hand was wrapped around a cloudy yellow drink. Homer smirked as he looked up at Jack.

"Drinking *Pernod*, what does it look like I'm doing? And I knew you'd need some help here."

Jack looked at him and only said, "Jesus Christ."

Homer laughed. "Don't flatter yourself, Devlin. Our friend Michelle is sending me to Geneva. Oil my boy, oil. Where the sheiks meet to fix prices. And the fastest way to Geneva is through Lyon, at least for a man who's not that fond of flying. And the Arabs don't start talking for a few days, so why not stop and see my old friend."

"God, you're an asshole," said Jack. He sat down and ordered a drink. Homer ordered another drink and Jack was surprised at how good his French was.

"Where'd you learn to parler?"

"An old draft dodger. You know. Well deserter, actually. The first night in Montreal I met a French girl. She liked *les Américains*. I lived with her for a year and a half. She was from the Beauce, and couldn't speak much English, so we spoke French."

Jack didn't bother to ask what happened to her. With Homer it was always the same. They tired of the booze and the indecision.

"So Devlin, what adventure are we off on now? I've only got a couple of days."

Jack thought to himself, what the hell. He only had one more name to see, the man Duclos had given him.

"I just spent the afternoon with someone even a draft dodger – excuse me, deserter – would be glad to shoot. Some guy who collaborated with the Germans during the war. You know the Vichy government."

Homer gave a short laugh and interrupted.

"Don't patronize me Devlin. I was three credits away from a history degree at Dartmouth when I got caught smoking dope, was kicked out of school and lost my student deferment. I know who Marshal Pétain and the fucking Vichy French were."

Jack figured he'd caught old Homer out. Details of his past, something he never gave out much. "The things you learn in a faraway place. Let's see, Dartmouth, I always figured you for a preppie. Dope, well that figures. And a deserter. If you were already over there, why bother to leave?"

Homer made a face, as if to say, 'why didn't I keep my mouth shut.' He lit another *Gitane* and passed one to Jack. "You like this French stuff?"

"Yeah, Homer. But what about deserting? Come on, you can't tease me like that."

"Promise you won't tell anyone."

"Sure, promise." Jack knew it was a lie as soon as he said it. He was already figuring out who he would tell. Homer of all people should know reporters can't be trusted with secrets. It's not their business. Talking and writing is their business, not keeping secrets. "Don't worry. Your secret's safe with me."

"Well the truth is I was less than a month away from ending my tour. And it wasn't like it was that tough. I never was in any firefights. I was a general's driver. He liked the fact he had a Dartmouth dropout as a chauffeur. We used to discuss history and politics. All the French colonial shit and how the Second World War finally ended the French Empire and the British Empire."

"Yeah," said Jack. "If the British Empire should last a thousand years..."

Homer interrupted. "This will be its finest moment. Christ knows what Churchill was putting in those cigars. The Empire didn't make it until 1960. Anyway that's when I started reading more about Marshal Pétain and the Vichy French. I then saw it was all related to Vietnam. The Japanese gave the Vietnamese a taste of freedom, though that's not the word. They showed them the white man could be beaten. So they beat him again and when they finished with the French, they did it to us."

"You want another *Pernod?*" Jack made a pre-emptive strike and ordered before Homer could speak.

"Sure."

"So why did you desert? The conversation with the general get boring?"

"No, one day I just got sick of it. Sick of the army, sick of the war. Shit, if you look back on it, the North Vietnamese were as imperialistic as the French. The South Vietnamese wanted nothing to do with them. No I just got sick of the whole thing. I put on my civilian clothes and took a cab to the airport."

"You flew back to the States? A deserter. Were you nuts?"

"God Devlin, you dumb fuck. Can you shut up and listen? Of course I didn't fly to Hawaii. I flew to Hong Kong and from there to Britain. Harold Wilson was in the chair at the time. They loved draft dodgers. *The New Statesman's* delight."

There was a short break in the talk, as Jack digested all of this. Must have been in 1968 or '69. When did Heath beat Wilson? 1970, maybe? Taxman Mr. Wilson, Taxman Mr. Heath. He stared straight ahead, drank and smoked. Homer did the same. It must have seemed an odd picture to an outsider, like two lovers having a silent quarrel.

"Then I went to Montreal. It's corny, but it was easier for my mother to come and visit me. It was only a three-hour drive."

Jack decided not to rib him. He almost felt sorry for Homer, almost. "There was an amnesty. Jimmy Carter did that didn't he? Seven or eight years ago. You can go home now."

Homer pulled at his moustache, like he was cleaning it with his fingers, then stretching it sideways. "Never been home once in 18 years. I'm not sure the amnesty applies to deserters. I'm not about to test it. Besides, I sound like an American, but I don't think like one anymore. I like it here. But enough of this maudlin shit Devlin, what are we up to tomorrow? It's too late to do it now. Let's just get pissed and do whatever it is we're doing tomorrow."

And that they did.

Breakfast came too early. The yellow in the eggs reminded Jack of the *Pernod* and he thought he was going to puke. Homer sat across from him smoking and eating something that looked like porridge. A chain-smoking vegetarian.

Neither of them said anything. Jack's head ached and he wished Homer had stayed home. After the *Pernod* they had moved to dinner and red wine. Apart from the expense, since Jack seemed to be doing most of the paying, there were the cigarettes. Non-stop smoking. And Jack had been off the weeds for three days, well almost three days.

Homer was affecting the foreign-correspondent look this morning. He had a kind of low-end safari jacket, a lightweight thing in off beige. The buckle on the belt was plastic. He had blue corduroys that were worn a bit thin. Around his neck was a blue polka-dot scarf, the kind skiers sometimes wear, and desert boots on his feet.

They presented a bizarre picture to the six or seven other diners in the small room. Jack was wearing jeans, black loafers and a blazer. He had gone to the trouble of putting on a tie. He'd heard the French were formal. A woman at the next table glanced over from time to time and then mumbled to her husband. So far they hadn't said anything, only nodded and grunted at the waiter.

All of a sudden Jack noticed the discreet looks they were getting from the rest of the room. He looked over at Homer, who was still dealing with his porridge, staring at it, poking it with a spoon and sprinkling it with sugar after every third or fourth bite, dribbling parts of it on the *Tribune* he was reading. They must think we're a pair of homos, thought Jack, and he started to smile.

"So what time do you want to leave?" Jack asked Homer in a loud voice. On hearing English spoken Jack watched the provincial French woman at the next table and saw her prejudices light up her face. Now she was sure. *Pédés*, as the French call them.

The sound of the words jolted Homer who wasn't interested in talking for at least another half-hour.

"Can't we wait? You only have one person to see." Homer looked up from his paper. "It's not healthy to rush with your food. Your diet, Devlin. It's going to kill you."

Jack looked at Homer Lamont. A chain-smoking functioning drunk whose only healthy quirk was a diet that might save his bowels if his lungs and heart didn't give out first. "Jesus, Lamont. Save me the lecture. Hitler was a fucking vegetarian. So deliver me from the moral high ground."

Homer was slapped awake by that remark and changed the subject. All of sudden he wanted to get on with the day.

"Well, come on Devlin, let's get on with it," and as he spoke, got up and walked around behind Jack and shook his shoulders, almost massaging them as he spoke. "Up and at 'em. Ready downstairs in 15 minutes."

At the sight of the in-restaurant massage, the woman at the next table gave her husband a smug closed-lip smile and knowing nod, so certain was she that she had uncovered a nest of English perverts.

"I've been here before so I should be able to help us get there," said Homer. "I used to be in rallies when I was a kid. It's all very easy."

Jack was hung over and annoyed with Homer. But he said nothing. Duclos had suggested the man they were going to see. His name was Bentonville. He too lived in Oingt, a town north and west of Lyon. It was on the edge of the area that Henri Foix covered in 1943 and 44.

Homer was studying the map and he'd found where they were going. "Odd name for a town. Why are we going there again? Oh, you're on the right road by the way."

Not a word as Jack concentrated on his driving. He was thinking how he would find Bentonville. He had his address and phone number, but there had been no answer when he called.

"This map is amazing. Beaujolais, Macon. Everything sounds like a bottle of wine. So you didn't answer me, why are we going to a place called Oingt?"

"Oingt," said Jack correcting Homer's pronunciation. "It sounds like went. And we're going to look for a guy named Bentonville. He was a collaborator. Duclos says he only came back here a few years ago. He had been living in South America."

"The boys from Brazil. Like Eichmann and the other Nazis?"

"Well this guy went to New York first, then took the train to Montreal. That was in 1946. A court in Lyon had sentenced him to death, so he was reluctant to come back. He managed to hang on in Quebec until 1955 when it looked as if Canada might deport him to France, so off he went to Brazil."

Homer thought for a while. "Well I'm sure he deserved it. But you know my government, old Dick Nixon, wanted me back in jail. For 20 years. Thank Christ Canada takes its time about this stuff."

Homer lit a *Disque bleu* and coughed at the strange taste. "Shit, I wish I'd brought a carton of Rothmans. Imagine smoking this junk for the next two weeks. Hey, where did you hear all this stuff about Bentonville? This guy Duclos knows all the details?"

"Well he knew some. He was in Quebec for a while too. No, he gave me a book. Well he sold it to me. It even had some pictures, so if we see Monsieur Bentonville, we should be able to recognize him. Good-looking prick, or at least he was."

Jack reached into the back seat and pulled the book from under his coat. "Here Lamont, read this. And I'm still a bit queasy so do me a favour and don't talk for half an hour. Just read."

"Cranky fucker," and Homer went straight for the pictures in the middle.

25

The field outside the village had a clear view of the open country on all sides. It reminded Henri of the place he had landed. It was odd in that it seemed sheltered, so that neither the Germans, nor anyone else, could make a sudden appearance without being seen from a distance.

Even with the favourable terrain, Henri insisted on a lookout. Even better than that, he had a telephone. Since he began the fight with the Germans, his organization of sixty men, and fifteen women had kept busy laying telephone lines. Henri had sent a radio burst to London asking for more equipment, wires and headsets, to be shipped in canisters.

A couple of days earlier, the Germans had stumbled across two of his men working on a phone line. Both ran, one was shot while the other made it to a copse. It was almost dark at the time, so he hid there and escaped five hours later.

Now it was 6:30 PM. In fifteen minutes there would be an exchange, three German soldiers for two children. The children would arrive with one man, at the edge of this field. Henri would be alone with three soldiers who were trussed up in the trunk and back seat of a big Citroen. Since it had been stolen from the police, they could have it back.

Henri's Luger was in a Wehrmacht issue officer's holster hidden by his jacket. The deal was that the man from the Gestapo would do the switch, not some flunky from the

Milice. He would be driven half a kilometre from the meeting point then walk the rest of the way with the children.

Both men had promised to meet unarmed. But Henri knew the Gestapo man would have a pistol. The prize of the catch was a German major with tape over his mouth and wire around his ankles and wrists. His rank had given him the soft spot in the back seat; seeing him alive would make it easier for the Gestapo man to make the trade.

The major had been beaten up, but not that much. Henri needed him as a bargaining chip. Florence had wanted to kill the lot; maybe she thought it would bring her husband back from Germany or wherever he was. Henri had stopped her.

"Are things on time?" asked Henri into the receiver.

"They are walking up now. He's alone with the two children. You should see them soon."

Then Henri saw three figures coming up the road, looking as if they were a family out for a stroll after an early children's dinner. Henri looked to the shed where his men were hidden with another vehicle. The sun was moving to the top of another hill and starting to change colour from yellow to red. It still had a way to go, half an hour, maybe more.

The Gestapo man was young, not 30, maybe a year older than Henri. He was dressed in a civilian jacket, a long sports coat similar to the one Henri was wearing. A bulge in the right outside pocket could have been cigarettes or a pistol.

The two men closed on each other and Henri stopped as the Gestapo man came through the open gate in the hedge. Henri nodded at the two children, a boy and a girl dressed in what looked like school clothes, each carrying a small case. It looked as if they hadn't slept much in the past couple of days.

"Stay there." The Gestapo man looked at them, with a theatrical, forced tenderness and then walked forward. He stopped and spoke in almost unaccented French.

"You have what I'm looking for?"

"Yes. The key is in the Citroen. The officer is in the back seat, the two soldiers are in the trunk."

Henri's hand moved for his pistol as the Gestapo man went for his pocket. He smiled. "Just a cigarette. Would you like one?"

"Yes." said Henri. He didn't mind wasting time as the sun went down. He could use the cover of darkness for what he had to do. And the cigarettes intrigued him. They were German.

"You're a brave man to come here on your own," said Henri.

"How gallant. Your accent. Pierre the Canadian. We have a price on your head. You're quite valuable you know."

"Really," said Henri in mock surprise. He motioned to the children. "Go over to that shed and wait for me there." He didn't bother to smile, he thought it might scare them after what they'd been through. He just acted like a tough schoolteacher.

"And how much how am I worth?"

"Oh just ten thousand francs. But after today I should think your value will rise. Maybe fifty thousand? One of your people will turn you in. You could come with me now. We'd treat you like a prisoner of war, not a spy."

Henri took a last pull of the German cigarette and gave the German a cold stare.

"I'm giving serious consideration to killing you, so take the Citroen and leave."

The sun was a ball of red. No chance of a strafing run now. The airfield was too far away. He walked over to the car with the German whose left hand moved toward the door and his right to open his jacket. Henri's commando knife was at his throat.

"Ah Monsieur, we said no weapons. But then we're both liars. I'll take that," and Henri slipped the PPK from under the German's jacket. "Very stylish."

The German smiled and got behind the wheel. The sun was almost down, but Henri warned him, no lights until the crossroads three kilometres away.

"Don't stop until you get there or the car will be shot up. We have you covered." A lie since most of the men were hidden right here.

The children were in the shed with Florence and two local Maquis. Florence had insisted on coming when she realized what he was planning. He had left a guidebook open. Henri argued, but in the end it made the train trip seem more normal.

The girl, a frightened eight-year old, was leaning into Florence and looking at the ground. The boy was quite cocky and had taken on the role of *père de famille*, the man of the house.

"My name is André and this is my sister Rachel." He addressed Henri, since it was obvious he was the boss. "Do you know where my parents are?"

"Yes," said Henri. "They have gone to Paris on government business. They might stay there for a while, at least until the Americans and the English come to liberate France. They are doing important work."

André Levy stared at Henri. The boy knew not to talk back to the Germans, but now he felt he could challenge this man.

"I think they were taken because we are Jewish. The Milice and then the Germans called us names. They were quite rough. One of them slapped my sister to stop her from crying. One of the children of the Milice made a sign, like a hanging and laughed at us, called us dirty Jews as we sat in the back of the truck."

As the young boy told his story Henri's face reddened in anger. He was furious with himself. He was an officer and had kept his word with the German, but he should have killed him. And the other men in the back of the Citroen.

"I am grateful, Monsieur, that you have rescued us. But I think my parents were taken because we are Jews," said the boy repeating himself in a speech Henri guessed he had prepared. "And if we hadn't been at school we would still be with them. So, if you could tell me where they are, my sister and I will join them."

Oh, no you won't, thought Henri. He knew the Levys had been transported and were in all likelihood in a holding camp in France about to be shipped to Germany. And unlike

Florence's husband, ordinary indentured labour, not even a political prisoner, there was little chance of them coming back.

"I spoke with your parents before they left. They are on a secret mission for the Resistance. They cannot be reached. The Germans were after you, not so much because you were Jewish, but because you are the children of brave and famous heroes of the Resistance. Now you too have to hide and you will live with a friend of mine. He has a farm. Florence will come and see you every couple of days."

Young André puffed out in pride as Henri told him the story of his parents. It was a lie and maybe even this young boy knew it, but he wanted to believe it. It was much better than the truth.

"And you Monsieur. If you don't mind my saying so, you speak an odd French. Are you from the north?"

Henri wanted to tell the boy the truth, but he couldn't.

"Yes I'm from the north, the far north."

26

The gate at the edge of the village was all that was left of the wall that once fenced in the medieval town of Oingt. Homer had given Jack the history of Oingt for the past 15 minutes, telling him about the church they had to see.

"A chapel from the 14th century, Devlin. I studied this stuff at Dartmouth, but I never really saw much of it on our field trip to France. Too pissed."

The streets narrowed and Jack decided to look for a place to park. It might be easier to do this on foot. He hoped Lamont was up to it. He didn't bother to ask.

They started to walk, Jack studying a map and trying to find the street where Bentonville lived. Homer kept talking about the tower at the top of the hill and the things they should see. One thing they did see was a café and they popped in. Homer wanted a glass of wine, Jack a coffee. Both of them needed a smoke.

While Jack tore into a croissant, Homer made small talk with the woman behind the bar. He never stopped. Jack turned off the French part of his brain and didn't listen, only a couple of times switching the French ear back on just to marvel at how fluent Lamont was. Jack thought he would learn Sanskrit to get laid.

He then perked up at the mention of the name Bentonville.

"What's going on, Lamont?"

"Well Oingt is named after a saint, or at least someone who started a convent here in the 13th century. We'll have to go look at that later. You know, I should really go back to Dartmouth and finish my degree."

Jack exhaled. Then he took a breath. "No Lamont. For Christ's sake. Bentonville. What did she say about Bentonville?"

"Easy. He comes here every night at five o'clock. You can set your watch by it, apparently. So that leaves us lots of time to walk around."

"You walk. I'm going to read that book and sleep." Jack asked the woman behind the bar if she knew where they could find some rooms. One for now, another later if they stayed overnight. They were in luck. There were rooms upstairs. Jack paid for one room right away and asked her to reserve another one for his friend in case they decided to stay.

"That's not a problem, Monsieur. There are no tourists this time of year."

"Right, Lamont. You go off and work on the prioress. I'm going to kip. I'll meet you back here at four o'clock."

It was a little before noon. He took a bottle of *Perrier* and a sandwich upstairs. Before he started to read he pulled the portable alarm clock from his bag and set it for 3:30. He knew he would never last twenty minutes reading French.

Downstairs Homer made friends with the woman working behind the bar. It was a slow day and she could take a few hours off after one o'clock. She liked Americans and agreed to give Homer a tour of the village of Oingt and the history of Marguerite d'Oingt, the woman whose family gave the place its name.

Later Homer told Jack that he knew he had to have this woman after he saw her breasts when she bent over to get Jack's bottle of *Perrier*. He also told Jack he didn't know how he could have a nap when he could be walking around a village parts of which looked the same as they had more than a thousand years ago.

The book kept Jack awake for maybe five minutes, then he fell asleep until just before three, his hangover gone at last. He got up to shave. He threw a towel over his shoulder to catch any drops of shaving cream, since he had slept in his clothes. A shave always made him feel better even if it was the second one of the day.

He had almost an hour to kill so he wandered through the village by himself. He figured he'd see more if he didn't have to listen to a running commentary by Homer. He had read a bit about the town, how its fortifications had been torn down in the 16th century. All that was left was the gate. The streets were narrow and he had a vision of people in the middle ages throwing their night soil into the streets in the morning. He knew the English used to do that but wasn't sure about the French.

Why would an old war criminal live here? Bentonville had been with the Milice, the militia that did the dirty work for the Nazis. They fought the Resistance, rounded up Jews and shipped them to camps in France, then on to the death camps in the east.

Jack imagined Bentonville liked the place because it was so French, as if it had rejected all the vulgar modern ideas the Fascists hated. No McDonalds, no video games. Then Jack rather liked Oingt, as well. As with any new place he wondered what it would be like to live here. And he wondered how much the houses cost. As he walked the streets, he tried to look into windows, without being too obvious.

He could see how Bentonville could hide here. Maybe the people who lived here didn't care. Of all the stuff he'd read, and that long movie the *Sorrow and the Pity*, there were a lot of people in France who just gave up, and a lot who were out and out collaborators. People like Duclos and Bentonville who agreed with Hitler's vision of Europe.

As he surveyed the old streets he wondered if Nazi soldiers had ever marched through here or whether the Milice and people like Bentonville managed to keep order on their own. The New Order. That was the phrase. Now France and

Germany split another order, Europe, with Germany in the driver's seat. Jack thought what a waste those two wars were.

A clock tower rang four and he thought he'd better get back. He wanted to be there before Monsieur Bentonville arrived. God, he hoped he could keep Lamont under control.

The surprise was to see Lamont at the bar, with a silly grin on his face as the woman behind the bar – her name was Colette – spent a lot of time fussing at his end of the counter and looking all girlish, though she was 40 if she was a day.

Jesus, thought Jack. Homer is amazing. He's so goddamned ugly and he manages to pull these women.

"Can you pull yourself away, Romeo," Jack smiled, quite sure Colette didn't speak English, at least not if it was spoken in a hurry. "Let's get over to that corner seat. It's almost twenty to five; we want to be over there when our man arrives. Get your lady friend to give us the nod when he comes in, though I should be able to recognize him."

Homer spoke in quick French to Colette, all so fast that Jack had a hard time understanding what she said back. The gist of it was she would look over when Bentonville arrived. Jack drank *Perrier* and coffee; Homer was back into red wine, good local Beaujolais.

"This stuff is so cheap. And it's better than anything we ever get in London, at least the kind you and I can afford. Just taste this. Can you imagine ever getting anything like this in that fucking wine bar?"

Jack wasn't much of wine man but even he could tell the difference. He took a sip, nodded and made an 'uh-hum' noise of agreement.

Once again he and Homer were on the road to getting a little pissed. Jack had given some thought to drinking over the past little while. He wondered why he always ended up hanging around with guys like Lamont. The reason, of course, is that Homer was never going to give him shit about drinking. And he didn't have to explain to Homer what it was that was enjoyable about just plain drinking, as a thing to do all on its own.

Neither of them would ever drink alone, of course. That would make them drunks.

The red wine was better than even the most expensive stuff he'd tried at the wine bar in London. Then neither he nor Homer gave much of a shit about great wine. Volume was more important than quality. Jack held the glass up and wobbled it a little, trying to see if the wine stuck to the side of the glass. He'd read somewhere that was the mark of great wine.

One eye was closed, peering through the prism of the glass when he saw Bentonville, looking just a couple of decades older than the pictures in the book on his escapades after the war, dodging the French executioner, or the French mob.

Colette looked over to Jack and nodded, though she could see right away he knew it was Bentonville. He was dressed in a formal way for this village, a white shirt with a bold polka-dot tie, all under a pin-stripped grey suit. His hair must have been blond once, his face was round, but not fat. He was good looking in an odd way, except his nose was a bit flattened, like he'd been a boxer once. His shoulders were broad, his neck a bit thick for such a well-dressed man and his hands were big.

Two or three thick fingers waved at Colette, signalling for his usual. Jack was now standing right beside him at the bar. He was about an inch, maybe two shorter than Bentonville, whose formal name was Pierre André de Bentonville. Must have been some kind of aristocrat, Lamont said earlier.

"Monsieur Bentonville? My name's Devlin, I wonder if I could talk to you for a minute." Jack spoke French and Bentonville was startled.

"Pardon?"

"I said my name is Devlin and I wondered if you'd mind talking to me for a minute or two. I'm a writer." He thought writer sounded grander than reporter, and wouldn't put him off as much.

Bentonville switched to English. He spoke it even better than Duclos and didn't have much of an accent. You might have had a hard time picking him out as a Frenchman. Maybe a Pole or a rich Mexican.

"You're a Canadian. Probably an Englishman from Quebec, judging by your horrible French and your accent." He picked up his drink and looked as if he was about to crush the glass. His teeth ground, moving his cheeks from one side to the other like a seesaw in slow motion.

"No, I don't want to talk. But you're here, and I suppose I'm curious. What do you want?"

Jack looked straight at Bentonville. He wanted to look around and see what that lunatic Lamont was up to, but he didn't break eye contact with the old collaborator standing in front of him. Jack figured he must be 70 by now, maybe a year or two older.

"I'm writing something about a man named Foix. Someone told me you might have run into him during the war?"

"They did, did they?" Bentonville took a slug of his drink, a whiskey with water. He used the dramatic pause. Jack figured he was either trying to remember Foix or deciding whether to talk about him.

"Yes, I remember him. Little fellow. Caused us a lot of trouble. Odd for a French-Canadian, he was working for the English King. I always thought him a bit of a traitor."

And I'm sure he thought the same of you, Jack told himself.

"I only met him once. And I'm sorry I didn't kill him. Sentimental fool wanted to trade three hostages for a couple of children. I could have killed him and I should have. He caused us a lot of trouble later."

Jack's mind was racing. He couldn't think what to ask next.

"What kind of trouble?" Pause. Let him do the talking.

" A battle. One of the few set battles we've ever had around here."

"We? Do you mean the Germans or the Milice?"

Bentonville shot Jack a mocking look, as if to say what a stupid question.

"What do you know, you stupid boy. Something you read in a book or saw in a movie made by some Jew in Hollywood?"

Jack felt his face redden, part from anger, part from embarrassment. Bentonville was right; all he knew was from books. And not that much either. He focused. He needed something. A quote, for a magazine article. Maybe some colour for his obit.

If he thinks I'm dumb, I'll be dumb. A dumb fucking Anglais from Quebec. Make him show me how smart he is. Brag for me, dumbfuck.

"Yeah, I guess."

Bentonville nodded at Colette for another drink. She gave him one and poured Jack another red, without asking. From her body language it was clear that Jack was buying his own.

"You guess. You guess. Your friend Foix, Pierre he called himself. Thought he was clever. We ambushed his men one night. He wasn't so brave. He ran like the coward he was. We killed a lot that night."

Jack remembered the clipping from the newspaper in 1945.

"Rifle butts wasn'it?"

Bentonville looked at him, and didn't give Jack the pleasure of surprise, if there was any.

"We knew he was sentimental. After the children. He thought I was a German. He insisted on one, and so there I was. We promised them another trade, but they weren't careful. We had them."

Bentonville stopped talking and looked straight ahead.

"Did you ever see him again? In Canada, when you were there?" This was a shot in the dark. There was nothing about that in any book or article.

"Yes I did see him. One night in a club in Montreal. He was having his picture taken with a bunch of friends. He was holding a piglet by the tail. It was a trick they did at this restaurant, put a little pig up there. I knew it was him."

"Was that when you left for Paraguay?"

Bentonville snapped. "Brazil. He looked at me. I left and was on a plane the next day. I'm sure he recognized me, but he couldn't leave. Stuck with his friends, he was."

Jack had his piece of the puzzle. He smiled and took out a cigarette, offering one to Bentonville.

"You've been very helpful, Monsieur," said Jack switching back to French.

His hand came across the bar and slapped Jack hard in the face. Then the old man moved fast, grabbing a bottle from behind the bar, breaking it fast and moving it to shove it into Jack's face or throat.

A foot kicked the bottle from his hand followed by a fist thrust into his solar plexus. Bentonville sucked for breath. Jack stepped back to see Homer, standing there, daring the old man with his eyes to try something.

Jack looked at Homer.

"Well, Devlin, I said I deserted. But that doesn't mean I didn't fight before I quit. There were bars in Saigon you know."

"And Hitler was a vegetarian," said Jack.

Bentonville, still sucking for air, looked up, most perplexed by that last remark.

27

London, May 1944

Another agent sat in the back seat of the Buick. Jane had heard him speak and assumed he was a Pole. Tonight she was driving him to a safe house in the Midlands. She would stay with some other members of the First Aid Nursing Yeomanry at a house run by the Royal Air Force.

FANYs they called them. High-spirited volunteers looking for excitement. They all enjoyed their rude sounding name, which in British English had a more juicy anatomical definition than in American English. She had blushed when one of her friends told her what it meant.

Jane had a licence to drive anything and, for a while, she drove big lorries, huge military transports. But she preferred what she and her friends called the silk-and-cyanide brigade, chauffeuring spies from safe houses to airports.

At first the job was exciting. Driving all over England in a big car when most people didn't have the coupons for petrol, if they had a car at all. The last few weeks she'd been a little blue. For one thing she hadn't heard of Henri. Not that she expected to, but maybe she might have heard if he'd been killed.

And she felt like an executioner. On a dry run back to London from the field at Tempsford she started talking with one of the minders.

"What chance do agents have, the ones we drop off in Europe?"

The minder, the same one who'd travelled with Henri to Scotland and back, was more open than he was meant to be. The end was near, he knew the world of secrets would loosen up soon, at least for him.

"It depends really. We always tell them it's fifty-fifty. But so far it's been a bit better than that. Say one in three doesn't make it. But it depends on who it is and where. France is dangerous. You never know who the enemy is. It isn't just the Germans but the French. There are a lot of them you can't trust."

Just then he stopped talking to light a cigarette. The smoke drifted into the front seat and Jane knew it was French. Must have been something he picked up from one of the agents, or a pilot coming back in a Lysander, the little planes that could land anywhere. The minder knew Jane didn't smoke, so he didn't bother offering her one.

She spoke first. "French, I see?"

"Yes. They do have a distinctive smell, don't they? Not where we were," said the minder just back from France. All of this is hush-hush of course, but then I wouldn't tell you things if I knew you weren't the silent type."

Jane smiled.

"Still carrying a torch for our little French chap?"

She could feel herself blush, but didn't answer.

"He's still alive, in case you're worried. More than we can say for some other operations. God knows what's happening in Holland. But it's the Poles I feel sorry for. The Russians are coming the other way. They'll probably kill our agents if they catch them."

Jane was shocked and she looked into the mirror to try and make eye contact with the minder. "Why? We're on the same side, aren't we?"

"Yes. But Stalin will want to claim he did it all himself, without any help. And most of the people we drop in were in the Polish army. Most of them tell me it was the Russians not the Germans that liquidated the Polish officer corps. But we're not even allowed to think that now."

A pull of the cigarette and a look out the window.

Jane thought about the conversation with the minder as she looked back at the determined blond man in the back seat. She knew he was set to be dropped into Poland. Maybe tomorrow, maybe next week. The drive to the execution.

That night Jane and two of her friends walked down the lane from the RAF women's barracks to the pub in the village. Walking back the other way was her blond Pole. He didn't notice her or her friends. He was too busy trying to speak to some giggling local girl who hadn't gone out with an English boy in two years.

At the pub the three of them sat alone in the corner. When airmen or soldiers approached them they just nodded and said no thank you. Odd, but they were left alone. Not one of them was married but all three were in love with men who were away, one on a ship, the other with the army in Italy.

Jane couldn't even talk about her man, since she wasn't meant to know who he was, where he was or what he did. She was happy enough to know he was still alive.

"I've struck it lucky, Peter's coming home on leave in a few weeks," said the friend with the man in the navy. The other two were jealous, but they smiled and pretended they were happy. They knew shore leaves were a regular thing for men at sea, and her lover was commanding a frigate somewhere in the Atlantic.

The other friend changed the subject and started talking about cars. She'd just been given a new Bentley, snapped from its owner somewhere in Shropshire.

"It has two advantages. It's unreliable, which means I spend less time driving it. And the top brass want to be seen in a Bentley, so I really don't have any long trips. Not like you Jane. Who wants to ride in a Buick?"

They laughed, and after one more drink, Jane decided to walk. Late May. The sun was still out even though it was almost nine o'clock. She crossed the street to avoid three American pilots who were coming towards her.

She wondered if the sun had gone down yet in whatever part of France Henri was in. When she returned to her flat it was almost dark. There was a note, telling her in a rather cryptic way that she and the Buick had work to do tomorrow.

28

Spring brought a fresh crop of Germans, or at least soldiers in German uniforms. They came from different parts of the new German empire. As they walked through the centre of Lyon, Philippe and Henri had a new game: try and pick the languages or dialects of the men from the Waffen SS, the most polyglot of the German fighting units.

They pretended to look in the window of a shop as they listened to three SS men in their grey tunics. Henri looked at the blonde hairline of the soldier with his back to him as he and Philippe headed to their favourite café.

"They were Germans, no guessing there," said Henri. Right away he could tell from the thin smile on Philippe's lips that he was wrong.

"Too guttural. Even the harshest German isn't that harsh," said Philippe. He was still recovering from the beating the Gestapo gave him. His ribs were weak, three of them had been broken, and there were still scabs on his face from the cuts when his head was shoved through the window. There was nothing wrong with his mind.

Henri was puzzled. He could speak French, English, Latin and some ancient Greek. But unlike Philipe he hadn't traveled across Europe, or been to a university for a year in Berlin. He thought of the map of old Germany and the new Reich.

"I'll give you a hint. They could have been speaking two languages, one so close to the other."

"Czech?" Henri thought the other might be Slovak.

"Not even close. Dutch. It's so guttural that they have a word they trap the Germans with. Scheveningen. A suburb of The Hague, I think. Even the Germans can't say it if they're pretending to speak Dutch. Czech? Where did you come up with that?"

"Well you said another language. I thought Czechoslovakia."

"Flemish. The Belgians who hate the French. The enemy of their enemy is their friend. Easy to recruit to the SS, I should think. Who doesn't like to think they're part of a master race? And the Dutch and the Flemish can look more German than the Germans."

At the café, another part of the same game, though neither Philippe nor Henri could guess the language. It was so foreign they felt they could talk in French about the men at the next table who were busy flirting with some French girls. Unlike the Dutch SS men, they were not in battle dress.

"I've heard that language before," said Henri. "There was an old couple, White Russians, I think who kept a small hotel in St. Sauveur. When they spoke to each other it sounded like this, but maybe not as rough. He said he was a duke."

"Every Russian is a duke," said Philippe with a laugh. He thought for a minute, and then whispered the name, as the sound of it might be the only thing the men next to them might pluck from a French conversation.

"Ukrainians. Another case of the enemy of my enemy. Kulaks. They hate the Russians more than Florence hates the Germans. The Galician SS I believe they are called. I've seen them at the newsreels. And they are said to hate the Jews almost as much as the Germans do."

Henri and Philippe were not here to play geography. The new batch of soldiers coincided with a crackdown on the Resistance and a roundup of Jews. The torture chambers were working overtime and both men knew the Germans feared the coming invasion in the north.

Today they were meeting a man from the post office, whose interest was not stamps but telephones. And his side-

179

line was radios, or a least radio traffic. The airwaves were jammed with signals to Paris, London and Berlin and all places in between. The man from the post office was a notch or two up from the *fonctionnaire* from the railway.

He walked into the café and sat two tables away. He carried a brown leather satchel, scuffed with age, from which he produced a stamp album. Corny, but it worked as code to identify him.

After a short wait Henri looked over and said, "I see you are a philatelist, Monsieur."

"Yes, do you have an interest?"

"Yes," said Henri. "Corsica is my speciality."

Corsica was the key word and within a minute the three men were poring over the stamp collection, discussing stamps in voices that had nothing to hide. At one stage one of the Ukrainian soldiers looked over and gave a shrugging kind of laugh, with a lift of his chin and neck as if to say 'No wonder we're running the show here.'

Talk of stamps went on for a while and Philippe bought a Greek Hermès stamp from the collector. It was from 1880 and didn't cost much. On the back was a series of lines, a micro map of a wood to the east of Lyon, in the heart of a kind of no-man's land the Germans and the Milice liked to keep to themselves.

The trip to the forbidden territory took place that night. Henri, Philippe, Florence and ten other members of the Maquis, dressed in black, stood in the trees examining a row of military vehicles parked at the side of the road. What made them different was they were white, with both swastikas and the red cross on them.

"Ambulances. They've been here for three days. They never move, and people walk in and out of them," said Florence who had been here while her make-believe husband was in Lyon. "And they do walk. No one is wounded. What is it?"

Henri thought about what they might be. With the red cross on the side, not even the Resistance would attack here.

"Wait here, and don't shoot unless someone is about to shoot me." He stared at them, looking around as if to drill in the point. "Don't even aim your guns and to be safe, only shoot on my command."

He walked along the edge of the woods until he was past the last ambulance in the line. Then he waited a few minutes as it got just a bit darker. He dropped to the ground and crawled across the strip between the woods and the road, then rolled into the ditch at the side of it. He then crawled until he was just behind the last ambulance.

The back door was no more than six feet away and the door opened away from the ditch. His dark clothes were partly stained with grass. Henri stuck his head above the ditch and scanned along the line of seven ambulances. All their doors were closed, and he knew from his reconnoitre in the woods there were no drivers or guards.

All of sudden he stood up and walked to the back door of the ambulance and grabbed the handle. It made no noise when he turned it. He pulled it open maybe two inches and the light from inside hit his eyes. There were two soldiers inside with headsets on, each monitoring a radio. He closed the door, but this time the latch made a click.

He rolled back into the ditch and pulled his commando knife from its sheath. Maybe they hadn't heard. The click had seemed like a cannon shot to him but the radio operators were wearing headsets. Then he saw the top of the door open and a soldier with a drawn pistol came down the stairs.

The soldier said something in German, which Philippe later told him was "Who's there?"

He moved toward the ditch but then went around the other side of the truck. He put his pistol away and made a remark, which Philippe said showed the soldier thought his friends in the next ambulance might be toying with him. He moved back to the door, and took one look toward the ditch but couldn't see Henri.

The top of the door was all he could see from the ditch and he turned and crawled back ten yards. Then he rolled out of the ditch and moved in a kind of walking crawl.

"Radio vans. They're monitoring all the traffic in the region. They're trying to read it and triangulate where it's coming from. Hospital vans. They'll need some tomorrow."

They retreated back into the woods where they had a stash of explosives. Working with portable torches they wired up the four small bombs they had. The plan was to blow everything at once so the wires to the bomb under each truck were connected in the ditch and then back to the detonator at the edge of the woods.

"We'll place them under trucks seven, five, three and one. That will make the most of what we have," as Henri gave a bomb to three Maquis. Florence insisted she go, and Henri gave in since he didn't have the time to argue. "Make sure these are right under the van."

As the three men and Florence lay in the ditch Henri attached each bomb to one main wire which ran in the ditch behind the vans.

The four of them spread out behind each of their targets. Henri signalled and they crawled ahead, covered by a moonless night. As they got close to the vans they could hear the radio chatter in one or two and talking in another.

Florence shook as she pushed her package under the ambulance, hoping there wasn't a muffler or some kind of plating to protect them from mines. As she was under her van, the truck moved and she could hear boots on the floor as someone walked inside. She froze for a second, then took a breath and left her bomb under what she hoped was the weakest spot on the floor.

They met back in the ditch, and left for the woods as Henri checked the connections before joining them. The other Maquis joined them, armed with Sten guns, only 20 or 30 yards from the trucks.

The second van from the end had the most violent explosion, as the fuel tank ignited. Diesel fuel tanks resisted fire better than gasoline, as the Americans and British found fighting the Germans in North Africa and Italy. The German radio operators who weren't injured in the blast, ran from the rear doors, pistols drawn.

At first the Germans didn't know where to fire but soon saw the flashes form the Sten guns at the edge of the woods. Of the fourteen radio operators only three survived, but they were inside the ambulances and never came outside. One Maquis was hit in the leg with a round from a Mauser.

It all lasted only a minute or two and Henri and his band disappeared into the woods.

29

ESSEN, LATE MARCH 1986

The weather was odd, cold all of a sudden. It meant the restaurant was overheated, and there was even some steam or mist on the glass. For Eric von François, it reminded him of something, or at least it reminded him of something he wanted Jack to know about.

"This is like the warming rooms we had after the war. That first winter, and even the second one, there were few whole buildings left standing in cities in Germany. Take Essen. It had been bombed into the Stone Age, as that American, Barry Goldwater used to say."

The waitress came by and brought them some coffee. It wasn't noon and it was too early to start drinking, though Jack was tired and thought beer might do him some good. He restrained himself. He didn't want to be appear a barbarian.

"I'd never heard of anything like a warming room," said Jack. He had only been speaking with von François for twenty minutes, maybe less. He had taken a series of trains to get from Lyon to Essen, leaving his friend Homer to go on to his assignment in Geneva.

"Yes. They were common. We would come into these places and huddle to keep warm. They were like soup kitchens, except it wasn't just the food we were after but the heat."

Huddle. That was an odd word for a German to use, thought Jack. He must have worked for the Americans or the

British. His accent seemed more British, but then a lot of older Europeans spoke with a British accent. The younger ones spoke American.

A telephone message from his friend at *The Gazette* in Montreal told him there had been a letter to the editor of the paper from a small group of Germans. The letter was never published but he thought Devlin might be interested. It took Jack just a few hours to track down this man and two phone calls to set up a meeting.

"Of course we weren't in a warming room in Essen. We had been in the east and had spent months travelling across Germany to get back to my mother's home near Munich. By then my father was dead. He was killed in May of 1944, in France, just before the invasion."

Neither of them seemed to want to get to the meat of the matter, that Jack was writing a piece, and knew a great deal, about the man who might have shot von François' father during the war. And they wouldn't talk about it now. The train from France had arrived at a little after three. Herr von François had to return to work for a few hours.

"I don't mean to be rude Mr. Devlin, but it's something I've been working on for weeks and we have a final meeting at five. Why don't I pick you up at your hotel around 7:30. Not all of Essen is this bleak," he smiled as he rose. "We'll find a quiet spot for dinner."

As he looked at his card, Jack said. "Seems an odd pairing. The von and the François. German and French.

"The explanation is easy, Mr. Devlin, and I've been making it all my life," smiled von François. "Our family were Huguenots in France. And we came east to find a Protestant home when the French started persecuting the Hugenots. More of that later."

Bleak. As Jack walked back to his hotel, a rather bleak American chain, it was hard not to notice the effects of the bombing, even more than thirty years after the end of the war. So different from Lyon. Almost all the buildings were new. The office towers were so ugly, but then Jack thought most of the new architecture in London was horrible.

London had it easy compared to Essen. Jack's father was in bombers and might have unloaded on Essen one night. He was brought up to be pro-British and was filled with the stories of the war. The Germans started it, true, and the Blitz was worse than anything the British dished out, not true.

There were 20,000 Londoners who died in the Blitz. Bomber Command could kill that many Germans, or more, in a night. There were many reasons why Germany lost the war and that was one of them.

Essen was so close to the British airfields and so industrialized it was one of the first cities to get nailed. And it got nailed over and over until there was just a skeleton of a place left, if you looked at the pictures from the summer and winter of 1945.

The story in the von François family was that he had been executed in France, shot by the Resistance while he was a prisoner. That was why Jack was here to find out if his father was one of the men on the bridge, one of the German soldiers *The Montreal Star* said were shot in the late winter or early spring of 1944.

Jack felt a little odd being here. He'd come to like Henri Foix, even idolize him a bit. His side had the moral high ground. The Jews, the French, Klaus Barbie, the Gestapo. Still, he felt a little uncomfortable meeting with a civilized middle-aged man about to discuss whether a Canadian executed his father.

That night they went to what Jack figured was a suburb of Essen. Mr. von François drove an old Mercedes sedan, and Jack knew what it was by listening to the exhaust as it drove up.

"Nice car," said Jack as he got in. "I didn't get a look at the back but is it a 6.3 litre?"

"Yes," said von François.

Before von François could ask how he knew, "Fastest production sedan ever made. Probably a 1972, am I right?" He loved showing off.

"You amaze me Mr. Devlin, how did you know?"

"Well I know the years they made this car and the body style, so that's pretty easy. And then the sound. There's no sweeter sound than a big V8. I owned a 4.5 litre, a 1971. I love German cars."

It was like mentioning the name of the local home town in a visiting celebrity's speech. Eric von François was won over and the rest of the night he spent talking to Jack as if he were an old friend. It was a simple technique, but easy to pull off since he was a German car nut.

The neighbourhood they drove into had lots of trees and roads with low light. It was rather English in a way and the restaurant was in a converted house that seemed a kind of mock Tudor. They shared the dining room with one romantic couple in the corner.

"I have a rather unusual war history. For a young boy, I saw plenty. I've explained my odd name and my family came from Prussia, the Protestant heartland. We haven't owned land for a while and my mother ran an art gallery in Berlin. My father was rather Bohemian and thought about going to California after the Olympics, but he was in the reserves and was called up."

Jack interrupted. "Do you mind if I smoke?"

"No, I smoke as well, at least in the evening. Gauloise? Do you always smoke French cigarettes? I rather like them myself."

They both lit up. "No it's just that I was in France, as I told you. But keep talking. You understand I know a lot about the war, but most of it is from our perspective."

"The winners always see things in a different way," said von François, with no irony or bitterness and with a slight smile.

"My father was away and after 1942 we moved to the country because of the bombing. We lived on a farm and I remember the American planes. There were prisoners working in the fields, I remember, near the end of the war. One of them was a Yugoslav soldier and he wore his uniform. I don't know why this story came into my mind, but it did."

"Go ahead," said Jack who hadn't even brought a note-book.

"Well my job was to sit on top of the hay wagon and watch for planes. Then one of those American twin-engine fighters came by, you know the ones with the split tail?"

"A P-38. Lightning."

"Yes right, that's it," said von François, almost excited at the memory. "Well I yelled and we all ran to the woods at the edge of the field. But this Yugoslav stayed behind and started waving at the pilot. I remember seeing the bullets smash into the earth."

"Canon," said Jack and he picked up the French Cricket lighter. "Each one about the size of this cigarette lighter."

"Well the ground was very dry and the bullets pushed up the dust and and you could see almost in slow motion. He was waving to the Americans yelling 'I'm on your side!' The bullets went either side of him, but he did void himself."

"That must have been a dangerous place to be, with the Russians coming?"

"Yes, we started to move back towards my mother's family's house in 1945. They lived outside Munich. We had a cart and we moved, sometimes at night. Then one night we were just outside Dresden, about fifty kilometres. We heard the bombers coming and went to the basement."

He took a sip of wine, but was unemotional.

"Boom boom, boom boom," and he moved his hands up and down. "Like a kettle drum. For hours we stayed in the basement. Then the noise stopped and we went outside. It was night, but the fire from Dresden was so bright it was like the sun."

Jack remembered a book he had read, something by a Lithuanian princess who lived in Berlin during the war. That was the first time he had felt sorry for Germans on the receiving end of a bombing. This was the second.

The waiter came over and von François ordered for both of them. Jack didn't say much.

"I must be boring you," said von François.

"No it's fascinating. I always hear things from the other side, as you can imagine. Most of what I do for newspapers is write death notices and these days half of them seem to be people who fought in the war or at least lived through it."

"And that is what you are interested in here, I assume? How my father might connect with the Canadian colonel who died a few weeks ago."

"Right," said Jack. "Where did you go after Dresden? Weren't you worried about the Russians? I don't mean to pry but in particular the women in your family. "

"We did make it to my mother's family house. But I remember just after the war, a week or two, there were lots of prisoners around. The Americans were there, but the prisoners were wild. I remember a Polish woman. My sister had a ring, a cheap thing, but she lost it. She accused the Polish woman of stealing it."

He leaned forward and took a sip of wine.

"Well I saw she was bringing these people back, men who were drunk. I ran to my mother and with my sister we went upstairs. There were bars over the windows, but the door was flimsy. We pushed a dresser up against the door and then my mother put a bed against the dresser and the wall. They came up about three or four of them with the woman. They knocked the door off the hinges but they couldn't get in. After half an hour they stopped and went back to drinking."

A pause.

"I don't know what would have happened."

Jack changed the conversation. They talked about food and cars. He also noticed that von François had a wandering eye when any woman under 50 walked by, so for a while they discussed women. Both were putting off what they really had to discuss.

In the car on the way back to the hotel, von François brought it up.

"So do you think the man you're writing about killed my father?"

"He might have. There's a newspaper article from 1945."

"Yes, I've seen it," interrupted von François. "An investigator we hired in Canada dug it up."

"Well, he could be the man. Then again there was a lot of bragging and macho talk that went on after the war. Though I must say I was shocked to read it. Imagine anyone saying that out loud," said Jack. "I think what you said, about things being different for the winning side and the losing side is so true."

The Mercedes turned into the street where the hotel was and parked in front.

"It looks as if he's the man, but I can't know for sure. If I find anything more, I promise I'll call you. No, I'll call you no matter what happens."

"I'm convinced he's the man. Knowing the story may be enough for me, but may not be enough for the other people in our group. We'll see. I might leave it alone from here."

Jack shook hands with Eric von François and walked into his hotel, though he was now less confused than he was in Lyon.

30

A grey uniform hung over a chair in the corner of the room. Beside it a French girl hung over the edge of the bed as she made short work of the soldier standing behind her; he might not have seen a woman, or at least a naked woman, in months.

He fumbled as he tried to stuff his oversized penis into her. She reached back through her legs and guided him in, though with some dexterous use of her hands he didn't get too far before he moaned and shot inside her.

As she washed off she looked at his uniform and regiment. Her sister had taught her what to look for. She kept a small notebook under the towels and made some notes. The young whore could speak a bit of German, but this one wasn't German.

It would be a busy night. The older woman who ran the brothel had been out drumming up business with the soldiers, in particular the new SS regiment that had just moved into the area.

Florence told Henri about her sister the whore without a trace of embarrassment.

"Jeanne works in a brothel just at the edge of Lyon. She's very useful to us and she and her girls will come in handy on Saturday night." Florence went on to tell Henri that her sister started working in the brothel just at the start of the war.

She was saving money to get married to a man in the French army. He had never come home and, until she heard whether he was alive or dead, she would keep on working.

The plan for Saturday night was to kidnap or kill a man suspected of selling war materials to the Germans. Tonight Florence would play the whore to try and lure the man they were after.

Every Saturday night that he was in town, the man from the concrete business went to the whorehouse. He liked it because it was close to the city, but far enough away from where he lived. There were two sides to the building, like the saloon and public bar in an English pub, and the business-man went to the whorehouse version of the saloon bar. The girls were better looking and the madam hinted there was less chance of getting the clap on the expensive side.

Henri walked with Florence to the brothel. It was only half an hour from her house. As they walked they went over the plan.

"I hope you don't really have to sleep with him," said Henri trying to be gallant. He was also more prudish than the French were, at least the ones he had met so far.

Florence gave a shrug, with her shoulders and her mouth. "It doesn't bother me. He'll get his money's worth for the first few minutes." She laughed. "Tonight the bastard will get more than he bargained for and with any luck tomorrow morning he'll be in an English jail."

Or dead thought Henri. He hoped she was right but it would be tricky. Only he had some idea why they wanted this man and Henri had to work it out for himself, no one in London was radioing him details. Seems the concrete man from Lyon produced a special formula that made bunkers stronger. His firm had plants throughout France and Henri guessed the invaders wanted to know what they were up against when they started pounding the coast in an invasion.

A few hundred metres from the whorehouse, Florence stopped to light a cigarette and Henri moved ahead. In a few minutes he walked into the working man's side of the old house and the madam led him upstairs to a room. She made no sign she knew him, and treated him with some contempt in front of the soldiers waiting downstairs. They laughed at the French working man heading for the cheap beds.

Upstairs Henri was alone in a room. The house was in an old bourgeois neighbourhood that had fallen on hard times. The closet in the old servants part of the house connected to a small dressing room next door. That was where Florence was to play her part as the whore.

Downstairs the madam put her girls in action, keeping the soldiers busy. Tonight, she told them, don't make them come too soon. Tease them for a while. Within a few minutes the front room was empty. The next shift wasn't set to arrive for maybe half an hour.

The girls knew what do.

"Keep your hands, your mouths and your asses busy from seven to seven-fifteen," said the madam. Monsieur Cement had made an appointment. And he was a man who was on time for his appointments.

London wanted him alive. If he were killed someone else in his company would do the deals with the Germans. But alive they could get at formulas inside his head. Henri was not supposed to know any of this, but he had guessed.

Inside the closet he thought how easy it would be to make him talk. But that wasn't his job. Coming up the stairs, the madam had told him when he would be there. She would now get a message to Philippe who would have a truck from the brothers' farm outside the whorehouse at seven twenty-five on the dot.

Henri checked his hunting bag. Inside was a bottle with enough chloroform to put him out for half an hour and some gauze to soak it up before it went over his face. He knew he could kill him in an instant, but he wanted this one without a scratch. The light went on in the other room and he could see though a rather large peephole in the door. He was too naive about the world to know why it was there. It was in fact his first visit to a whorehouse.

Henri watched as Florence undressed and put on the slip she had in her bag. At first he was embarrassed, but like so many other customers who had watched this room from the closet he was fascinated. Florence had breasts shaped like cones, the flat stomach of a young woman who hadn't had children and what Henri thought was a perfect ass.

She pulled the slip over her head and lay on the bed and waited. Though she knew Henri was behind the door, she didn't know he could see her.

Just then Henri heard another noise behind him. The door opened into the room and Henri could hear voices, the madam's and a German speaking in thickly accented French.

"I'm not one of those Ukrainian peasants madam. I am a German officer and I'll take my pleasure on my time, not yours."

Henri was now trapped in a cupboard between the two rooms. He was amazed to see there was another peephole in the door into the German's room. He was a major and took off his clothes while he waited for a girl from downstairs. Henri hoped she arrived in a hurry. Then in the other room Monsieur Cement walked though the door.

Florence sat on the edge of the bed, her legs crossed, her nipples pushing against the silk of the slip. She spoke first, with a smile Henri hadn't expected.

"*Bonsoir, Monsieur.*" She then went on to ask what he was interested in.

"You decide, mademoiselle. I leave the artistic side in your hands."

A door opened in the other room and a girl arrived. The German was already naked and lying on the bed. He motioned to the girl who came closer. He pulled up her slip, slapped her loudly on the ass as he pulled her on top of him. Henri was glad the German was busy. He noticed the girl being playful, trying to make sure the major got his money's worth and didn't have time to hear any noises through the wall.

Henri felt for the blade along his leg in case he had to kill the German officer. Then he turned to the other peephole to be shocked at the sight of Florence massaging Monsieur Cement's stiff penis with her hands and then her tongue.

Florence was not wasting time. She wanted the quarry in a position where he couldn't see the cupboard door.

"Follow me, Monsieur," she said in a soft voice. And he stood on the floor while Florence knelt on the bed in front of him. For a moment Henri was distracted by moans from the next room. The girl with the major was doing her job well.

Henri took out his bottle of chloroform and soaked gauze. He held his breath to avoid taking in the fumes in the tight space. He moved the door handle and slid the door open enough to pass through. Florence was panting in exaggerated grunts to cover any noise.

In a second or two Henri was behind Monsieur Cement. One hand moved fast, pressing the chloroform rag to his face, the other grabbed his hair and held it tight. He yelled into the rag, but no one heard it, or if they did, it would have mixed well with the other animal noises in the house that night.

"It's about time," said Florence who crawled off the bed and into her street clothes as Monsieur Cement slumped to the floor. The two of them then dressed him. They would carry him down the stairs as if he were a drunk. Henri looked at his watch. It was seven twenty-three.

Monsieur Cement didn't weigh much, maybe a hundred and forty-five pounds. They had no trouble taking him down the stairs. The waiting room was empty, except for the madam. One of the downstairs doors opened and a soldier started to come out. The madam laughed and so did the soldier after she made a sign to show he was drunk.

As Florence and Henri moved toward the door, the madam said in French to the girl who'd just been with the soldier.

"Give him another one. On the house. And fast."

The girl grabbed grey sleeve and with a coquettish smile pulled the soldier back into the room. He was probably 22 and was ready for another go-round.

Just outside Philippe was fussing with the back of the truck. He moved over, grabbed Monsieur Cement by the feet and the three of them put him in the back of the truck. Florence got into the back; Henri joined Philippe up front.

They had a fifteen-minute drive, maybe more. They should get it done before dark and the curfew, when driving a farm vehicle on the road meant they would be stopped. Up front Henri found two Sten guns under a blanket and checked to make sure they were working. He pressed the skeleton-like stock of the gun against his thigh, ready to use it if he had to.

There was maybe another twenty minutes of light. The roads were empty. Farmers were at home, and there was no patrol, either of Germans, or more common, the French police, more dangerous than the Nazis since they were quick to spot anything out of the ordinary.

In the back of the truck Florence had tied the hands of Monsieur Cement behind his back, then tied that rope to a beam in the front of the compartment. She sat in front of him and waited for him to wake, holding one of Henri's Lugers in her hand. She knew that even if she had to shoot, she should only wound him.

Florence and her kidneys felt the bump as Philipe turned off the road, really a lane, on which they were driving and headed into a field. The light was low but Florence could see Monsieur Cement's eyes starting to flutter. He could call out now but it wouldn't do him any good. And his voice might not come back for a few minutes.

The truck came to a halt and Henri jumped out running to the back to let down the door and pull out their captive. Philipe went over to the pilot and minder standing beside the single engine Lysander sitting in the flat field.

A big glass canopy sat under the wide overhead wing fifty feet across to give the Lysander lift on a short airstrip. Under its belly was what looked like a bomb but was an extra tank to allow this tiny plane to fly to England and back without refuelling. It was light, with no armour and no guns, only radios to keep in touch with home base and with the Resistance on the ground.

Henri noticed its wheel covers were painted black as was the fuel tank and the whole underbelly of the plane. From the ground it was invisible. It was faster than it looked with a top speed of 212 mph, capable of cruising at 190 mph. Faster than a bomber and able to get them back to England in a little more than two hours.

Monsieur Cement was just coming to. He staggered under the direction of Henri and the minder who stuffed him on the plane. Just as he went in he looked at the face of the woman he had been humping from behind before the lights went out. His expression showed a man who had no idea what was happening to him and no doubt not a clue where he was headed.

Steel handcuffs and a leg iron were snapped on Monsieur Cement for his trip. As the minder locked the cuffs and leg iron to a bar inside the plane, the pilot started the engine. The plane turned into the wind and started taxiing almost straightaway. There was a strong wind and the little Lysander lifted off in less than 150 yards.

31

A TRAIN TO ST. ALBANS, APRIL 1986

The train to St. Albans was a joke. It only took 50 minutes. And, thought Jack, they have the nerve to call St. Albans the country. He'd expected a two-hour ride. Since it was a Saturday, he bumped up to first class. It didn't cost much extra and there were certain things worth spending money on and first class on English trains was one of them.

There was some green separating London from St. Albans, but most of what he could see from the train was pretty suburban. He pictured the type of people who lived there. Solid English types voting the straight Margaret Thatcher ticket. As the train pulled in he saw Michelle standing on the platform waiting for him. If she voted for Thatcher she'd have to keep it a secret at work. Voting Tory was unfashionable at any TV network.

Michelle had spent the night with her parents. Over the phone the other night he thought she might have hinted he could have spent the night at her place, but he could be quite thick about reading these signals. Jack always flirted with women, but sometimes he was lost when they decided it was the real thing. He was getting this feeling with Michelle.

She smiled and gave his lips a light dusting with a kiss. "How was France?"

"You know, French." Michelle laughed. Jack found that with the English, you could never go wrong making fun of the French. Almost all Englishmen had a deep suspicion of all things French, in particular the people.

Well, almost all. Michelle's father's name was Harry and he was as English as you get, right down to the cardigan over the checked shirt and tie. But right away Jack could see Harry loved France and he loved the French. Jack looked around the house and there were bits and pieces of France in paintings, photographs and maps. And of course he had named his only daughter Michelle.

"*Bonjour* young Jack," said Harry. "Michelle tells me you come from Montreal, so I guessed you might be French."

Jack hated to disappoint him, so he didn't bother telling him his own father's favourite line about French, which was 'You have to squeeze me before I can say *Oui*.'

"Well I'm more from the English side than the French side," said Jack.

"But I would have thought Devlin was Irish?" said Harry.

Oh shit, thought Jack. I hope he doesn't have a thing about the Irish. Jack couldn't stand professional Irishmen from the States and Canada, but he knew there were English people who hated the Irish. "Well anyone who isn't French calls themselves English. Even the Greeks and Italians are English. The French call us *les Anglais*. Not always a term of endearment."

That sidestepped things.

Just then Michelle's mother came out of the kitchen wearing what Jack called an apron, but what the English referred to as a pinnie. "Hello there young man, Michelle has told me so much about you."

Jack could feel himself blush. He was starting to wonder whether the war was the reason he had been invited for lunch. Harry rescued him and motioned for Jack to come into his war room, as he called his study. On the wall maps of Europe and photographs of some of the planes from Bomber Command. The picture of the Halifax was right over his desk.

Harry walked over to it. "Signed by Bomber Harris himself. We went to a reunion in the mid-1950s. I knew he would be there and I brought my Halifax picture, rolled up. A cranky old bastard, but he couldn't refuse me, not in front of all those people."

Thank Christ we're off the French and the Irish, or at least my French and my Irish, thought Jack. Time to move where he wanted to go. He had a train to catch late that afternoon.

"I had lunch with someone the other day who was ranting about Harris. Called him a mass murderer. A Canadian guy, named Dolan. He was doing something on Hiroshima and what a bad idea it was. His next target, if you'll pardon the expression, is going to be Harris."

Jack thought that should send Harry through the roof, but he surprised him. He was calm.

"Well there are lot of people who agree with your friend. Even if it's only on the bombing of Dresden. After the war the Labour government snubbed him and he never got the peerage you might have expected. Butcher Harris they called him in Bloomsbury," and he reached into a pile of books and extracted an old *Time Magazine*. "Harris had a 'them or us' attitude to the bombing. But he knew what he was doing. He even saw what the Germans did wrong in the Blitz in London. They used explosives instead of incendiaries. Harris changed that. He figured, let the fire do the work for you."

Jack thought of his friend Eric and Dresden lighting up his eight-year old night. He might bring that up with Harry, but then he might leave it alone. It complicated things.

The old *Time Magazine* Harry held in his hand mesmerized Jack. "Where you'd get that magazine? Isn't that Harris on the cover?"

"There he is," said Harry, holding up the magazine. "June 7, 1943. I picked this up in a sale along with a whole raft of magazines from the war years. Pretty good stuff, even if they did get his title wrong. They called him Air Marshal Chief instead of Chief Air Marshal."

This guy's a bit of gold mine, thought Jack. "What did you mean when you said he knew what he was doing?" Better to warm him up before getting to the stuff he was really after.

"Here listen to this. A quote from Harris after the Americans joined the war. He broadcast to the Germans telling them just what to expect, though I don't know how many heard him and given how they fought to the end, I doubt many cared."

"I will speak frankly to you about whether we bomb military targets, or whole cities. Obviously we prefer to hit factories, shipyards and railways. It damages Hitler's war machine the most. But those people who work in these places live close by them. Therefore we hit your houses and you."

Harry passed over the magazine to Jack who looked at a drawing of Harris on the cover. "Great war propaganda. I guess we needed the Americans, I mean the Brits and the Canadians needed them. The Americans must have started doing all the heavy lifting."

Harry shook his head and reached for another volume on a higher shelf.

"I think I have this committed to memory, but I'll check it out. The fact is that on a ton-mile basis the RAF really carried the battle against Germany in 1943. For every ton the Eighth Air Force dropped on Germany, we dropped four."

Jack could see where this was going, the same way it did at North Weald with Mason. He decided to help it along a little. "Really? I thought the B-17 was the best bomber of the war."

Harry was too polite, and not as jingoistic as Mason, so he just trotted out the facts. He laughed. "I've been around my daughter's newsy friends for too long to fall for that trick. Feed them a provocative line and watch how high they jump. Well, I think you'll find our Lancasters carried eight tons against three for the B-17. More at the end of the war, of course. And the Lanc had only eight crew members while the B-17 had ten."

The talk went back and forth for ten minutes. Jack moved it round to the Halifax and what Harry did during the war. He got in just one sentence.

"You know I'm not supposed to tell you a thing."

Just then Michelle walked in. "Enough talk, it's time for lunch." Jack looked at Michelle who was in full domestic mode. He wondered if he was being trotted out for approval. Claire was rather jealous that he was off to lunch alone with a woman and her parents. Maybe she was right.

Roast beef. Michelle's mother was solicitous. Jack was starting to get a little terrified. He couldn't wait to get back to the war room.

Lunch took under an hour. There was wine in crystal glasses that Jack figured were trotted out eight times a year. Conversation centred on a trip Harry and Judy, that was the wife's name, were planning to South Africa a month from now. Harry had an oddball reason for wanting to go, but it was one Jack could understand.

Harry said he didn't like the sun, or the cheap South African wine. He wanted a last look at how he thought the British Empire must have been.

"Things are going to change there. I'd like to see apartheid before they get rid of it. I don't agree with it, but I want to see how it works. It's like getting into a time machine and seeing how colonial Africa must have been a hundred years ago. It makes you wonder how people can keep order in a place where they're so outnumbered."

Michelle disapproved. "I don't think you should support it." Jack tuned out since he heard this South Africa rant about twice a day in London. Instead he thought about what Harry had said and how parts of his trip to France were the same. A time capsule into the life of Henri Foix.

"What did you mean secret," asked Jack when they were back in Harry's war room.

"Well there's an Official Secrets Act in this country. And when we were assigned to those missions in the Halifaxes, flying agents all over Europe, we had to swear to keep it all secret. During the war they said they could have you shot for talking about what we did. But they didn't even shoot German spies. They hanged a few, but not many."

Jack was sitting on a couch in the war room. Harry was at his desk, and he leaned across it to grab another book. Jack caught a name on the spine of the book and thought he recognized it.

"But no one is going to shoot me now," laughed Harry. "And you didn't come to St. Albans to sample my wife's roast beef. Now according to this, there were about sixty French-Canadian soldiers parachuted into France ahead of the invasion. Their job was to train the rather disorganized members of the French Underground and turn them into a fighting force."

"Sounds simple enough," said Jack.

Harry got up and walked over to a shelf where he kept his pipe. It seemed to go with the cardigan. He put up his finger for emphasis as he walked. "Simple in theory but in practice only fifteen of them came back. I met one when we flew to France one night."

Jack leaned forward on the couch. "Really?"

"He must have been one of the first to go. It was February, I think. Cold as hell. A full moon though. It was a blind drop, I think."

Jack interrupted. "What does that mean?"

"It means no one was there to meet him. He drops blind to an open field. We drop a few canisters first, filled with Sten guns and ammunition. He leaves with just his parachute, a pistol and his knife. I could see he had a money belt on. Probably carrying all kinds of money. Later I found out they could be marks, francs and American dollars."

"Did he tell you he was Canadian?" asked Jack.

"Oh God, no. We weren't even meant to talk to them. Just sit there and fly with someone for a few hours and not say a word. He was a nice enough bloke. I could tell from his accent he was French, but it was different. I had lived in France and Frenchmen have a certain way of speaking English."

Jack laughed. "Like Maurice Chevalier."

"Right," Harry laughed back. "Like Maurice Chevalier. Except this man didn't speak like Maurice Chevalier. We had a cigarette together. It was one of those French jobs. The SOE must have given him that. You couldn't get those in England. But I tricked him, or at least I think I tricked him."

"How? What do you mean?"

"I said something to him in French. He answered me back. I was almost sure it was the accent of Quebec. It sounded a bit Norman, but it was different."

"How do you know so much about French accents? I mean this isn't exactly France here in St. Albans."

Harry moved back behind his desk. 'My father worked in France for ten years. I went to a French school, all my friends were French."

Jack slipped his question in while Harry was taking a breath.

"What did he do, your father?"

"Wine. He was an agent for a big wine importer. His face looked it too. Red and full of claret. We lived in Tours. My best friends were French boys. My first girlfriend was a beautiful dark-eyed French girl. We were fifteen."

"Was her name Michelle?" asked Jack.

"Good guess. Judy doesn't even know that. She just liked the way Michelle sounded. But that's why I knew accents and that was why I was certain he was a French-Canadian. After the war I read about them, the French-Canadians in the SOE. And this book, it's by a Canadian diplomat, gives the details."

Harry pushed it over to Jack. "Here, borrow it. And give it back to Michelle."

"Did you ever guess what his name was? I mean from reading the books?"

Harry pursed his lips, and took a pause before speaking. "No. I think I might know which one he is, but I can't be sure. So I don't know if he lived or died. Odds are he died."

"What did you think his name was?"

"Foix. Henri Foix. There were a few stories about him in the Canadian's book. The photographs weren't clear enough. And it was dark in the Halifax."

"Well he died alright," and Jack watched the expression sag a bit on Harry's 66-year-old face. "But he died last week. And it sounds to me like you were carrying Henri Foix that night."

Harry looked at Jack as if he were crazy.

"And how, my young friend, would you know that?"

"Because I'm writing Henri Foix's obituary for my paper. I've read about him too. And I just got back from France where it appears your Monsieur Foix did things not even you could imagine."

Harry's face formed a simple smile, where his lips spread out at the ends, but stayed closed in the middle. He looked as if he might cry.

32

A FIELD NEAR LYON, LATE MAY 1944

A surprise package dropped from the sky. Henri received a message to bicycle out to the farm, where the one remaining brother had dragged the latest shipment under a covered hayloft at the edge of a field.

Inside, the oddest collection of Sten guns he'd ever seen. It was a crude weapon to start with, and ugly. But effective. It looked like a pistol with plumbing attached at either end. A stark tube of metal that was the stock, welded to the barrel at the business end of the Sten. The clip with ammunition in it came down at a ninety-degree angle from the barrel and made the Sten easy to hold.

A nasty weapon close up, the Sten could spray a wide area with metal, killing a lot of people in just a short burst. It was named for the two men who invented it and the place where they did it. A Mr. Shepherd and a Mr. Turpin working at Enfield made the acronym S-T-E-N and all this done at the Royal Small Arms Factory.

Henri left his bicycle beside the cellar where he had spent the boozy night with the two brothers. The farm they worked on was divided into a small vineyard and some croplands, mostly kept clean for shooting, when there wasn't a war on.

"What's so urgent?" asked Henri.

"A new shipment of Sten guns," said the farmer. "Philippe told me to send for you."

Henri looked at the Sten guns and knew straightaway what type they were. He had seen them, and used them, at the camp in Scotland.

Just then Philippe walked over. He and Henri grunted greetings of exchange. The bad blood from their first meeting in a field like this was now long behind them, but they were both short with words and concentrating on the job at hand.

"What are those things at the barrel?" asked Philippe.

As he pulled one from the canister, examining it, Henri explained, "They're silencers. Usually used by commandoes. Get the killing done in a hurry and do it without a sound. We can use these."

For the next three days Henri trained a large group of Maquis, maybe a hundred and fifty of them, in a clearing in the centre of the woods. It was an odd place, used to shoot game that had been flushed out of the thick copse of trees.

He drilled them for the closest thing they would have to a set piece battle. They had two American bazookas, two light machine guns and a heavy machine gun someone had taken from the Germans. Henri knew the risks involved. Hit-and-run tactics were one thing, but it was almost always suicide to face the German army head on with partisans.

The reason for all this drilling was a new addition to the neighbourhood in the last couple of weeks, a radio operator who had landed in a Lysander carrying one suitcase that weighed about ten pounds. George, they called him, or Georges in French. He worked by day in the railway yard and by night operated the Mark IV radio hidden in his case.

The Mark IV was a marvel of miniaturization for 1944, built by the specialists back in London but using new smaller tubes made in the U.S. It could send and receive messages over a long distance, and lock in a signal, something the earlier radios had trouble doing. It could run off batteries or plug into the wiring of a house or office.

The radio and the operator did their best work at night, sending and receiving signals that travelled 459 miles each way. At least that was George's estimate. In London they measured his 'fist,' the electronic fingerprint that identified him. And if a German were to hold a Mauser pistol to his head, he could run a pre-set security exercise to let the home base know something was wrong.

Henri was glad George was on the scene, since it freed him up from radio duty. He knew now he had to have these men ready to fight in three days.

It was late May and the signals from London were telling him to step up attacks on German targets, especially trains and troop columns. That morning George told Henri of an order to attack a German armoured column moving north through their sector.

The plan was to start a fight near dusk with the woods behind them so they could retreat.

The day after the Stens with silencers arrived, London had sent a new batch of supplies in as bold a move as any of the Resistance had ever seen: there was a drop by ten Halifax aircraft, and they were escorted by a flight of new RAF long-range fighters, the North American Mustang with the British engine.

"We're getting close to the invasion if they're stepping up the pace like this," said Philippe, smiling because he hoped the war in France would be over in less than a year. In fact it would take 89 days after the invasion before Lyon was liberated. They were 10 days away from the invasion. If anyone had told them that in 99 days they would be free, they would never have believed it.

Henri agreed. It might even be weeks.

"The Germans must know it too. They're desperate, but they have their back to the wall. That will make them even more dangerous."

These new canisters contained more than Sten guns. There were heavy machine guns and PIATs, the British version of the American bazooka. Both worked on the same principle. They were hollow-charge weapons, using a trick discovered by an American inventor in the 1880s and perfected by a pair of Swiss scientists in 1938.

Surprise, surprise, the Swiss sold them to the highest bidders.

The PIAT allowed infantry to shoot a jet of molten metal through the wall of tanks, searing its crew, setting off their ammunition and fuel or a combination of all three. Henri had trained with these weapons, the bazooka in Helena, Montana, the PIAT in Scotland.

Now he had just a few days to teach his men how to use them. Lucky for him the weapons were not hard to master.

The sun stayed out late in May, and Henri had to hold back the Maquis who were anxious to join the fighting involved in the invasion across the English Channel which they knew had to come soon.

Henri had no way of knowing whether this was just a ruse, another version of the big commando raid on Dieppe in August of 42, or the real thing.

For the Maquis, and many of people in the surrounding towns, it was the real thing. And many people who once thought about siding with Laval and Pétain were now trying to join the Resistance. Best to be on the winning side at the end, even if at ground level the Germans seemed unbeatable.

The idea was to stop a division racing to the coast through this sector. And the best time was later in the day, since the men of the Resistance could never last in a real battle with the Germans. Just kill enough of them and destroy enough equipment to keep them out of action and away from the coast, even if for just a few days.

Philippe led one band of about 75 Maquis at the head of a road where a German formation was set to pass around four-thirty in the afternoon. Henri moved another 130 or so into position about five hundred yards away. Both groups were equipped with heavy machine guns and each had two PIATs, in addition to submachine guns and pistols carried by the men.

The idea was the wait until the head of the column reached Philippe, when he would open fire with the heavy machine guns and small-arms fire. The PIATs were to be held in reserve in case of armour. The message from London had no detail on what kind of troop movement it was meant to be.

The sight of dust and the sound of motors alerted Henri to the approaching column. But it was the squeaking noise of tracks that made him take a deep breath. Were they half-track troop carriers, or panzers? He was soon to have his answer.

It would be a short battle. The tracks were those of two panzer IIs, and Henri recognized them as soon as they came into view. Light tanks built for reconnaissance, they were still powerful weapons. Behind them were trucks filled with troops followed by more armoured vehicles. He had a wired telephone connection to Philippe.

"You hit the first tank with the PIAT we'll get the second one. Kill as many soldiers as possible, and then move back through the woods. There's sure to be more armour in the rear."

"Right." Philippe's last word.

The PIAT round hit the first panzer in the side, making its turret useless. The second tank exploded as the round hit the ammunition inside. Philippe's troop fired a second round to make sure the first tank was disabled.

The German troops, used to guerrilla warfare in the Balkans, were out of their trucks on the safe side, though the machine gun fire killed dozens in the first seconds. Henri now moved with some of his men back towards the other end of the column, though he couldn't see it.

Soldiers and armour were moving to outflank them and trap the Maquis in a circle of death. Henri took the PIAT and fired a round into a half-track, so it blocked movement. A tank behind it fired a shell straight back. It was a Panzer IV, fitted out for battle with extra armour protecting its tracks. Time to retreat.

"Tell Philippe to leave."

He fired the PIAT at the big panzer but it was not enough to break the neck of armour reinforcing its turret. The tank waited for the half-track to empty, and then headed straight over it. Luck. Henri fired a round at its undercarriage and disabled it.

Heavy machine-gun fire from the Maquis kept the German soldiers busy. Henri took over a big gun, which he knew he would have to leave behind. He ordered his men to retreat to the woods. Less than a minute later Henri threw a grenade at the advancing Germans, and left one primed, propped up against the heavy machine gun.

As they left they dragged two dead Maquis, and four wounded men. They didn't want to leave the dead men for fear of reprisals against their wives, parents or even children. Two young German soldiers, almost certainly new recruits, approached the heavy machine gun. Henri watched as they were torn to pieces by the grenade.

Rather than retreat he sent the dead and wounded through the woods and moved parallel to the column, coming out near the end of it where it was stalled. The Germans were on alert, but they thought the fighting was about a mile down the road. The two PIATs fired into half-tracks followed by sustained machine-gun fire. There were no panzers here and the fight continued for 10 minutes.

As soon as they saw a tank approaching, the Maquis increased their fire as the PIATs moved to a different angle to try and disable the tank. The German tank driver fired his 75-mm canon into the woods, killing ten men at once. A shot from the PIAT disabled the track of the tank but it continued firing, its turret still moving.

Henri left the dead behind this time; none of them were recognizable. In a fifteen-minute fight he had lost almost half the men he set out with, a toll as devastating as the trenches of the First War. But he had stalled a troop movement on its way to the coast, where the Germans expected an invasion at Calais.

Later Henri would discover his losses were even greater than he thought.

33

"**W**hen is this Foix person going to be ready?"

Langton was polite but there was a certain urgency in his voice. For one thing, Henri Foix died almost a month ago. The due by date on dead people was two months, tops. He knew Devlin did other things with his life, but ten days was a long time. He would be shocked to know that Jack had done almost nothing but work on this one obit that whole time.

"Sorry. I'll file tomorrow. Overnight, I'll file it to the queue."

Langton gave a half-smile in response and went back to his work. The obit editor was an odd-looking character sitting there in a bright checked shirt, a wool tie and a well-trimmed beard that looked as if it should be worn by the captain of an early ocean liner. After 20 seconds or so he looked up, as if the picture of Jack's face had just registered.

"What happened to you? Your face took quite a scrape."

Jack didn't want to give him details but he didn't want to lie. And he knew it would be bad form to retell any heroics.

"Scrape is the word. Bit of a problem in France."

Langton almost looked worried. "Part of this Foix story?"

"Yes. Met a man in Lyon who didn't like answering questions. An old fan of Pétain."

"Well take a few extra days if you want."

"No, no. It's almost all done anyway. Don't worry. It'll be ready tomorrow."

"Why don't you see the doctor about that bruise?"

Langton had never been so solicitous. This had to be the longest conversational volley in months. "Don't worry. It's fine. Should clear up in a couple of days." He smiled and walked over to the stringer's desk he used.

Financial suicide, thought Jack. Ten days on one obit, eleven days if you counted the first night he worked on it. It might pay him a hundred pounds, a hundred and fifty tops. And he'd spent more than that on the chase across France. The side trip to Essen was a killer, in particular since it included a one-way air trip back to London. His American Express bill would cripple him next month.

He sat down at his desk and pulled out the printed copy of what he had so far.

Lieutenant Colonel, Henri Foix, who won a DSO for parachuting into France to help organize the French Resistance in the months ahead of D-Day, has died in Montreal at the age 69.

The desk at the office wasn't the place to finish this. He had almost everything he needed, but before he finished it, he had to check out one last bit. About the killing of the soldiers. And he needed to start acting like a reporter instead of an historian. Tomorrow was the deadline. It was already 10:30 in the morning.

"Is Tom McColl there please?" As Jack waited on the phone, he thought about that name. It sounded so plain, a name they would pick for a book or movie. Almost ordinary. But there was nothing ordinary about this Tom McColl. He was a career diplomat who wrote books on history and he'd done one on Canadian spies and agents.

"McColl here."

The phone conversation was almost as short as that answer. McColl would meet him just before noon, 11:45 to be exact, at the house in Brook Street, the one where the Canadian High Commission was about to lose its long lease. The Duke of Westminster could get more cash leasing it to someone else.

Jack was worried about taking so long to do this story. God knows how much other work, obits and radio, was farmed out while he was away. But he'd find out later that he hadn't missed much. There had been a fine crop of English dead to keep the pages full. Foreigners, even foreign war heroes with a DSO and *Croix de Guerre avec palme*, could wait.

He closed his Death book, packed his briefcase and prepared to slip out without saying a word to Langton. Then the phone rang, and he couldn't resist answering it.

"Where have you been, for God's sake? You haven't phoned me in a week. How long have you been back in London?" It was Claire. "And what have you done to my mother? She's *en colère* with you. So, what happened?"

What a pain in the ass. But Jack brought up a picture of Claire in his mind, mental snapshots of thick lips, a beautiful face and exquisite round ass. Curly blond hair. Passion. He'd have to deal with all this.

"Well I just got back," a lie he hoped he could get away with. No use explaining things, he'd just go and see her. "I've got a meeting in Brook Street a little before noon. How about lunch at Brown's. Late, say 1:30?"

He knew she couldn't resist Brown's. She mumbled in French on the other end of the line. Jack broke in. "I'm running late. See you there." He put down the phone so fast, she could have accused him of hanging up on her.

On his way to the tube he stopped at a bank machine and took out 50 pounds. His mini-lunch with Claire would cost at least 20 of it.

McColl, the man at the Canadian High Commission, was irritable. Jack could tell right away that for whatever reason, McColl didn't like him. They weren't the same type. McColl was as English-looking a Canadian as you could get, almost too perfect in the way he dressed, and acted. He wasn't stupid enough to affect an English accent, the vowels never worked no matter how hard they tried, but his speech was clipped and he used words that they would never understand back in Saskatchewan.

The first few minutes were spent impressing Jack with his knowledge of the war, and the SOE, which he called SOE, leaving out the article as the British did. And he seemed to dislike Henri Foix almost as much as he disliked Jack Devlin.

"There were a lot of things Foix did that upset London. He was much too chatty after the war," said McColl, looking out at the street while he spoke to Jack. "All that talk about executing Germans."

Jack stopped writing.

"I'd read about that. I think in *The Montreal Star* in 1945. It was right in the headline and they went into some detail in the main story. Are you saying it wasn't true?"

"London didn't like the publicity. It's hard to imagine it was true. Why would anyone tell such a story, even if it were true?"

"Maybe he was proud of it," ventured Jack.

"Well he shouldn't have been. And you won't be doing him any favours telling that story in your obituary. By the way, he's been dead for some time now. Don't these things ever go stale?"

"They do, but in this case the body's warm enough." Jack made small talk for a while and McColl gave him a copy of his latest book on the war, signing the inside page, careful to scratch out his printed name before signing in ink.

He must have wondered why Jack was still there. He'd found out what he needed in just a couple of minutes, the rest was stalling to be polite.

A little past one. Jack could take his time walking to Brown's. He passed by The Audley, one of his favourite pubs. It sat at the end of a row of buildings made of reddish stone. He wished he'd asked Claire to meet him there; for one thing it would have been cheaper. Brown's was closer to her shop, but then she was the one who wanted to meet.

To make his lunch with Claire a bit easier he went into the pub and ordered a bloody Mary.

"Make it a double."

"Right, sir." The only pub in London where they don't call you mate, thought Jack. No matter what Claire wanted it was going to be complicated. Maybe it had to do with her mother? Well of course it had to with her mother.

"Another one, please," and Jack passed a ten-pound note across the bar and waited for his change. What a day, he thought to himself. The paper's pressing me for an obit. A meeting with the smuggest Canadian diplomat in captivity and now a possible scene with Claire. No wonder he needed a drink.

To relax he made small talk with a woman at the bar, around 50 maybe, but dressed too young in one of those pink Puffa jackets. She seemed more interested in booze than men. Jack was curious about her story but he had to go. He left money to buy her a drink.

She nodded and gave a smile that aged her and told Jack she was a hopeless drunk.

As he walked he thought what a complete prick the diplomat had been. Rude and pompous. And so old-fashioned for a man just a few years older than he was. Jack liked English shirts, but this man was a fop, over the top. Today he'd been wearing a striped shirt with a detachable white collar with a wide spread. The cuffs were white, and the tie was from Hermes.

The shoes were the real killer. Hand-made, thought Jack, who'd done a few stories on the shops in Jermyn Street and St. James's Street. The shoes had a buckle, and came from John Lobb or someplace like it. The other day he'd seen a picture of General Eisenhower with those shoes on in 1944 and he thought his English driver/mistress must have picked them for him.

Jack thought they'd beat up a guy like McColl if he showed up all tarted up back in Estevan, or wherever it was he came from.

Even with his dawdling he was five minutes early. Since Claire had to get back from lunch she might be on time. He ordered a bloody Mary and a package of Marlboros. He had decided to quit that morning but the day was becoming too much for him.

Claire came in an obvious rage, *en colère* as she would say. Jack stood up to kiss her but she presented just her cheek, keeping her full rouged lips to herself.

"What did you do to my mother? She's threatening never to speak to me again."

Jack felt a little cowed, but since he hadn't done anything to Claire's mother, he wasn't going to apologize.

"I didn't do anything to your mother. I went to your house, talked to her, and asked her some questions about the war. I don't think she liked me bringing up the Jewish thing. You're the one who told me she was part Jewish."

There was a silence, one of those long silences lovers have. After what seemed like an hour, but was in fact just a minute, Jack weakened and spoke.

"You never told me you had such a nice house. Christ, people will think I'm hanging around with you for your money." It was said as joke, but she didn't laugh. When she did speak she wasn't angry anymore, but solemn.

"My mother went through a lot in the war. The Germans captured her then the Maquis rescued her. She and her brother were traded for some German soldiers. She's not ashamed to be a Jew, but she's still scared to be one."

The waiter brought over a plate of sandwiches. Claire ordered a second glass of white wine and Jack nodded for another bloody Mary. He lit up a cigarette even before eating.

"Sorry if I caused any trouble with your family. Well your mother, really. Your father wasn't there."

Claire looked as him as if he were an idiot. "Of course he was there, he just didn't want to see you. He stayed in his study with the door closed. My mother told me about it."

As she talked his mind drifted off. He remembered a book review he'd read in the *New York Times* a few years ago, something about children of the Holocaust. Some Jews became almost anti-Semitic, or at least denied they were Jews.

Jack watched the vacant look on Claire's face. She finished her wine in a hurry. He thought he knew what was coming.

It was the same sort of thing ever since his first girl-friend in high school.

"I don't think we should see each other anymore."

The bowling ball dropped in his stomach. The same feeling he'd had at least a dozen times before. He wasn't ready for this, he didn't want her to leave, but he wasn't going to beg. He might make her talk a bit though.

"Oh, why?"

"Death. All this death. Your obsession with war and dead people. I can't stand it anymore."

She leaned over and kissed him on the cheek and left.

34

A high-pitched shriek cut through Jack Devlin's ears as he ripped the headset off, too late to avoid what he was sure was permanent damage to his eardrums.

"Jesus Christ," said Jack. "Take it easy."

"Sorry," was all the sound technician said. He had pushed a switch too far producing the screaming noise. He sent out a tone again and Jack held the headset away from his ear to make sure it wasn't about to happen again.

Desperate to earn some money, he was in the radio studio doing a news hit just before noon. That made it just before seven o'clock in the morning Eastern Standard Time, and would give listeners from Newfoundland to Winnipeg a fresh take on the top story of the day.

"It is two months and two days since the disaster at Chernobyl, but the damage caused by the catastrophic failure of the Soviet nuclear plant is still being felt. Today a group of American scientists are expected to visit the site in the Ukraine to assess the damage and to offer advice, if not help, in cleaning up the world's worst ever nuclear disaster.

SOUND UP AMERICAN SCIENTIST
At the same time, scientists meeting in Oslo say the damage to Northern Europe is now even greater than was thought at first. One Swedish physicist said the people of Chernobyl were exposed

219

to one hundred times the radiation given off at Hiroshima. And the cloud poisoned much of Northern Europe.

SOUND UP SWEDISH PHYSICIST

Nuclear power accounts for forty per cent of the Soviet Union's electricity generation. In spite of calls for a shutdown of other nuclear reactors using what is seen as the faulty graphite reactor technology, it seems doubtful the Soviets would cripple their economy to satisfy a meeting of scientists in Oslo. This is Jack Devlin in London."

Two minutes on the button with the sound clips. A real money earner. And he would update for the newscasts later in the Canadian morning. Jack needed the cash and he knew how to make it in hurry.

As he told Homer in one of their economic discussions, "Daily newspapers print every day. That means they need material. But radio needs new stuff every hour or two. The best little earner there is."

Now another sound came through the headset. "Good work Jack, how about lunch?" It was Michelle and since he was now a single man again, he might fire this up, even though it could be dangerous, since she was the source of so much freelance work.

"Sure," said Jack.

"I have a few calls to make. Why don't you meet me in the wine bar? Whoever is first snags the table."

Michelle flipped the key for the studio. "Forget the wine bar. It's Italian today. I've already booked the San Marco. 12:15. See you there."

Aggressive, thought Jack. I might not have to do much work.

The first call was to Langton. There had been a fresh crop of deaths, including a prominent U-boat commander, one of the few who had survived the war. That took the pressure off Jack for a day or so, and he could churn out cash at the network.

As he walked past the front desk he noticed the cockney sexpot bending over a box of tapes. The network was Canadian but almost all the people who worked here were English, with a few Scots thrown in for balance. Local hires. They were cheaper than sending live Canadians over. Jack was cheaper too. No one had to pay for an expensive flat.

Foix. Henri Foix. He thought about what McColl had told him, and thought about what he knew. Should he put everything in the obit? He thought about the German and whether it was Henri who killed his father or whether he'd killed prisoners at all. Hard to know and maybe he didn't want to believe it.

"I'd leave that out if I were you."

If anyone but McColl had said it he might take the advice. Jack hated capital J journalism. It was one of the reasons he left Canada. He couldn't put up with all the moralizing. But now he had a real problem. Leave it in, or leave it out.

The decision had to be made by tonight, when he should file, tomorrow morning at the latest. Jesus, he thought, what happens if Michelle wants to get laid?

"Just *San Pellegrino*," said Jack. "If I have to refile that Chernobyl shit all afternoon I'm going to need my head and my voice." He handed Michelle his pack of Marlboros. "Here keep these and don't give me any, even if I beg."

Michelle had undone a button on her dress and her eyes were sleepier than usual. Her long legs were crossed and she leaned into Jack as if she'd been drinking all day.

"So I hear you dumped the French girl." Jack was shocked at how people found out about these things so fast. He clicked through a mental short list and figured it was Homer. Blabber mouth. Then Homer had to suck up to Michelle for work, so it was a trade-off. Gossip in exchange for buying a couple of stories from Switzerland, or maybe Ireland.

"Yeah," said Jack, not wanting to admit how it was Claire who dumped him, and for an odd set of reasons. An obit ghoul. "Looks like it's over."

"What was her name again?" The not-so-subtle demolition of a doomed rival.

"Claire."

"She works in a shop or something?" Put down number two.

"Sort of. She manages PR for a jeweller in Bond Street. Anyway, there are no hard feelings." Translation: I'm not about to dump on her, so why don't we just drop it.

She switched the subject to work, and to the regular correspondent, a man she despised, and whose name she tried never to mention if she could avoid it.

"Old-what's-his-name is out of town."

Jack interrupted. "Ireland again?"

Michelle laughed. "No, even better. Called back to Canada. They were unhappy about him getting drunk and going missing in Geneva last week. Thank God we had Homer there and I never thought I'd hear myself say that."

"Do you think they're bringing him back for good?"

"No such luck, I'm afraid. A little brainwashing. Scare him; maybe try to dry him out. But they love his stuff, God knows why. He'll be back."

Jack thought one of the reasons Michelle didn't like Old What's His Name was that he was English, or at least part English. Not from London or the Home Counties and he just got up her nose. He thought sometimes it's almost impossible to know what makes the English tick. Jack couldn't see much of a difference, but it seems she could.

"It's all good news for you Jack. You're my number one stringer. They like you in Toronto. You should do pretty well. Could last two weeks, even as long as a month."

She caught something in Jack's face and decided to be rather blunt.

"And don't worry that we're friends," said Michelle. "No matter what happens, I'll never let it interfere with my work, or our work."

Christ, thought Jack.

Lunch arrived. Veal done one way for her, the simpler way for him. Sear the meat and put some lemon on it.

Sure, thought Jack. He was in it now, no way out. Well things could be worse, he always fancied Michelle. Now it looks as if he was going to learn a lot more about her.

"How's your obit going? The French one you spoke about to my father."

"I have to have it finished by tomorrow." Now her face changed. "It won't be that tough. I have almost all of it done. The trouble is I worked too hard on it and I have too much information."

"What do you mean?"

"Well I found out some things in France, and in old newspaper articles. And in Germany. I'm not sure whether to include them all. Things look different in 1944 and 1986, we don't see things in the same way. Now the Germans are our friends, then they were the devil."

She kept listening; he paused for a couple of seconds.

"I wouldn't mind talking to your father about it. Is he going to be at home tonight?" He also wanted to talk to his old Air Force buddy, Mason. He could call him this afternoon between Chernobyl hits.

"He's in all day every day. He retired last month so he'll look forward to a problem. What is it anyway?"

Jack didn't want to tell her everything. "Well just something my obit man did during the war. Let's say it was against the rules. Anyway, I never met him, but I like him. I feel as if I know him and he's become my friend. Weird, but it's true."

"I'll give you his number when we get back."

Late spring and a surprise burst of sun and heat made the London streets seem almost as hot as Montreal in July. Jack threw his jacket over his shoulder and they slowed down as they walked back.

"Why don't we got out celebrate the end of this obit, tomorrow night. Another deadline, it'll force me to get it done."

'Sure, but you can work here tomorrow?"

"Yeah as long as I don't have to be in here before one."

"Shouldn't be a problem. How about eleven?"

"Alright."

As they got to the door the Scottish audio technician was heading out for his second pub break of the day. A complete piss tank who tried to pretend he was an ordinary human being and not a functioning alcoholic.

"There's a new clip on Chernobyl. Some Canadian do-gooder in Oslo complaining about radiation crossing the Atlantic."

Jack smiled at the local angle and repeated the motto of *The Toronto Star*, the biggest daily in Canada.

"What does it mean to Metro?" He said it out loud, remembering the sign over the desk of *The Toronto Star* in the press gallery in Ottawa.

'What did you say?" asked Michelle.

"Nothing. Just some piece of Canadiana."

35

Henri would find out later that his attack on the German panzer column was one of a series coordinated from London from intelligence picked off German radios. There were thousands of Maquis at eight locations picking at the same soldiers over the long road north.

The band of one hundred soldiers under Henri's command had slipped back, crossed the road behind the Germans and surprised them from the other side. But a third of his men were dead, or so wounded they couldn't fight.

In the last light of the day they met near the spot where they trained. A messenger from Philippe's group came back just after dark.

"Where are the rest?" asked Henri.

"Some got away into the woods, but they caught us in a pincer movement," answered the young man who Henri assumed had also studied Latin and Greek. He began to describe the battle using words not taught by army strategists but by classics professors.

The look on his face told Henri he was in shock, horrified by what he had been through. And he wasn't telling the whole story. Henri grabbed him by the shoulders and gave him a light shake.

"Relax. Tell me what happened to the men. How many are left and where are they?"

The young man composed himself and readied himself to tell the whole story.

"When they surrounded us some of us managed to get away, about half of us I guess. But there were a lot of wounded. They were lying on the ground. It was a small area, not bigger than a large clearing in a forest."

He reached over for a flask another man passed him and took a long pull of brandy to steady himself.

"We tried to give covering fire from the woods, the way you showed us. But there were too many and there were two panzers behind the Germans. We only managed to drag two of the wounded away."

Henri was now breathing harder.

"What happened to the rest?"

The young man looked at the ground, ashamed that he couldn't stop what had happened.

"They killed them. They used rifle butts and smashed their heads into the earth."

Henri didn't speak for the longest time.

"What happened to Philippe? Is he here?"

"No. He pulled out his pistol at the last minute, but they crushed his skull like a grapefruit."

The muscles in Henri's jaw moved so fast they almost distorted his face. He took a long breath and walked away. Later that night he would find out thirty-three of his men were killed by the Germans.

In the morning there were reprisals in the nearby village of Oingt. Eighty hostages, men of all ages, fifteen women, were hanged from balconies, struggling as the ropes garrotted them to death. They were executed in groups of seven or eight and it took almost half the day.

The fighting that spawned the executions had now split the German column in two, the heavy panzers moving north and the lighter vehicles staying behind. The night of the massacres in Oingt, Henri and sixty Maquis members moved to take their own revenge.

The soldier that was first to die had polished his French at night, in cafés and in bed. Six mistresses in two and a half years. Only one of them a spy, and he had killed her himself. Reporting her would have meant too many questions.

She was the smartest and had taught him the nuances of grammar and accent. They would play games in restaurants in Lyon. She would point out someone and ask him to listen to his or her speech and then identify where in France they came from. It got so he could not just pick out someone from Paris but could spot Marseilles with ease. He even learned to pick out strange accents from Northern France.

His biggest coup was when he guessed someone was not from France at all. He was a Swiss. Tonight he was stumped. The rapid fire French was strange. The accent maybe from the north, but then it changed and there were words he'd never heard before. They almost seemed like old words, something from a play, not modern speech.

The man was carrying a Luger at his side. The questions were about men killed two nights ago, thirty-three of them clubbed to death with rifle butts, their heads smashed in as they groaned for mercy. The dead were Maquis, French Resistance, and the German soldier knew they had to die, just like the whore he had strangled in a field outside town. When he killed two of the wounded men it reminded him of duck hunting, crushing the neck of a bird brought down with buckshot.

It wasn't breaking the rules of war since they hadn't been wearing uniforms. And it was something this funny sounding Frenchman wouldn't do. "They were spies, like you," said the uniformed German soldier.

The Luger moved up in a flash and the German's face was a bloody pulp. The man with the strange accent moved forward and pushed the body over the low railing of the bridge, using its own weight to do most of the work.

The German soldiers froze as if to attention and the man with the Luger shot another who looked at him. The third man he approached said it was against the Geneva Convention to shoot prisoners in uniform.

"What about the Maquis you killed with rifle butts?" asked the man with the Luger.

"We're sorry," said the soldier confessing. "I didn't want to do it."

He pulled the German soldier aside, and told him to stand at the end of the bridge and not move. The soldier had seen this before, men executed in reprisals. He had done it in Yugoslavia and to men in uniform. But he had never seen it done to Germans. The man with the Luger shot two men dead in less than a few seconds and then, on his signal, the Maquis fired rounds into the forty-seven German soldiers on the bridge. The bullets tore through their uniforms, deforming their young bodies. Blood sprayed back at the French gunmen. They lifted or kicked the bodies into the river.

"Now you understand French," said the man with the strange accent.

"Yes," said the young German, his eyes dry from fear behind his wire-rimmed glasses, his own shit running down his leg to his boots.

"Go back and tell your commandant if he does that again, I'll kill twice 51."

The German left and the man with the accent raised his Luger at one of his own Maquis, a silent warning not to shoot the German who was staggering off in the direction of Lyon.

36

Jack sat in the spare office at the network reading the front page of a three-day old Vancouver newspaper. The lead story was about a hunt for old Nazis in Canada and it focused on Ukrainians, the Galician SS, who had worked with Einsatzkommando, killing squads which roved the countryside executing Jews.

Chernobyl was today's Ukrainian story and he walked to the studio to record the latest version of the nuclear horror story. There was a new top to the Chernobyl yarn but by this stage the whole thing was just about memorized. So, as he sat with his headset off, waiting for the half-drunk Scottish soundman to get his levels right, Jack thought about the atrocity story and how he had one of those on his hands, an atrocity story that is.

"In five, Jack." Jack put on his headset.

"A Canadian scientist has sounded the alarm on Chernobyl and what it could do to human and animal life in the Arctic..."

The read was over in a couple of minutes, the Scottish soundman happy because Jack didn't make any mistakes. The technician, smarter than he appeared, would slip in the clips and send the item to the main Toronto newsroom on the next feed. Unlike most of the competition, the sound would be crisp and sharp, no cheap phone connections, and the interviews clear.

Easy work for Jack. The interviews came from the BBC, and the clip from the Canadian scientist was provided by an enterprising stringer in Stockholm who did a long interview with the Canadian. She would get paid twice, maybe three times, as the clip ran on newscasts and the long intelligent interview used for a weekend program.

The phone rang as Jack walked back into his office, or at least the office he was using this week. It was Nick Mason returning his call.

"I was hoping you were planning a visit out here. I could use a trip to the pub," heard Jack who knew Mason made that trip just about every day, if not twice a day.

"Well, I'm in a bit of a hurry. I have to have this obit filed for tomorrow. It's about a Canadian who served with the SOE."

Mason interrupted. "I'm afraid I can't help you there, dear boy. RAF, remember?" He said it with a laugh.

Jack laughed with him. "Of course. But this is different. This fellow I'm doing an obit on worked in the south of France near Lyon, for several months before and after D-Day. He saw a lot of action and one night some of the men he was fighting with were wounded and then beaten to death with rifle butts."

Mason made a noise at the other end of the phone. Breathing, not words. Jack paused then kept going.

"There were reprisals in a village. People hanged from lamp posts or balconies really. The commanding officer was executed for it after the war."

"And a good thing too," said Mason. "Bloody war criminals. They used to shoot some of our chaps when they landed. Sometimes you couldn't blame civilians after what we'd done to their cities, but soldiers. They're meant to know better."

"Well that's the trouble," said Jack. "My man did the same sort of thing a day or so later. He captured some Germans outside a whorehouse and executed them. All but one of them that is. He let him go to report to his commandant."

Not a word from Mason. Jack took the silence as a sign for him to keep talking.

"It worked. The warning, that is. The killings stopped, the retaliations and shooting of the Underground's wounded anyway. Though I think they still sent a lot of them to camps in Germany."

Mason came to life at the other end of the line.

"So what's your question?"

Jack thought he knew what the question was.

"Well, should I put that in the obituary or leave it out?"

"Christ man. It's pretty simple. Leave it out."

Jack interrupted. "But it's a war crime isn't it? Same as what the SS man was hanged for after the war."

Mason had the final word.

"He hanged civilians, your man shot soldiers. The bastards got what they deserved from the sound of it. And we won the bloody war."

A pause.

"Come out for Sunday lunch at the pub. Noon. I'll have read your piece by then."

Jack said alright and hung up the phone, still not decided about what to do.

37

The different sized wheels of the locomotive telegraphed clicking noises as they passed over each joint in the rail. Back in the dining car Henri looked out the window at the smoke from a glass factory down a snow-covered hill. He thought about how much he missed the odd sort of freedom he left in the spring and summer of 1944 in France.

December 17, 1945, was the date on the newspaper. Things had returned to normal in a hurry. Few of the stories were about the war except for a Japanese prince who had committed suicide rather than face a war-crime tribunal. Henri looked out the window and thought they would soon be hanging Germans after the Nuremberg trials. He hoped some of the SS murderers in France would hang or face a firing squad. He pushed a picture of Philippe out of his mind and returned to the paper.

There was the weather. It was going to be cold, 13 degrees above zero, Fahrenheit of course. That would be minus ten degrees back in France, though it almost never went that low, not even on the coldest days. A look at the weather in the U.S. showed a snowstorm hitting Buffalo. Henri knew that could mean a blizzard in Montreal in a few days.

He had just finished breakfast and was now waiting alone with the paper. It was a little before 8:30 in the morning and the train from Halifax was half an hour late. As it pulled around the corner Henri could see the front of the train and the special car filled with fish, two back from the engine. The railway attached the fish car to the faster passenger train to bring the cod, mackerel and lobster fresh to the fishmongers on the Main.

"We'll be arriving in Montreal in twenty minutes," announced the black porter. Henri was ready. He had shaved and washed at six in the morning. He was in uniform, the ribbons from his DSO and *Croix de Guerre* on his chest. He planned to carry his greatcoat over his arm. He had already given the porter the money to take all the luggage to the cab rank, with the address he needed it sent to, his mother's house near McGill University.

The train was stopping now just two stations before Windsor Station, the place he had left in 1942 to go west to the American training camp. On the platform outside were wagons piled high with milk cans, bringing this morning's milk to be bottled at a dairy a couple of blocks away.

"Hello," a voice taking Henri back to the real world. He almost blushed as he saw her face and thought of the night of passion in the tight sleeping compartment. At least he had been given a private roomette. The army was about to use him for a major propaganda coup, so it was the least they could do.

Jane leaned over and kissed his cheek, just one side. She touched the other cheek with her fingers then sat down across from him. The kitchen was closed, but the waiter brought her a cup of coffee. She drank it to be polite. She'd grown used to tea.

As they spoke, a young man in a captain's uniform approached them. Henri noticed no campaign ribbons on his chest. He had taken the morning train from Ottawa, a man from Defence ready to help Henri in his meeting with the press.

"Major Foix?" Henri's promotion had come earlier that year.

"And Madame Foix?"

Henri stood up and the young captain saluted him.

"We'll be arriving in Montreal in just fifteen minutes," stating the obvious as the train pulled out of the station. "Is there anything you need to know?"

Henri answered. "Well I've never met the press before. We were trained not to talk." He still couldn't even mention the SOE. "How much can I tell them? What will they want to know?"

The press officer smiled. "You can tell them just about anything. The war is over and we won. Talk about your life with the French Underground. They might want to know how you met your wife."

Jane smiled. She knew Henri would keep some of the secrets to himself. She wondered if they might want to speak to her. She looked at the press officer, who was still standing beside their table.

"Will they be asking any questions of me?"

"They might well do. What they want to hear about are your war experiences. You were a driver, I believe. Talk about London during the war. Canadian woman braves the Blitz and returns to a life of domesticity with war hero. That's the kind of thing they're looking for."

Henri interjected. "My wife has a few medals of her own," a dig at the young captain. "She was in some pretty tight spots, raids on airfields, bombs in London. Let her talk all she wants."

Jane laughed. They had only been married since August and she still found it odd to be called a wife. When she got up the young press officer was startled by her limp and Henri passed her a cane. She was still recovering from the blast from an air raid in London and hadn't driven a car since. It had been touch and go whether to amputate her leg. She hadn't told Henri, but he knew. Still, she was better off than her two friends in the pub; the explosion killed them both.

The flash and pop from a big Speed Graphic camera startled Jane as they walked out unto the main concourse at the station. There were four photographers and half a dozen reporters, along with members of her family and his.

Along the platform Henri saw other packs of newsmen waiting for their assigned war hero. He swallowed and felt a nervous twinge in his stomach, which surprised him.

"Gentlemen. I'd like to introduce Major Henri Foix and his wife. Major Foix as many of you know received the DSO and the *Croix de Guerre avec palme* from the government of France, all in recognition of the work he did with the Resistance."

The army man paused and then turned to Jane. "And Mrs. Foix was a driver during the raids on London and was decorated for her part in rescuing pilots at an airfield while bombs were still dropping. They are both willing to answer your questions."

The first reporter put up his hand and Henri saw the yellow nicotine stains around his two first fingers and thumb. His eyes shot down to his feet and saw his unpolished shoes encased in toe rubbers, known in French as *les claques*. The cuffs of his trousers were crusted in salt, picked up from walking in the slush.

An older man, with the prejudices of his time, he started out by slagging France.

"How did you feel helping the French, when at the start of the war they could hardly help themselves?"

The muscles moved in Henri's cheeks, but he answered the man in a calm voice. "I fought for Canada, not for France. Britain was our ally. You know my compatriots, people I grew up with, say you fought for England. I say the hell with England, I fought for Canada. And I didn't go there to fight for France."

While scribblers scribbled, Henri paused then finished his thought, looking straight at the dissolute older reporter, a man from *The Montreal Star* it turned out.

"There were seventy of us French-Canadians who dropped into France to help the Resistance. I am one of the lucky fifteen who made it home."

A reporter interrupted with a standard question on how it felt to be back home, and he replied with a standard answer. Jane was asked about her war work.

"Women drivers were needed because men were doing the fighting. We used big cars, requisitioned from their owners for the duration of the war. Strangely enough, I drove a Buick for much of the early part of my war."

"What about the air raid? Wasn't that what you were awarded a medal for?"

"Yes. Well it wasn't anything anyone else wouldn't have done at the time. We started out from London before dawn. Our lights were covered so they were just slits. It was hard to see where you were going I can tell you. When we arrived at North Weald, which is just outside London, the sun was up and German planes were strafing the field. I helped some pilots who were wounded..."

The reporter looked up form his notebook. "Had you done this before?"

"Well I trained as a nurse here, at the Royal Victoria."

The old newsman in the front was now pulling on a Buckingham and somehow managing to take notes at the same time. Henri almost smiled as he watched him.

The older reporter then got off what he considered a big picture question, rather than the how-do-you-feel-kind-of stuff he might have thought better relegated to the women's pages. "We've seen a lot of pictures, even movie newsreels, coming out about the concentration camps. Were the Germans busy with that kind of operation in France, and did you come across any of it?"

"The Germans were very active in France in rounding up Jews. No one knows the final numbers and we might not for years. In our sector, near Lyon, we helped many Jews escape. And some of our bravest fighters were Jews."

Cigarette in the mouth, pen on the pad, the old reporter spoke without looking up. "Can you think of any particular incidents?"

Henri paused, not knowing which one to pick. So it's drama they want, he thought. "There was one incident where we captured three Germans, an officer, about the rank of what we would call a major and two of his soldiers. We got them while they were out in their car. We exchanged them for two

Jewish children, about nine and ten. I remember the boy was particularly brave. He was the older one. We couldn't bring ourselves to tell him his parents had been shipped off to a camp. But he knew. I can tell you it took everything not to shoot the Germans after the exchange."

Feeling he was on to a good line of chat the old reporter managed to flip a page in his notebook and light another Buckingham with his Zippo and still keep other reporters from asking the next question.

"Was there a lot of that?"

"A lot of what?" asked Henri.

"Anger. Hatred, the urge to kill people."

"Well I can tell you one night the Germans killed thirty-three of my men. In fact two of them were women. Killed them with rifle butts as they lay wounded after a fight. We weren't wearing uniforms, but it was still a cowardly thing to do. At times like that you almost lose control."

"What did you do?"

"The next day we captured a column of Germans. There were fifty-eight of them. We lined up all fifty-eight against the railing of a bridge and we shot them, one here and one there, until they were all dead. Then we sent word to the commandant that if he killed any more of our wounded we'd kill twice fifty-one Germans. It stopped. He didn't kill any more of our wounded."

There was silence for maybe twenty seconds as the reporters wrote down the words. Henri's cheek muscles were shifting back and forth in double time.

The meeting with the reporters took almost an hour. One photographer ran in front of them and caught a picture of them as they walked out of the station, the big flakes from the snowstorm covering them like confetti at a wedding.

Jane almost got in the front right door to drive, but Henri opened the back door to his brother's pre-war Lincoln and his brother drove them up the hill.

38

LONDON, MAY 1, 1986

The rain was so heavy there were no taxis. Jack had to walk home from South Kensington, ducking into doorways now and again. He turned down at the hospital and took refuge in the Princess of Wales, which had only been open for fifteen minutes.

"Why do they call them raincoats, they're useless in the rain," muttered Jack as he asked for a pint of Guinness. He figured it had food value.

"You need an umbrella mate, that's what keeps the rain off."

The barman was right, but Jack always forgot umbrellas as soon as it stopped raining. He thought he might have lost ten of them since he moved to London. Because of the rain the pub was empty, except for a couple of sullen regulars at the end of the bar.

Jack only had time for one. He had to finish Foix's obit fast, though he needed just a few hundred more words to finish it. The question is what would he put in it.

All of a sudden the rain let up. Jack took the rest of the Guinness down in two separate gulps. He kept his cigarette going to finish on the walk home.

It was damp inside his basement flat, and not too warm. As he ripped a fax off his machine, he laughed when he thought about proper central heating. Or an air conditioner for the middle of the summer. He would love to buy one but his friend who owned the house would have a fit.

The fax was from his friend at *The Gazette* in Montreal, anxious to know when he could have his week in the flat. With no Claire to go live with, Jack would have to make other plans.

He pushed all that out of his mind and sat down to write.

Henri Foix was one of about 70 French-Canadian officers who volunteered for commando duties in France in the months leading up to D-Day. Most were from the Royal 22nd Regiment, known as the Van Doos, men whose native language was French and who could blend into life in occupied France.

After the war, some of the young officers, none older than 28, some just 22, said they were treated as generals of the Resistance. They commanded thousands of men and women agents over wide areas of France. It was dangerous work. Of the 70 or so officers dropped into France, only fifteen returned.

Henri Foix first received commando training with the American Special Forces in 1942 at a camp at Helena, Montana. After further training in Scotland and England, the then Captain Foix parachuted into France in March of 1944. His sector was the area around Lyon, where Capt. Foix was put in charge of 3,000 members of the Maquis, the French Underground. They used weapons and equipment dropped from England to fight a guerrilla action in occupied France.

For almost six months his job was to disrupt the German army, destroying bridges, rail lines, and German military positions. He trained 600 members of the Maquis as a combat unit and used others to set up a 500-mile secure telephone line behind German lines. In one battle between the Maquis and German troops, Captain Foix reported German soldiers used rifle butts to club to death 33 wounded resistance fighters.

The assignment included the ambush and assassination of German officers. Since Captain Foix did not fight in uniform, capture would have meant being shot as a spy. The Gestapo searched for the slight, French-Canadian officer, at one point sending a pretty blond Polish collaborator to trap him. But she was discovered, and it was she who was shot as a spy.

While in France, Capt. Foix was known to the Resistance as Pierre le Canadien.

"They were amazed that a French-Canadian would come back and help them," said Capt. Foix after the war. His cover story included a platonic wife, a French agent named Florence. "She shot a German officer down like that." Capt. Foix told a reporter just after he left France.

The sector around Lyon was not liberated until September 3, 1944. France then awarded Henri Foix its highest military honour, the Croix de Guerre avec palme, with the medal presented by General Charles de Gaulle.

Henri Alsace Foix was born in Richmond, Quebec, on April 9, 1917, the son of a lawyer. His unusual middle name was not from a family connection but rather his father's patriotic affiliation to the French territory occupied by the Germans since the war of 1870. Henri attended a Jesuit classical college in Montreal, a training ground for French Canada's elite. His schoolmates included a future federal prime minister and a future separatist premier of the province of Quebec.

Henri Foix trained as an engineer at the Université de Montréal, where he was also in the Army Reserve unit. He joined the Canadian Army at the outbreak of war and was commissioned in 1942.

Jack put in some other facts of his later life, but left out the detail from the Montreal newspapers of 1945. He told himself he wasn't sure, so why put it in.

He married Jane Orpen, whom he met when she was working as a driver for the FANYs, the First Aid Nursing Yeomanry. She was created a Member of British Empire (military class) for bravery under fire when she went to the aid of wounded and dying pilots during an air raid on a fighter base just outside London at North Weald. They had three daughters.

Jack read it over and made a few corrections, putting the {bt and {et at each end of the piece to let the computer know where things started and ended. It was almost nine o'clock. He logged into the paper's computer and sent the message through to the ATEX system.

Once it was filed he switched from exhaustion to almost light-headedness. He was thirsty and horny. Claire was out of the question. Or was she. He picked up the phone.

"Hi." A short wait.

"I'm going over to the Princess of Wales. Jump in a cab and meet me there. It shouldn't take you long. Keep the receipt. I'll pick it up."

He laughed and walked out the door.

It had stopped raining.

Acknowldgements

Thanks to two women of Knowlton, Quebec, who helped me: Jean Wooton, who told me of her experiences as a driver in wartime Britain and Jacqueline Grenier who picked out my many typos and errors in English and French. To my CBC colleague, Amy Olmstead, who was patient enough to read through a couple of versions of this; to my literate neighbour, Martin Dwyer, who caught many last minute clangers. And to my friend David Twiston-Davis, chief obituary writer of the Daily Telegraph, who taught me a lot about obit writing over the years.

April 2004